SKY WALKER

The Author would like to thank;

My Editors and fellow literature enthusiasts;
William V. York
James R. Woestman

Tech Support;
Robert J. Hornickel

Chris and Claire at @EightLittlePages for doing an awesome job on my formatting and cover design.

All my Beta Readers!

And finally, my Caleb and Cammie for your patience and encouragement, while your mom spent hours behind my laptop. I love you endlessly!

To my Friend Dillion
Reach for the stars!

SKY WALKER

Cynthia L. McDaniel

Love,
Cynthia L McDaniel

SKY WALKER

ISBN- 978-1-7325796-0-6

This book is a work of fiction. Names, characters, places, and incidents are either the product of the author's imagination or are used fictitiously, and any resemblance to actual persons, living or dead, events, or locales is entirely coincidental.

This book is lovingly dedicated to my three sisters, Debby, Tammie, and Kimi.

My very best friends, who are always on my side, and my biggest cheerleaders.

I love you more than words can express.

PREFACE

"Once you have tested flight, you will forever walk the earth with your eyes turned skyward, for there you have been, and there you will always long to return."

-Leonardo da Vinci-

AUGUST 20, 2017

My heart pounded in my chest, and I felt my breath deepen in the terror of the moment. I glanced over my shoulder, trying not to be too obvious, and saw two scruffy men walking behind me. The sun had just gone down, and the darkness was getting thicker, as I approached the tree line that would lead me safely into my neighborhood. All I had to do was get through the treeline. I heard the footsteps grow louder and increase their pace.

"Hey, come here," one of the scruffy voices said.

"We're not going to hurt you," laughed the other.

I knew I was in a lot of trouble, and had to get out of there immediately. The next thing I knew I was running. Running as fast and as hard as I could to the tree line. I glanced over my shoulder again, to see the two men chasing after me. They were so fast, and before I knew it, they were right behind me. I again set my sights on the tree line. Just 100 feet away. As I began to run faster, it happened. I felt something strong clutch the inside of my chest, and pull me from the ground. I was still running, but my feet no longer felt the earth beneath them. Up and up, higher and higher, I went above the towering trees. My arms and legs flailed, unsure of what to do, or how to respond to the lack of gravity on them. I looked down behind me to see the scruffy men frozen, their mouths opened wide, and their eyes full of terror, watching until I disappeared over the trees. I gasped trying to catch my breath, my heart pounding in my chest. How can this be real? I was flying!

ONE

WILBUR WRIGHT ONCE said, "*More than anything else, the sensation (of flying) is one of perfect peace mingled with an excitement that strains every nerve to the utmost-if you can conceive of such a combination.*"

I'm pretty sure Mr. Wright must have not only been an aviation pioneer, but also a fortune teller as well. I think he looked 100 years into the future and saw me coming, because this has been my life over the past year. Perfect peace mingled with an excitement, that has strained my every nerve to the utmost.

Ok, before you get the wrong idea, this is not a superhero story. In no way do I claim to be a superhero, or possess the bravery that it takes to fill that role. I'm only seventeen. In fact, I'm ashamed to admit it, but I'm a 17 year old scaredy cat. I refuse to go anywhere at night by myself, and I run and jump in my bed after I turn off the lights, just in case something is creeping underneath it. Before I go to sleep, I check all the doors at least five times, before I'm convinced the house is a close second to Fort Knox.

I'm pretty sure at some point in everyone's life, we all wish we had some kind of superpower, or at least have thought about it. Whether it be supernatural strength, teleportation, invisibility, or xray vision, we all dream of what it would be like to be plucked out of the ordinary and thrown into a life of the extraordinary. I know I have. But who am I, and what are the chances of any significant thing like that ever happening to me? I'm just another teenage American girl, mixed in with a million other girls. Definitely not a stand out, or anyone who would go out of my way to have attention drawn in my direction.

Before this year, I had never flown a day in my short life. In fact, I had barely left my hometown of Clarksville, Tennessee, except for the occasional trip to Nashville, where my fellow high school teammates and I go to battle the best basketball team in our division. (Well, all the teams we play are the better teams from our point of view. We suck so bad.) But I've been fascinated with flying for as long as I can remember.

My family's tiny white house sits on the edge of a tree line, that lies in a direct flight path to Ft. Campbell, Kentucky, a large army base on the outskirts of my city. My little sister and I listen for the thumping sound of the large Chinook helicopters coming in the distance. No matter what we are doing, we drop everything to run outside and watch as many as 6 fly over! They come in so low, you can see the soldiers inside and sometimes they wave down at us. Our dishes rattle on the shelves and our little house rumbles, and I soak up every minute of it. But that's been pretty much the extent of flying and excitement in my life. Until this year. My senior year. The year I began to fly. And when I say fly, I don't mean in a plane or an air balloon. I mean, I can fly.

When I was 8 years old my life changed dramatically. My dad, Ken, had a massive heart attack and died at the young age of 39. Until then my family life was totally normal. My dad owned a successful mechanic shop in town, and his income was more than enough to provide us with a beautiful home and a comfortable life. My mom stayed home and took care of me and my three sisters. I'm the third girl in the family. I have two older sisters, Danielle and Tessa, and one younger, Kassie. My name is Claire. My mom let my Aunt Betty name me, because she was running out of ideas by the time I came along.

All my sisters were born with beautiful golden blond hair, and big brown eyes. I don't know what happened with me. I have the big brown eyes, but my hair is a rich curly brown, and when I was born, I looked like a porcelain baby. They tan to a golden brown in the summer, and I tend to burn and lightly freckle. I remember my dad telling me not to hate my freckles when I would complain about them. He said one day they will join together and I will have a nice tan. Hmmmm...I'm still waiting for that one to happen.

After my dad passed away, we were forced to sell the shop, and pretty much broke even. With the money my mom had left, we purchased a small white frame house in a quiet, retirement-type neighborhood. Our home is in a busy section of the city, somewhat to itself at the end of a cul de sac, hidden by a large tree line. My oldest sister Dani, moved to California with her best friend about 7 years ago to escape an abusive relationship. My second sister Tessa married a soldier, and they are stationed at Ft. Bragg, so it's just me, my baby sister, and my mom now.

My mom's name is Mary. If you ever want to meet a perfect person, you definitely should meet her. She's always sweet, and always kind, and my friends like spending the night at my tiny little house just because they like to be around her. She works a full time job at Clarence's Thrift Store, and gets the biggest thrill out of finding Kassie and I nice clothes from there. She tries to bring us something new to wear every Friday when she gets paid, so while we don't get to shop at the mall too often, we are still able to dress nice. Thanks to her, Kassie and I have a pretty impressive wardrobe.

So here I was, the summer before my senior year, where the biggest concern on my mind was where I was going to attend college the next year, or if I was even going to college at all. I hated the thought of leaving my mom and Kassie alone. I work at Sonic

Drive Inn as a rollerskating waitress, and my income though very small, is a help to my mom. Plus I felt somewhat responsible for Kassie, even though we are only a year apart.

It's funny how your life can change so dramatically in one moment or in this case, one night. How one chance meeting can change everything. I think about that night, and how things would have been so different for my life if I had never met Johnny Angel. Yes, I know it's a weird coincidence, and sort of corny, but his name is Johnny Angel.

Everything began in July, the summer before my senior year. July 7th to be exact. Up to this point I had never been on a date a day in my life. I had plenty of crushes, but at 17, I had never even kissed a guy. And let me just clarify, it's not because I hadn't had the opportunity, but the guys I went to school with never interested me. Most I had grown up with, and they seemed more like brothers than anything.

That Friday night my best friend Alicia was coming over, and since we both had the night off, we were going out. We usually have no idea where we are going or what we are doing, but we like it that way. It's more of an adventure to not plan and see where you end up.

I heard Alicia's car pull into my gravel driveway, as I sat at my vanity putting the final touches on my red lipstick. I was clasping the gold heart necklace on my dad had given to me, when I heard my mom in the living room talking to her. I put my white sailor hat on, the one Alicia despised. I couldn't help it. I loved it. My mom had brought it home from Clarence's one day, brand new, still in the bag.

It looked really cute with my long curly hair, white tee, jean shorts, and big silver hoops.

"If you're wearing that, you'll be riding in the back seat." I turned around to see Alicia leaning against my door jam, with a snide grin on her face. She looked so adorable in her cute hot pink tee and denim skirt. Alicia's parents were Hispanic, giving her a beautiful creamy mocha skin color. She now flashed the most perfect smile I had ever seen, thanks to two years of braces in junior high.

Alicia and I have been inseparable since we first met in the preschool class at church. We had seen each other through everything. She was there for me through the death of my dad, and I had sat and entertained her in the hospital for days after her knee surgery. I could talk to her about anything, and I knew she would never judge me. She gives great advice, and is always the first to welcome a new stranger into our circle of friends. The girl is almost too perfect.

"Don't be hating Mony," I laughed. (Mony is the nickname I've been calling her since grade school.

It's after the Mona Lisa. Mona Alicia..get it?) "You know you're just jelly, because this hat is one of a kind and you don't have one."

"One of a kind?" she laughed. "Claire! There are a

million sailor hats out there! In this military town, I'm sure I could dig one up if I tried."

I laughed and threw my furry, white decorative pillow at her. "I can't help it! I love this hat! It's my signature style."

Alicia caught the pillow with ease, and chucked it on my perfectly made bed. I'm a neat freak and can't stand to have a messy room. To make matters worse, I'm pretty sure I have OCD and all my clothes are arranged by color, as are my shoes. It's my blessing and curse at the same time.

"Well, are you ready to go?" I asked Alicia, as I tried to nonchalantly straighten my pillow she threw on my bed.

"Let's go neat freak!" she said grabbing my hand and leading me out the door.

I kissed my mom goodnight, as she reminded me of my 11 p.m. curfew. I wouldn't have been home late anyway, because Alicia had to be home by 10:30.

Alicia and I headed out into the humid Tennessee evening. It was almost 6:30, and still 84 degrees out. We had about three and a half hours until we had to get back in.

"So where are we going?" Alicia asked as her little red Nissan roared to life.

"Hmmm..." I said lifting my right hand pointing to the road ahead of us. "Let's just drive, and let the night take us where it wants to."

Alicia rolled her eyes, laughing. "You're such a drama queen, Claire."

I opened the moonroof, and cranked up Michael Buble on my playlist as we headed out of my neighborhood. Nights with Alicia were some of my favorites, and I knew all too soon they would be gone.

We cruised down the big hill that led into the city of Clarksville. The lights coming up over the river were beautiful.

"Clairey, (her nickname for me) we need boyfriends. We're 17 years old, and neither of us have ever been on a date."

"Alicia, don't start with that again," I giggled. "Unless you want to date someone at school, I don't know what to tell you. And what about Jason? You guys had something going on."

"Me having a crush on him since 5th grade is hardly something going on. Plus he's headed to UT next month, and I will pretty much never see him again. And what about you? You almost had your first kiss with Joey Ragoza in 9th grade."

"Yeah," I sighed looking off into space and remembering that 9th grade dance. "He was so adorable. I know he would have followed through if I didn't have that big piece of cilantro stuck on my front tooth."

Alicia and I laughed so hard, that she almost swerved off the road in our hysteria. We finally calmed down, and she continued on.

"But anyways, look at us. We live in a town that has a major university, an army base, and 5 high schools," she argued. "There has to be something wrong with us. We've never even kissed a guy."

"Something wrong with us as in we're ugly?" I asked.

"No, I'm not saying we're ugly," she laughed, then looked at me concerned. "Why, do you think we're ugly?"

"Mony, it was a joke," I said rolling my eyes and smiling.

We spent the next hour cruising up and down Riverside Drive, singing and playing our music as loud as we could. There were so many people out, that at some points the traffic crept along. I was busy yapping about our upcoming basketball season, when I noticed Alicia's attention focused beyond me at the fairgrounds in the valley below.

"Clairey, look at all the cars down there," she said wide eyed.

I followed her gaze past me to what had caught her attention."Ahh, you mean the meat market?"

"Seriously?" she laughed. "I heard Jason hangs out there. Wanna go check it out?"

"You really think we're gonna find Jason in all of that?"

"It's worth a try," she shrugged.

"That's totally fine with me," I smirked, "but lock your doors."

I turned down the radio as we took a quick right turn into the fairgrounds. Every weekend night, some of our friends, along with half the population of under 21's hung out there. Alicia and I had never been, because we were usually busy with our basketball team, or we had to work. Plus our moms had casually warned us to stay away. I don't know what they had heard about the fairgrounds at night, but it obviously wasn't good. Anyway, they had never said we couldn't go, they just said they would prefer us not to go, so it's not like we were completely disobeying.

Inside the fairgrounds, we followed the long stream of cars into the circle 8. The circle 8 is basically a road shaped into a big 8. It spans the whole fairgrounds, and is at least two miles long. I had never been there at night, just in the day for picnics, rodeos, fishing on the river, and once a year when the fair comes to town. It looked so different at night.

As Alicia and I drove through, I couldn't believe how many people were there. All of them hanging out on their cars and overflowing into the street, making traffic come to almost a standstill. Different kinds of music came blaring from all the cars parked on the side of the road, that had their bumpers backed up to the Circle 8. College students hung out on one end, high school students on the other, and soldiers were basically all over the place.

"Oh my goodness Alicia, have you ever seen so many people? We are never going to find Jason in this crowd."

Alicia shrugged, her eyes big, intently watching the traffic in front of her, and the crowd of people all around. She suddenly gasped, and slammed on her brakes. I looked up to see what startled her. A guy had stepped out in front of us. He smiled broadly into the car at me, and started doing some kind of a dance in the middle of the road. I don't know if I could even call it a dance. He pivoted to the left, and then back to the right. He obviously didn't have an inkling on how to dance, but I laughed at his failed attempt to.

He looked up at me, laughing too. I was glad he found himself funny.

"What the heck, Claire?" Alicia laughed. "Now that's a dork right there."

"He's so funny, Alicia. Bless his little dorky heart."

Alicia smiled as the adorable dork approached my side of the car. He leaned into the window and smiled. "Hey girls. How's it goin?"

"Fine," I smiled back, feeling myself shaking inside nervously. "Nice Dance."

"Oh, thank you! I made it up myself." He stuck his hand inside of the window to shake mine. "I'm Johnny."

"Nice to meet you," I smiled shyly shaking his hand. This is exactly why I'm 17, and have never been on a date. I have no game when it comes to guys.

I looked over at Alicia, who was turned and talking to Johnny's friends at her window. Other cars began to honk impatiently at us, and Johnny asked if we wanted to pull to the side.

"What do you think Alicia?" I almost whispered.

"I guess it's ok. They seem pretty harmless."

"Ok, well just for a few minutes," I said to her, and looked back over at him. "Ok. We'll pull over."

They directed us to the side of the road by their vehicles. Alicia continued to talk to the other two guys, while Johnny held my door open for me, taking my hand to help me out of the car.

"So, are you in the Navy?" he smiled. Good grief, his smile was beautiful. I know that some people don't believe this, but I can tell a lot about a guy from his smile. If it's genuine, and what kind of heart he has.

Side note- I can also tell a lot about a guy just from the shoes he wears and how they look on him. If he's active or lazy, goofy or serious, smart, or overall unorganized. I've said no to many guys, just because of what shoes they wear. Some people may call that shallow, but I've dodged many bullets by that method.

Johnny had a perfect pair of white Nikes on with khaki shorts, and a blue Hurley tee. His white baseball cap that he wore backwards, matched his Nikes. He definitely passed my shoe and smile test.

"No, I'm not in the Navy." I laughed. "I just like this hat."

"Oh yeah? Well, I think it's really cute."

"Thank you."

I was blushing so hard. Johnny's smile was killing me, as well as his bright green eyes and dark hair. I could feel myself breaking out in hives like I do when I get nervous or upset. I was so glad it was dark out except the car lights, and few street lights in the area.

"So, are you going to tell me your name?" he asked.

"I'm Claire."

"Claire. That's a pretty name. Are you in college?"

The dreaded question, because I could tell, even with his baby face, he wasn't in high school.

I cleared my throat. "No. I'm actually starting my Senior year in high school. Alicia and I both are," I said pointing back at Alicia, who was laughing loudly at the very handsome black guy who had her attention.

Johnny noticed me looking at his friend. "That's my buddy, Shawn. He's my barracks mate. We are both stationed at Ft. Campbell, and just got here a few months ago."

"Oh," is all I said. My mind was numb, and I couldn't think of anything else.

"So high school, huh?" He leaned against Alicia's car. "So that would make you...?"

"17. 18 in April." I sounded more sure of myself now.

"I'm 19," Johnny said. "but I've been 19 since last November."

"So you joined right out of high school?" I asked leaning on the car beside him. I was starting to feel more comfortable with him already.

"Yeah. I want to be a helicopter pilot, so basic took me a little longer."

My eyes lit up immediately when Johnny mentioned flying. "That's so cool! Chinooks fly over my house all the time."

"Well, maybe sometime I can take you out to the airfield, and let you get a close up of one."

"That would be great. Thank you!"

Talking to Johnny was so natural for me. He told me everything about himself that he possibly could, and I soaked it up like sponge. He was from Tampa, and spent most of his life on the ocean, where he excelled in windsurfing, and had actually won quite a few competitions. His parents were still together, and he had one older sister, Janey. His dad was retired from the Air Force, and his mom was a school teacher. For an 19 year old, it sounded like he had already lived an amazing life.

When Johnny asked about me, I did my best to sound just as interesting. He seemed genuinely sad when I told him about my dad, and laughed when I told him about my terrible basketball team.

“Maybe I can come cheer you on sometime,” he smiled.

“I would love that,” I smiled back. I couldn't stop smiling. My eyes started hurting from squinting with all the smiling.

Two hours later, we all sat together on the tailgate of Johnny’s truck, talking helicopters, and what there was to do around Clarksville. Alicia leaned over and whispered, “Claire, we should probably go. It's almost ten.”

“Already?” I sighed.

“You guys have to leave?” Johnny asked, his eyes slightly frowning.

“Yes. We still have curfews,” I cringed through my teeth.

“Ok,” he sighed, “but you can't leave here without

giving me your number."

I pulled my phone from my pocket, and Johnny Angel and I exchanged numbers.

"I'm calling you tomorrow, Claire," he smiled and opened my door, while Shawn opened Alicia's.

"Awesome," I said smiling up at him.

"Put your seat belt on," Johnny said authoritatively pointing down at my seat.

"Yes sir," I saluted Johnny with a wink as we pulled away.

"Alicia, don't forget to call me!" Shawn yelled after us.

"I'll think about it," Alicia teased as we headed out of the fairgrounds. "Did that really just happen?" she asked in disbelief.

"It definitely doesn't seem real," I said shaking my head. "Shawn seems like a nice guy."

Alicia was grinning uncontrollably. "He is so sweet, Clairey. He's from New York, and he's training to be a helicopter pilot."

"He's adorable Mony. Johnny said they are roommates."

"Johnny seemed like a sweetheart."

"You have no idea!" I gasped. "And you're not going to believe what his last name is. Angel. Johnny Angel."

She stared at me in disbelief.

"Seriously," I said laughing.

"Well, of course that would be his name." She smiled, "They all look like they fell out of heaven."

I rolled my eyes, and we laughed at the all too familiar pick up line.

TWO

I WOKE UP the next morning to the sun shining through my sheer white curtains, and the sound of my text dinging. I rolled over lazily wiping my eyes, expecting to open my phone to Alicia's usual, "Good Morning Dollface." To which I would always reply, "Good Morning Muffin Cakes," or some kind of sweet food. But it wasn't Alicia. It was Johnny. I stared at the phone trying to register his name in my sleepy head, and then all at once the events from last night flooded my mind. OH. MY. GOODNESS!

"Good Morning Claire. I hope this text isn't too early for you. I wanted to tell you how very glad I am that I met you last night and if it's not too soon, if I could see you again tonight. Maybe we could see a movie?"

I held the phone in my hand as if it were gold, not wanting to answer too quickly, and sound too desperate. But at the same time I didn't want him to think I was lazy, sleeping in too late. I pulled the covers over my head.

“Ok Claire,” I said to myself out loud. “If you text him back right now, you're going to seem too desperate. But if you wait, it's going to look like you're not very interested, and then he might make plans to do something else.”

“Text who back?” I heard Kassie's muffled voice from outside the covers.

“Kassie, don't you knock?”

“I heard you talking to someone when I walked by. What am I supposed to do, ignore you? Someone could have broke in for all I know.”

I sat up in bed, throwing back my perfectly white comforter.

“Sure Kass,” I teased her sarcastically, “that’s the first thing I would have thought of. Someone in my room at 10 am on a Saturday morning attacking me.” I grabbed my neck, plunging backwards into my pillows, making the most horrible choking noises I could.

Kassie sat down on my bed, hitting my legs on top of the comforter. “You're overly dramatic episodes are not going to distract me Claire. Who is texting you?”

“None of your business,” I said almost in a desperate whisper as I continued to choke myself. Alicia was right. I am dramatic.

“Oh, come on,” she pleaded. “I tell you all about my guy adventures.”

This was true. Kassie was so beautiful. She had many guys asking her out all the time, so she had many guy adventures. I'm pretty sure that since she turned 16 in April, the age we're allowed to date, she has been on at least 10 dates. The last guy Kyle, has kind of stuck, and they are a full month into dating now. Kyle is a junior like Kassie. He is also the star quarterback at our school, which is no easy feat for a Junior. He's completely sweet and adorable, and mom and I like him a lot.

"Ok," I said after pausing for a long moment, "but I'm not ready to tell mom yet, so please keep it quiet."

"I promise."

"So, Alicia and I went out last night and we met these two guys. They were so sweet, Kass."

Kassie sucked in a deep breath that turned into a small scream as it came out. "What's his name?! Where does he go to school?! Where did you meet them at?!" Her questions came tumbling out all at once, as she exhaled.

"Goodness!" I giggled. "Hang on a minute." I paused a moment and looked directly into her wide eyes. "The Fairgrounds."

"The Meat Market!" she exclaimed.

"Yes," I said slightly annoyed, "but don't tell mom. I want her to think I met him through friends or something, when I finally do decide to tell her. And he's not a meat market kind of guy, Kass."

"I don't think that Claire. It's just that you're so picky, and I definitely could have never imagined you meeting some random guy at the meat market...uh, I mean the fairgrounds."

"Me neither. But I don't know. I just have a good feeling about him."

"So, who is he?" she asked eagerly.

I spent the next half hour telling Kassie as much as I could possibly remember about Johnny. Every detail of how we first met with his little introductory dance episode, to where he was from, what he was interested in, and his job in the army. Her eyes lit up especially bright when I told her about his ambition to be helicopter pilot. Kass was just as excited as I was when they flew over.

"Well, what did he text you?"

"He wants to hang out tonight," I said as I got out of my bed, and began straightening my sheets as perfect as I could get them.

"Don't you have to work tonight?" she asked standing up and helping me as best as she could.

"Yeah. I thought about calling off, but I don't want to miss out on the money." Sonic Drive Inn on a Saturday night was crazy busy. I made in one Saturday night, what it would take me three weeknights to make.

I finished fluffing my pillows and placed each one in a perfect formation on my bed. Just as I put the last one in place, Kassie plunked back down on my bed and stretched her body across it, yawning as loud as she could.

"I know!" she said staring up at ceiling and throwing her hands up to further convince me of her idea. "Why don't you guys hit a late movie?"

I looked at the big wrinkle Kassie's body was making on my bed and tried to focus on her question, and not so much the fact that my bed was now a mess again.

"No way Kass! I don't want to go on my first date with him smelling like fried tater tots."

She was just about to argue her point with me when we heard a familiar thumping sound in the distance. Kassie and I glanced at each other, and then scrambled to throw on our flip flops. We ran outside just as 4 Chinooks appeared over the field to the south.

"There's four!" she yelled over the loud popping sound of the rotors.

The dust from the field began to swirl, as the tree limbs swayed downward and the ground shook underneath the massive, army green machines. I looked up as they flew overhead, feeling a tremendous amount of pride and patriotism. I wondered if Johnny was on board now, or if he had ever been on any of these Chinooks.

We watched them slowly disappear into the distance, until all you could see was four tiny little dots.

"So what was that you were saying about working tonight?" she teased. "Text him back now! That was a sign. At least let him know you're working."

"Fine," I smiled as we went back inside, and I grabbed my phone.

Saturday night at Sonic was just how I expected it to be. Almost every parking space was full of young people hanging out on the tops of their car hoods, and walking from one car to the next. Loud music blared from the outside speakers as Alicia and I, plus three more carhops, did our best to cover all 50 spots. By the time 8 o'clock rolled around, I was exhausted and trying not to sweat too much in the humid July air. I took a short break in the back store room to tie a loose lace on my white roller skates, pull up my 70's knee high socks, and squeeze my hair tighter in my ponytail.

"Clairey!"

The door flew open and Alicia rolled into the room, coming to a complete stop only when she hit the storage shelf in the back, almost knocking over a large jar of pickles. She had only learned to skate this summer out of desperation for wanting this job. I, on the other hand, could skate circles around the most seasoned pro, having perfected my skating abilities on the skating rink floor of Magic Wheels most of my middle school career. I worked so hard to teach Alicia how to skate to no avail. Alicia's lack of balancing skills had always been an issue with her in everything she does, thus prompting me to call her "Grace," any chance she gave me. And boy, did she give me a lot of chances.

"Whoa! Slow down there, Grace!"

"They're here," she mouthed out of breath, and hanging onto the shelf.

"Who?" I asked, but I instantly knew who she was talking about.

"The guys! Shawn, Johnny? Last night? Hello?!"

"What the...?!"

"I told Shawn where we worked," Alicia interrupted me, and then instantly covered her mouth.

"Mony!" I whined. "What did you do that for? Look at us! We're a mess!"

I rolled over to the only mirror in the room hanging on one of the lockers. My curly ponytail was frizzy with tiny tendrils of curls falling in my face. My red lip gloss was pretty much gone, and my eye liner had faded into a smokey dark smudge beneath my eyes. I quickly tried to pull myself together as Alicia nudged me over with her hips attempting to share the slim mirror with me.

"I thought you couldn't wait to see him again," she said wiping underneath her eyes. "Besides. We look hot!"

"Yeah, hot and sweaty. Not to mention the chili dog sauce on my shirt," I said pointing to the stain on my Sonic tee.

"Seriously! Quit whining! There are hot guys outside, and they are here to see us! This is a good thing."

Alicia grabbed my arm, and attempted to pull me out the door almost slipping. I, in turn, grabbed hers and guided her gently outside.

I saw them immediately, leaned casually up against Johnny's navy blue Ford F-150. Johnny cocked his head
sideways, his eyes lighting up when he saw me. I rolled over to him a little embarrassed by the way I looked.

"Nice wheels," he smiled.

I giggled. He was so funny.

I looked over to see Alicia trying to stand up as casually as she could beside Shawn. He held her arm trying to steady her.

"And...how did you get this job, girl?" he laughed. Shawn was so adorable. His smile was so big, and his skin a perfect dark mocha. He and Johnny oozed that charisma that few guys own, and for those that do own it, have a hard time not tipping it into the arrogant zone. Alicia had told me that Shawn was from New York, and his mom had practically forced him into the military to escape a group of friends headed down the wrong road. I could tell by the way he looked at Alicia, he was as smitten with her, as she was with him.

"Claire tried to teach me.." I heard her begin to explain.

"So, I'm sorry to just show up here," Johnny's smooth voice caught my attention again. "I know we we're planning to see each other tomorrow, but Shawn was coming to see Alicia anyway. Plus I just didn't want to wait another day."

I tried not to smile so big, but I couldn't help it. How could I be falling for someone in just one day?

"No, Johnny. It's totally fine. I'm so excited to see

you." I was blushing hard. Now he was the one smiling big.

"So what are we doing tomorrow?" I asked as I leaned up against the bumper of his truck.

"Well, I thought I would take you somewhere, but it's going to be a surprise."

My eyes lit up with excitement. "Really?" I squeaked through my big smile.

"Yes," he laughed. "But just us. Is that ok?"

"Oh yeah. That's definitely ok."

"Claire! Pick up!" Mr. Arnold, my manager, yelled from the window.

"I guess I better go." I gently grabbed his pinky finger without thinking about it.

"Ok. I'll text you tomorrow, Claire."

I flipped around giving him a quick salute and wink, like I did Friday night. I could tell he really liked that.

"Put your seatbelt on Private Angel," I teased and rolled away.

THREE

"SO TELL ME a little more about this fella, sweetie. And where are you guys going?"

My mom sat on the edge of my bed Sunday afternoon, as I combed a leave in conditioner in my hair to try and tame my curls from the humidity.

"Mom, you'll like him. He's so nice. I wouldn't be going out with him if he wasn't…and he's going to come in and meet you."

"Well, that's a start," she said meekly. "Where did you say you guys are going?"

"I didn't," I replied almost apologetically. "He said it's a surprise. But mom, seriously. He's a great guy. You don't have to worry."

"I trust your judgment Claire," she said gently placing her hand on mine. "I just want to make sure you're safe. It makes me so nervous with you girls. I don't know what I'd do if anything ever happened to one of you."

I looked at my mom sympathetically. I understood all the hurt that came wrapped up in that statement. I had heard it a thousand times since dad died. She held tight to us girls. I didn't want to ever hurt my mom, or to ever be a part of her hurting. She worked so hard for us, and deserved every happiness this life could offer. That's why I did my best to obey her, make my curfew on time, work to help pay bills, make good grades, and be the best example I could be for Kassie. I didn't want to add to her stress. It was so important to me that she liked Johnny too, for that very reason.

"I know mom. I promise it will be fine," I said giving her a hug. "He said he wants to come in and meet you. Trust me, as soon as you meet him, you'll know what I'm talking about."

Mom squeezed me back, and then looked at me inquisitively.

"So did he pass the shoe test?" she teased.

"Yes!" I laughed. "That's the first thing I noticed."

Mom giggled, and I heard Johnny's truck pull into the driveway.

"Claire!" Kassie yelled from the living room. Kyle was over hanging out with Kass, and I was grateful for that. I knew Kyle being there made my mom more comfortable too. Kyle was a towering 6'3, and she felt Kass and I were safer with him around. Kyle had picked up on my mom's hesitation for me going out with Johnny, and he promised her that he would "take care of Johnny," if he hurt me in any way. I just laughed him off, and rolled my eyes. What a Barney Fife.

I heard Kyle answer the door, and introduce himself to Johnny. Mom and I walked into the living room, and my tummy fluttered as soon as I saw him again. He was taller than I originally thought, coming pretty close to Kyle. He had to be at least 6'1. His shoulders seemed so broad under his black tee shirt, and he passed the shoe test again in his beach ready leather flip flops tucked neatly under his weathered jeans.

I looked over at Kassie who was staring at me with wide eyed approval.

Johnny confidently shook hands with everyone. He oozed confidence and kindness, which in my opinion is not an easy balance. He quickly made friends with Kass and Kyle, and I could tell they really liked him. Johnny was especially kind to my mom, and I saw the worry melt off her face immediately.

"You've got a great family," Johnny said as he opened the door to his truck, and helped me climb inside.

"Thanks. You definitely put my mom at ease."

"She's a sweet lady, Claire."

Johnny got in the truck beside me, and shut the door.

"So, I'm glad you dressed casual," he said, checking out my tank top, jeans, and chucks. I had put my hair up in a high bun to keep it out of the way. "We are going to be moving around a lot."

A half hour later Johnny pulled through the gates of Ft. Campbell. After a short security check at a second gate, we drove onto an airfield and up to a large hangar. I knew immediately where we were. I jumped out of the truck unable to contain my excitement, and ran around to open the door for him.

"Well, alrighty then! I thought you southern girls liked the door opened for you, but whatever makes you happy," Johnny laughed as he jumped down from his truck. "Are you ready to check out some Chinooks?"

"Absolutely!" I said grabbing his pinky finger. I pulled him toward the hangar, and he beamed in my excitement. "Are you sure it's ok for me to be here?"

"Oh yeah. We have visitors here all the time." Johnny slid back one of the tall hangar doors. I gasped when I saw two large Chinook helicopters sitting majestically in the sunlight that was pouring through the natural light windows in the ceiling.

"It's so different looking at them from the front, instead of underneath," I said in awe.

"They are pretty awesome," he agreed.

We walked around the helicopters as I checked out every part of them, from the wheels to the blades.

"Do you want to take a look inside?"

"Oh yes, please!"

Johnny lightly took my arm, and casually slid his hand down to mine. My heart pounded inside my chest, as his fingers very gently laced between each of mine. He didn't let go, and I didn't mind. Holding hands with him felt new and exciting, but very comfortable at the same time.

The next hour Johnny and I spent walking inside the helicopters, as he explained in precise detail all of the functions of the Chinook. He was so patient as I kept throwing questions at him. He took time with me, and answered every one.

"So how close are you from being able to fly one?" I asked, as we sat in the pilot seats of the Chinooks.

"Well, that's actually a lengthy process. I have to work my way up through the ranks, go to flight school. I have a lot of hurdles to jump, but I'll get there."

"Johnny, that's so wonderful. You're only 19, and you have such drive and direction."

"Thank you. It was easy for me. I love flying." He leaned over closer to me. "So what about you

Claire? Do you know what you want to do?"

I turned my attention away from the flight board. He was staring at me intently waiting for my answer. I took a deep breath feeling my neck turn instantly hot. I knew I was breaking out in my usual nervous hives.

"I'm probably going to school here at Austin Peay. I want to be a teacher. Second grade to be exact."

"I could definitely see you doing that," Johnny said, grabbing my hand with both of his, and gently squeezing my fingers. "You are one of the sweetest girls I have ever met."

Not that I'm a guy expert, but I pretty much knew what was coming next. At least it did in every romantic movie I had ever seen. He was holding my hand, leaned in close, and he complimented me. A kiss should have come next. But it didn't. He leaned back in his seat.

"So are you hungry?" he asked.

"Sure," I replied, biting my lip in frustration. It would have been so cool to have my first kiss in a Chinook.

He took my hand and led me out of the hanger. The sun was setting, and cast a bright glowing light all around us. Johnny opened the truck door, and helped me inside. I tried to not read too much into him not kissing me. After all, even though it seemed longer, I had only known him for two days. But just the same, after he shut my door I checked my smile for cilantro.

The next few weeks of my life leading up to school was so busy. I was balancing work, Johnny, my friends and family. I didn't know how I was going to manage when school started. At least I would only be working Saturdays then.

But I loved being with Johnny. I spent every moment I possibly could with him. We did everything from double dates with Alicia and Shawn, to movie nights with Kass and Kyle. He would come and hang out in his favorite parking spot at Sonic just to watch me roll by. I was really falling for him, and I could tell he felt the same about me.

On the Saturday before school started, I was looking forward to a big date with Johnny. We were going to Nashville for the night. Finally, I was going to get some time alone with him. For the last three dates we had been with either Shawn and Alicia, or Kyle and Kass. He had told me gently the last time that he wasn't trying to be rude, but he wanted to go out with just me this weekend. I was all for that.

I was in my room getting ready for our date when my text dinged. It was Johnny.

"Hey beautiful. I'm so sorry to do this to you, but I got stuck with guard duty at the last minute. The guy who was supposed to do it got sick, and I was next on the list."

I stared at my phone screen. This sucked so bad. My whole weekend was full. Sunday I was supposed to go shopping with Alicia before school started on Monday. Now I wasn't going to get to spend any time with him until next weekend.

"Hey Mr. Perfect. (My new nickname for him.) It's ok. I'm definitely disappointed, but I understand."

"Me too. But I was thinking, if you want to come hang out with me for a little while tonight, you can. I'm guarding the hangar."

"I would love that! Are you sure it's ok?"

"I'm pretty sure. No one ever said I couldn't have a visitor there. lol"

"OK. What time?"

"Is 6 ok?"

"Sure!"

"You will need to get a pass at the front gate to get on, but

you should be ok. Just have your ID and vehicle registration on you."

"Yes Sir!"

"See you soon."

Two hours later, I pulled my car into the back parking lot of the airfield. Johnny came out, and guided me to park behind a huge army truck on the side of the hangar. He would later tell me the truck was called a Cougar, and that he only had me park there to keep my car out of the way. I was so excited to see him. Every time I saw him, even if I had seen him the day before, my tummy fluttered in anticipation. And now he was helping me out of my car, looking so great in his uniform. I was going to spend the next hour with him walking the airfield and I couldn't wait. This was just as great as any date in Nashville to me.

"I'm so sorry about this," he apologized again. "I tried to get to out of it. No one would switch with me on such short notice."

"It's really ok. You know how much I enjoy being here."

Johnny and I walked the airfield as I chatted on about school, basketball, and how sad I was summer break was over. I listened to him tell me about his week at work, as we walked through rows of airplanes. He checked each one to make sure the doors were locked. I was so impressed with his thoroughness. He was so responsible.

"That sky is looking pretty dark over there," he

nodded toward the west as we rounded the last row of airplanes. I followed his glare to a mountain of dark clouds rolling toward us.

"So how long do you have to stay here?" I asked as we headed quickly toward the hangar. "I didn't see anyone else out here."

"Well, hopefully I'll be done at midnight. That's when the next guy shows up."

We approached the hangar as thunder rumbled the sky in the distance. Johnny suddenly grabbed my hand tightly, and turned me towards him. I looked at his green eyes that flashed with intensity. My hand hurt in his strong grasp. Was he finally going to kiss me? It had been almost a month now.

"Claire, there is a large storage closet in the back left side of the hangar across from the bathrooms. I want you to go there, and don't come out until I tell you, ok?"

"Johnny?" I questioned him nervously. The sound of a loud engine interrupted my question. I looked behind me in the distance to see two headlights from a humvee quickly approaching the airfield.

They were far enough away they couldn't have possibly seen me, but I went inside the hangar and found the large closet, just as Johnny had instructed me to do.

I opened the door to the dark closet that was about the size of my living room, and walked inside quietly shutting it behind me. Obviously it wasn't ok to be here. Lightning flashed through the sky light, and in the short moment of light I saw a wooden crate in the corner I could sit on. My hands guided me in the direction of the crate, fumbling over beams in the unfinished wall.

Then it happened. The moment that changed my life forever.

I turned to lower myself down, and felt my left foot slip from beneath me. Falling back I crashed into the crate. The sound of wood cracking and glass breaking enveloped me. A sharp stinging pain shot through my left arm and very quickly after, a burning sensation. A strong metallic smell filled the air and I gagged slightly. Frozen for a moment on the cold cement floor, I was more terrified of whoever it was with Johnny outside hearing me, than whatever the extent of my injuries were. I remained still and quiet for what seemed like an eternity. At last the door handle rattled and slowly opened.

"Claire?" I heard Johnny's soft voice, and the click of a light switch. Fluorescent lights filled the room and I looked around me to see a vibrant pink liquid covering my left arm and leg, with thin slivers of glass on the floor. Blood tinted the pink substance covering a slice in my arm right above my wrist.

Catching my breath, I tried to explain what happened to Johnny. "Umm...the crate broke. I was just going to sit on it. I didn't realize how old it was." I grabbed my arm that was burning more intensely now.

"Oh man, Beautiful. Let me see." Johnny knelt beside me, and gently inspected my arm. "Well, it doesn't look very deep. I just need to get this liquid cleaned off you. Whatever it is."

"It looks like Pepto Bismol," I tried joking to hide my fear.

Johnny smiled and lifted me off the floor. We went across the hall to the bathroom where he soaked my arm under the running water until all traces of pink were gone. He left and returned quickly with a First Aid kit.

"So, who were they?" I asked as he bandaged me up.

"It was my Sergeant. He forgot some paperwork he needed for tomorrow. I mean, I think it's fine you being here, but I just thought it wouldn't be a good idea to surprise him."

I looked down at my arm that he had so professionally wrapped up. The pain was not as intense now, but throbbed lightly.

"I hope you don't get in trouble for whatever it was in there that I broke."

"Oh, no way," he assured me. "All that stuff is so old. It's from the Gulf War, I think. We are actually scheduled to do a clean up this week of all the storage rooms here."

I looked around at the blood and bandage wrappers everywhere. It had taken a bit to get the bleeding stopped. "Well, at least let me help you clean up my mess."

"Not with that arm, Missy," Johnny laughed and lifted me off the sink that he had turned into a patient table. "I have at least four hours here, so I'll need something to do until this storm passes over."

I walked with Johnny to the door of the hangar trying to hide my feeling of lightheadedness. The storm had pretty much passed, though I could still hear the light sound of raindrops on the metal roof. Johnny popped up an umbrella to walk me to my car.

"Thanks for cleaning me up," I said slightly embarrassed. "I'm so sorry."

Johnny laughed. "At least you're not boring."

I giggled, and turned to open the office door that led outside.

"Just a minute Claire." Johnny lightly grabbed my good arm. "Before you go..." I felt his left arm slide around my waist, and pull me in closer to him. I looked up at the height difference between my 5'3 and his 6'0. "Is this ok?" he whispered.

"Definitely," was all I could get out, as I tried to catch my breath.

Johnny leaned down and softly touched his lips to mine. I moved my right hand slowly over his arm tracing every muscle, all the way up to his shoulder, lightly resting my hand on the back of his neck. He pulled me even closer careful not to bump my bandage, but by this time I couldn't feel anything but his lips on mine anyway. Every wonderful thing I had imagined about my first kiss happened in that moment. All my worries of messing it up never happened, because kissing Johnny came so natural for me. At last he pulled away, almost setting me on the ground.

"I've been wanting to do that since the first day I saw you, Claire."

"Goodness. What took so long?" I softly teased him. "I thought there was something wrong with me."

"It was your first one. I didn't want to rush you, and I wanted it to be special."

"It was perfect mister. Thank you."

I drove home, unable to think about anything except Johnny's perfect kiss. I went to bed and had almost forgot about my arm, except for the weird dream I had. Have you ever had a dream that felt so real that you actually feel your body experiencing it? That night, I did. I dreamed my arm was glowing a bright pink, just like the stuff that was on it. I felt my body rising off my bed, and then woke suddenly as my body hit the mattress. I sat up straight in the bed sweating profusely. I went to the bathroom to dry myself off, and change my jammies.

After splashing cold water on my face, I looked down at my arm that was throbbing lightly again. I pulled the bandage back slightly, and gasped at the goriness of my scar. It was deep with white, almost pinkish puss oozing from it. I gagged slightly re-sticking the bandage back on the best I could. I was definitely keeping this one from my mom. She would have me at the ER for sure, and I didn't feel like spending my whole Sunday there.

FOUR

SUNDAY AFTERNOON ALICIA and I sat outside the mall at a cafe talking, exhausted from two hours of shopping.

"So, you fell on a crate and cut your arm?"

"Yes, but it feels fine now. I was thinking I might need stitches, but Johnny said I don't."

"Clairey, let me see."

"No Mony. It's really gross. I peeked at it this morning and it's scabby and oozy."

"Did you show your mom?"

"No way. And give her something else to worry about?"

She looked at me frowning. "Oozy and scabby are not good adjectives for a wound. Let me see it Claire."

"Alicia..."

"Now." She lightly slammed her hand down on the table.

I rolled my eyes sighing and put my arm on the

table, slowly pulling off the bandage. “Only so you'll stop talking about it.”

I unrolled the bandage waiting for the pain of unsticking it from the wound. Down at the last layer, I cringed in anticipation of the burn. Alicia leaned over the table looking earnestly at my arm waiting for the gross spectacle. She loved stuff like this. She wanted to be a nurse, so this was right up her alley.

“Get ready for the gore show,” I warned her.

“Good thing we already ate,” she giggled.

I pulled the final layer of bandage off, and we both stared down at my arm. It was very quiet for a moment despite the busy cafe around us. I looked up slowly at my bewildered friend.

“Is this some kind of joke?” she almost whispered.

“No,” I said trying to catch my breath.

“I thought you said you cut it. You didn't tell me you got a tattoo! Your mom is going to kill you!”

My eyes grew wider, as I stretched both arms out in front of me. My arm, still wrinkled from the bandage, now showed a dark, faded symbol just above my wrist where my wound should have been. The best way I can describe it, is as faded rings that looked like they belonged around Saturn. Mixed in the rings were bright pink streaks, almost like shooting stars. It looked so old and faded, like it had been on my body longer than I had been alive. Not one trace on my skin, indicated that I had even been cut.

I paused for a moment not knowing what to tell Alicia. What did it matter now anyway? There was no way I could even begin to try and explain it to her. Not knowing what to do, and with panic setting in, I lied to her.

"Sur..surprise. It...it was a joke," I stuttered. I was a terrible liar. "I got the tattoo last night and...I'm not ready to tell my mom so I thought I would try it out on you. I would try lying and see if I could get away with it."

"That makes absolutely no sense," she said folding her arms and sitting back in the chair in a huff.

"I know. It was so stupid of me. I'm...I'm sorry." At least I wasn't lying about that.

"That tat doesn't even make sense Claire. What does it mean?"

I paused again looking down at my arm. She was definitely going to know I was lying now.

"Well....you know how much I love the sky."

Alicia stared at me like she wanted to be agitated, but my answer made her laugh. "Good luck with explaining that to your mom, dummy," she teased.

I laughed in relief. Thank God that was the end of that. Alicia's phone dinged with an obvious text from Shawn. Her face lit up in excitement.

"Are you ready? Shawn's coming over to watch a movie this afternoon," Alicia said standing up and grabbing her mountainous pile of shopping bags.

I nodded my head looking over my arm. My outside facial expression smiled, but I felt every inside muscle of my face frowning in worry. My arm healing so fast made no logical sense, and even worse, how was I going to explain a Saturn ring tattoo to my mom? What was going on with me?

My mom, Kass, Kyle, and I, sat at the dinner table that evening. Mom had made her famous pork chops and potato salad, my favorite, but I wasn't hungry at all. I managed to cover my new body addition with some old makeup I had from 10th grade, that was two shades too dark for me. So far so good. I made sure I kept my arm under the table.

"Mom," I chimed in after Kyle had stopped talking about the football game that was coming on soon, "I think I'm going out for a run before it starts to get dark."

"Claire, I don't know. We only have about an hour of light left," she said.

"But, I'm only going for 45 minutes. I promise I'll be back before then."

Mom stared at me and finally consented. "Ok baby, but go now. If you're not back in an hour I will come looking for you."

"Ok! Thanks Mom," I said jumping from the table. I already had my running gear on in anticipation of going.

"Ohhh Claire," Kass reminded me with her sing-song voice, "Don't forget, it's your turn to do dishes."

"I know," I sighed, although I had forgot. Kissing my mom on the forehead, I headed out into the warm evening sunshine. This was my favorite time of day to run. I had just enough time to get past the business district, through my favorite Victorian neighborhood (that was filled with beautiful 100 year old houses), and back through the tree line to home just before the sun set. My routine was always the same; I started out in a slow pace that I would work into a quick jog, and towards the end slow down with a power walk. I had been into running since my dad had passed. Running has been therapy for me. It has helped me to not focus on the feelings of depression and anxiety I've felt since I lost him. I don't know what I would do without it. Being outside, under the big blue canopy of clouds and open sky, helps clear my head, focus on the positives in my life, and reminds me that there are so many great things in life to look forward to. At the grievance group Kass and I had attended together, I was able to share my story of how I've managed to get past the bitterness and anxiety through exercising. I believe without running, I would be a very depressed 17 year old.

I cleared the tree line and ran out of neighborhood towards the business district. I loved running the sidewalks and passing the old buildings that were so rich in turn of the century architecture. Some of the buildings still had etched in stone the businesses they held over 100 years ago. My favorite was the old bank that was now a hair salon. They had turned the vault into a manicure section, and the building fascinated me. I imagined what it must have been like for the people who lived in the Victorian neighborhood just to the east, to walk downtown on a Sunday afternoon like this one for shopping or tea.

Quickly picking up my pace, I made my way through the streets of the antique neighborhood, where some of the four way stops still had the original cobblestone streets. Breathing in the smell of fresh cut grass, I decided to add a few more streets to my run. It was so beautiful tonight and I wasn't ready to go home yet. Each house held its own personality, but by far my favorite was the large gray house with the white trim at the end of the street. Surrounded by ancient oak trees, this house had a large gathering porch with a white wicker swing, that looked so inviting every time I passed. If I ever got enough money and could design my own house, that's the kind of house I would build.

Circling the block, I headed towards home and with that came all the reality of life in this century. I looked down at my arm worried about the strange mark that was now showing through after my humid run. It looked very healthy and still showed no signs of having been injured.

The sun set sooner than I thought and by the time I reached the business district it had gone down completely. I slowed my run to a power walk and headed to the deserted gravel road that would lead me to the tree line and into my neighborhood.

The gravel road stretched out isolated and dark before me. I wish I had paid more attention to the time, and had left a little sooner. My tummy fluttered, and for some reason I felt really uneasy. I removed my ear buds and listened to the sounds around me. Crickets were buzzing, and somewhere in the distance I could hear an owl's deep hooting, to add to the creepiness I felt. And then I heard something new. The crunching of gravel footsteps on the road, that did not match my own. My heart pounded in my chest, and I felt my breath deepen in the terror of the moment. I glanced over my shoulder, trying not to be obvious, and saw two scruffy looking men walking behind me. They both smiled snidely at me, and the taller one glanced behind him, as if he were making sure no one was around. And no one was around. I was still a ways from the treeline, and no one would hear me scream if they tried to grab me.

"Hey, come here," one of the scruffy voices said.

"We just want to talk to you. We uhh….lost our puppy," laughed the other.

A thousand thoughts flashed through my mind in a panic, as to what I should do in that moment. Then I remembered the hole in the fence that separated my neighborhood from the gravel road. If I could just get to that hole, I could get through it to safety. There was no way they would fit.

Without a second thought, I bolted toward the fence. Running as fast and as hard as I could to the tree line. I glanced over my shoulder again to see the two men chasing after me. They were so fast and before I knew it, they were right behind me. I turned again and set my sights on the fence. Just 100 feet away. Putting my head forward I moved my legs as fast as they would go.

Then something incredible happened. I'll try my best describe it, but I don't even know how to put it into words. Something strong clutched the inside of my chest, and yanked me from the ground. I was still running, but my feet no longer felt the earth beneath them. Up and up, higher and higher, I went above the towering trees. My arms and legs flailed, unsure of what to do or how to respond to the lack of gravity on them. I looked down behind me to see the scruffy men frozen, their mouths opened, and their eyes wide watching me until I disappeared over the trees.

"Oh my God! God please help me!" I screamed, but no sound came out. Flapping my arms hysterically, I tried to push myself to the ground to no avail. Over the rooftops of my neighborhood I soared, scared I was going to go higher, but stayed at a steady height of about 300 feet.

Unable to control my balance I flipped upside down and hung in the dark sky, finally coming to a stop high above my neighborhood. Flying in the air is terrifying enough, but hanging upside down looking at the tiny trees and houses below, is heart stopping. Something felt as if it were holding onto my ankles for a moment, then it was gone. I plunged toward the earth.

I screamed the first five seconds of the freefall, before coming to my senses. "Come on Claire! Turn yourself upright!" At least if I didn't fall head first, I might have some chance at surviving. I pulled my legs to my chest and tried to make myself bottom heavy. For some reason this helped, and my plunge drastically slowed down.

My eyes scanned the ground looking for a tree or something that could break my fall. The moon cast a bright glow over the neighborhood, and my eyes caught a sliver of something that looked like a diamond in the night. The Ellis house was lit up below and their backyard swimming pool was sparkling in the moonlight. I set my sights on the pool and despite my best efforts of slowing down, I cannonballed hard into the cold water, and straight to the bottom. My tushy hit the cement pool floor and I pushed myself up to the surface just as I ran out of breath.

Somehow, I made it! I was still alive!

Gasping, I swam to the side of the pool, and grabbed onto the ladder, my body shaking, terrified of losing gravity again. The water around me glowed a dull pink, and I looked down to see the specks of pink glowing on my Saturn rings. I rubbed my arm trying to get them to stop, to no avail. I clasped my hand over the tattoo as best as I could. What the heck?

Inside the Ellis house their Collie, Gus, barked and scratched at the door. The patio light came on and I heard the sliding door smoothly glide open.

"Gus! Quiet!" Mr. Ellis scolded him as he walked outside to investigate. I pushed myself up against the pool wall and under the ladder as much as I could. He walked around for minute and checked the large wooden gate to make sure it was locked, then headed back inside. "Nothin, but a cat again boy," he complained as the door slid shut and clicked locked.

I sat in the pool, scared to stay, but even more afraid to get out. What was that? Would it happen again? Next time I might not be so lucky and may end up in space somewhere. At last I climbed the ladder out of the water and made my way to the gate grabbing as many bolted down items that I could.

Once I was in the front yard, I went to the road and stood by a small tree holding onto it for dear life. My body shook in fear, and I looked up into the star filled sky afraid of whatever it was coming back again and sending me hurling into space this time. I didn't want to let go of the tree, but I had to get home.

I decided to try and get to the next oak tree by the stop sign. Starting out in a quick, soggy jog, I kept my eye on objects that could keep me on the ground and I could hold onto, should I lose gravity again. First a tree, then a stop sign, another tree, a fire hydrant. My eyes searched the diamond sky for any sign of the mysterious force that had taken over me. It was not easy running in my soaked sneakers that squeezed out water with every sloshy step.

Twenty minutes later I arrived at home soaked, exhausted, and dreading the barrage of questions I knew I had coming.

By the time I reached my house the weird tattoo thing had stopped glowing. I heard the football game on in the family room, as Kass and Kyle cheered loudly for the Tennessee Titans. My mom was in the kitchen and yelled at me through the door. "Claire is that you?"

"Yes Ma'am."

Mom peeked her head out the kitchen door, her glare turning from agitation to concern. She gasped at the sight of me. "Look at you! You are a sweaty mess." She leaned back as if to get a better view of me. "Are you ok Sweetheart? You look like you've seen a ghost."

"I know," I said, fidgeting with the bottom of my shirt like I always did when I was nervous. "Ummmm...it was so hot out there. I think the heat just got to me."

"Well, you should probably get in the shower, stinky girl," she said walking over and kissing my forehead. "I was just on my way out to find you, you know."

What was this? No fifth degree? I laughed nervously, and quickly headed to the bathroom for a shower, afraid it might occur to her to suddenly ask a lot of questions.

Inside the shower, I let the warm water calm me down as I grabbed soap and tried to scrub the Saturn rings off my arm again with no luck. They were only the size of a half dollar but still very noticeable, and I could tell they were permanently etched in my skin. I thought back to last night and the pink liquid that had burned into my cut. This had to have something to do with my flying episode.

At 9 pm my text dinged. I knew it was Johnny sending me his ritual good night.

"Hey Beautiful. How was shopping today?"

"It was fun. Alicia and I spent way too much money. Lol"

"Is your arm doing ok? I've been worried about it all day."

"Yes, it's fine. It's actually healed up really well."

"Great. It looked pretty bad last night. I thought for a minute there you were going to need a few stitches."

"Me too. Johnny, I'm just curious, did you ever figure out what that pink stuff was?"

"No. I did see on the crate that it was from my Brigade. And also a name, Kearney. Why, are you having a bad reaction to it?"

"No. I was just wondering. Do you know anyone named Kearney?"

"No, he served in the Gulf War, so I'm sure he's long since retired or he's stationed somewhere else."

"Ok. I was just curious."

"Are you sure you're ok?"

"Definitely."

"I'm so sorry that happened to you Claire. I was thinking about it all day today and I shouldn't have sent you into that dark closet alone. I feel like a jerk."

"Honestly, Johnny. It's fine. You made up for it with the world's best kiss ever."

"Same for you! I felt like I was floating all day."

(Oh the irony.)

"That's pretty much how I felt."

"I hope the first day of your Senior year is a great one."

"Thanks Mr. Perfect. Sweet dreams."

"You too, Claire Bear."

FIVE

I LAY IN bed most of the night unable to sleep. Fearing I would float out of my bed, I tied my wrist to the bedpost with my belt. I shuddered as I played the day over again in my mind, still feeling the clutch of powerin my chest, and the jolt of my body being pulled from the ground.

Maybe it was some kind of spirit taking over my body. Maybe I've been given superpowers from my dad who was looking out for me. Every possible scenario ran through my mind, but nothing made sense.

The last I glanced at the clock it was 4:20. I made up my mind to try and get back into the hangar, and figure out what was in the box. I was sure the crate I broke, and it's remnants were completely gone, but perhaps there was another one around full of the same thing. By the time I finally fell asleep, I had a plan to go back to Ft. Campbell for a major snooping job.

Monday morning Kassie and I pulled into the school parking lot, ready for the first day. I was running on three hours of sleep, but the adrenaline from last night had me wide awake. I felt like I had slept all night and then some. I paused after putting the car in park, a little scared to get out. Kassie was talking about her classes and something about football. I looked over at the door entrance trying to calculate how quickly I could get in the building. I was so terrified of being shot into the air again.

"Claire, are you ok?"

"Yes, Kass. You've asked me that like 10 times already," I laughed trying to sound nonchalant.

"Well, I'm sorry, but you're just acting so weird." Kass grabbed her book bag and got out of the car. She walked around to the front waiting for me. "Claire, come on!"

I reluctantly took the keys out of the ignition, and grabbed my backpack. My body felt ten pounds heavier as I pulled myself from the car, and slowly walked across the pavement. Kass skeptically watched my every move. Maybe I should have stayed home today.

We walked up to the school, and my tummy fluttered nervously. Now I felt like everyone was watching me. One step at a time, slow and steadily. My thoughts raced again. What if I rocketed in the air, right here in front of everybody? I would be labeled some crazy freak and they would institutionalize me. I would be locked in a hospital and studied like some kind of science experiment, and that would be only if I survived the fall. Last night I was so lucky to land in a pool.

"Claire! Kass!" I looked over to see Alicia and our friend Lexi, hanging out by the courtyard beside the front entrance.

"Hey Mony! Hey Lexi!" I said walking over and sitting beside them on the bench. I tucked my hand under the seat and held on for dear life.

"So Claire, Lexi wants us to set her up with one of Johnny and Shawn's friends," Alicia laughed.

"Oh really?" I smiled. Lexi had just moved from California over the summer, and we had met her in our church youth group. Alicia and I had taken her under our wings, although I didn't think she would need much help in the guy department. Lexi was a cute little typical California blonde, barely 5 foot. Definitely a head turner.

"You make me sound so desperate, Mony!" She laughed. I loved it that she called Alicia, Mony too. I could tell she was getting a lot more comfortable with us. "I am kicking myself for not going with you guys that night."

"Lexi, you were at Disneyland. There's no place, or no one better than that."

Lexi flipped her long ponytail back and leaned

closer to me. "I don't know about that. Alicia can't stop talking about Shawn, and she said Johnny is just as hot."

"He is pretty great Lexi," Kass chimed in. "Kyle really likes him too."

"Awww!" Lexi sighed. "You guys definitely need to introduce me to one of their friends! The pickings around here are pretty slim." Lexi slid her arm through Kass'. "Well, except for Kyle of course."

The bell rang and everyone grabbed their backpacks. I eyed the front door, and threw my backpack over my shoulder before letting go of the bench. I looked for a clearing and shot through the crowd to the safety of the building. At least if I went airborne in here, it would only be to the ceiling.

My heart raced as I entered my first class, in fear of what the day might bring. I did my best to concentrate on my class, but I couldn't take my attention off my new tattoo and last night.

As the day progressed I began to feel a little more confident about not taking off through the roof of the building. Who knows? Maybe it was just a one time event. After school I met Alicia in the gym for basketball practice. Our coach invited us to start warming up before the season started. We needed all the practice we could possibly get in.

At point guard, I had the responsibility of calling all

the plays, and this year I would co-captain the team with Alicia. After warm ups we set up for a practice game, so that I could get used to calling plays.

Running down the court I yelled out my favorite play. "Tennessee!" All the offense spread out while Alicia ran from her center position to set a pick for me. I ran around her, and dribbled towards the basket. The image of me flying flashed across my mind, and I had barely passed the the free throw line when I felt my chest tighten up. Oh God, no. Not again. My feet left the free throw line, and I began to soar towards the basket. Once again my arms flailed, and my legs continued to run in the air. Somehow I managed to keep the ball in my hand, and I almost slammed into the basket. Grabbing the rim, I let go of the ball and it bounced off the backboard and into the net. I hung onto the rim afraid of letting go, and flying into the rafters. The gym grew deathly silent as the ball bounced loudly on the gym floor, eventually rolling to a stop by the locker rooms.

"Claire?" I heard Coach Alexander call calmly from the sideline. I turned my head around and looked down toward his direction. The 12 wide eyed faces of my teammates were staring up at me in bewilderment.

I whispered to myself, "Alright Claire. Let go of the net and drop softly to the floor." This was it. Either I was going to fall to the ground or be floating in the rafters. I slowly let my fingers slip off one at a time and felt gravity gently pull me to the gym floor.

"What the heck Claire?" Tina, one of the tallest

forwards asked. "You looked like frickin Michael Jordan."

I paused for a moment fidgeting with the bottom of my shirt, and saw Alicia notice my nervous habit immediately. "It must be all the leg squats and skating I did over the summer," I tried to explain with my voice croaking nervously. "And I....I encourage all you girls to do the same. It really makes a difference." Again silence and lots of stares.

"Well," Coach Alexander finally interrupted clapping his hands together nervously, "Ummm...with that, we'll call it quits for the day. Don't forget tomorrow you need to bring your shoe money if you plan on ordering your game shoes with us."

Everyone turned and walked towards the locker room whispering to each other, with a few looking back at me. Coach Alexander patted me on the back. I could tell he was unsure of what to say. "Keep up the good work, Claire."

"Thanks coach," I murmured as he grabbed his clipboard and left towards the athletic office.

Alicia and I stood there, her stare cutting deep inside me. I raised my eyebrows nervously at her biting on my lip.

"Well?" she finally asked.

"I don't know," I shrugged. "It must be all the skating."

"Claire, you went from here, to here!" She pointed from the free throw corner, to the basket to emphasize her point. "Through the air!"

"I honestly think it was just all the adrenaline. Plus I've been eating extra healthy." I shrugged. I wasn't about to tell anyone anything at this point! Not even Alicia. She wouldn't believe me anyway.

"Well, whatever it is you're eating, you need to share it with me. I don't know if you noticed, but we suck worse this year." She put her arm around me as we headed to the locker room.

"Oh, I noticed," I laughed, thankful she dropped the subject at least for now.

Tuesday was a stormy day, both outside and inside my head. I didn't want to go to school. I faked a tummy ache and stayed home afraid of dealing with what happened on Monday. I didn't want to leave my house, or my bed for that matter. I was terrified of what was happening to me.

By lunch time I was getting texts from Alicia wanting to know if I was ok. I did something I never do. I ignored her. Later that afternoon my phone busily dinged with texts from Johnny. I didn't answer him either. I didn't want to talk to anyone. I layed in my bed most of the day, listening to the thunder, and the rain pounding on my bedroom window.

Kass came home from school and mom came home from work that afternoon. I stayed in bed still. I wasn't hungry. Depression set in more as the day wore on. All I could think about was the accident. The few times I fell asleep, I dreamed about the scruffy guys chasing and catching me.

Mom came in when she got home to check on me. “Claire, are you sure you're ok?” she asked

feeling my forehead. “You don't feel like you have a fever.”

“Seriously, mom. I'm fine. There's a bad flu bug going around at school. I probably caught that,” I lied again. I had been lying a lot lately, and I hated lying. Especially to my mom.

I managed to talk her into letting me stay home again on Wednesday and Thursday. The flu excuse helped keep everyone away and bought me time alone.

Wednesday evening I sat on my bed in my favorite tee and sweats with my hair piled high on my head, trying to catch up on school work Kass had brought home. There was a light tapping on my door and Kass opened it gently.

“Claire, can I come in?”

“Sure Kass, but just don't get too close.”

She didn't listen, but instead sat on the edge of my bed.

“I don't know what's going on with you Clairey, but I know you're not sick. I think I know you better than that.”

I looked down at my laptop unable to look in her eyes.

She slid closer to me and gently grabbed my hand. “I just want you to know that no matter what you're going through, big or small, I'm here if you need to talk. I would like to think I'm a pretty good listener, and non-judgemental."

I sat quietly for a moment trying to decide if I should tell her or not. I tell my sister everything. I can't think of one secret I've ever had that she didn't know about. I thought about how hurt she would be to know that I kept something so big from her. I know I would if she kept it from me. But this didn't feel like the right moment. There was so much about it all that I was still trying to figure out. When I could work through it a little more, I would definitely tell her.

"Thank you, Kass," I said quietly. "You know I tell you everything. I promise you, when the time is right I will tell you."

Kass smiled slightly. "I understand. I know you will."

"You know I don't like keeping secrets from you, right?"

"I know." She squeezed my hand and then held up her phone. "So, Johnny's been texting me. He's worried about you."

"I know. He's been texting me too. I'm going to text him tomorrow."

"Claire, I don't want you to mess up a good thing in your life. Johnny is definitely a good thing."

I didn't say anything, but nodded in agreement with her. She moved closer and gave me a tight hug, then walked towards the door.

"Kass," I called to her as she opened the door. "I promise. When the time is right."

"Ok." She smiled and closed the door.

SIX

LITTLE DID I know while I was sulking in my new superhero capabilities, at Ft. Campbell, Johnny was called to his Majors' office. Major Silva was a no nonsense man with a deep crease between his eyes from all of the hard glares he shot at everyone. His thick Spanish accent echoed loudly and commanded attention, no matter where he was.

Johnny entered his office with little apprehension as to what he might want. He and Major Silva had always had a positive relationship, despite the Major's rough exterior. In fact, all the guys teased him about being Silva's favorite, as a lot of the responsibilities were passed down from the Corporal to Johnny. In boot camp he was chosen as squad leader, a title that followed him when he was stationed at Ft. Campbell. Johnny was working hard to get to the next level of Specialist, and that would bring him closer to his dream of being a Chinook pilot.

Johnny entered the office, saluted the Major, and stood at attention.

"First Class Angel, at ease." The crease between his eyes became deeper as he stared Johnny down. "Let's talk about Saturday night."

"Yes, Major."

"How was your guard shift at the hangar Saturday night?"

"It was fine, Sir."

"Any trouble?"

"None Major."

"Did you notice anyone hanging around or any suspicious activity during your shift?"

"No, Major. There was no one suspicious there."

Another hard glare.

"I'm asking because it seems there are a few items missing from the storage closet. Just checking to see if you know anything about that, or if you saw anyone remove anything from the hangar that night, or lately."

Johnny took a deep breath. "No Major. I didn't see anyone remove anything."

"Ok Angel. I figured not, but I had to question you along with the other guys."

"What all is missing, Sir?"

"Well, there are a few parachute bags, a couple of tents, an old wooden crate, and from the shelf, a large box of rations."

Johnny nodded his head.

"Well, if you hear of anything, I want you to report

it to me immediately. No matter how big or how insignificant it may seem. I need answers here."

"Yes, Sir."

"How is everything else going?"

"Everything is fine, Sir."

"Well, I'm sure you know we are considering you for Specialist. Just keep up the good work and before you know it, you'll be sitting in that pilot seat."

"Yes, Sir. Thank you, Major Silva."

"You're welcome Angel. And you're also dismissed."

Johnny saluted the Major, waiting for his return salute. He then did a perfectly crisp about face and headed out into the warm evening sun. Johnny let out a long deep breath as he headed to his barracks. It would figure other stuff was missing, otherwise they wouldn't have noticed that old crate gone.

I had no idea all this was going on with Johnny. Otherwise I wouldn't have been so selfish and not contacted him. Sometimes I can become so self-absorbed in my own issues, that I have blinders on and everything else melts away. That's what I let happen with Johnny. In the enormity of my own problem, he was slowly fading away.

Thursday night I sat on my bed searching Google for any answers or history to a gravitational problem in humans, or whatever you would call what was going on with my body. Google offered a variety of issues from NASA and the effects of loss of gravity on astronauts, but it was nothing even close to what I was experiencing. I tried again with the name Major Kearney and Ft. Campbell, and finally had a hit. But all I was able to find on him was an article back in the late 1990's welcoming him to the air base. It further explained his family's legacy, and their role in the studies of prolonged flight effects on pilots. His father was obviously some sort of scientist, but that was it.

Snapping my laptop shut, I gave up on my quest and leaned back on my bed. I thought about my flying episodes both Sunday and Monday. I had not lost gravity since then, but then again, I hadn't left my room.

What was it that made me lose gravity? Sunday night I was running in fear when I took off, and then Monday I wasn't. It didn't make sense. And how was I able to bring myself down? Sunday night when I pushed my body to the ground that seemed to help. At practice, I calmly talked myself down from the basket. Maybe if I just set my mind to it, I could control myself flying.

I decided to give it a try. I got up and locked the door to my room and stood in the middle, away from all the furniture that could make my landing a disaster. I closed my eyes and thought of nothing but my body leaving the ground. As soon as I saw myself flying I felt my chest tighten again. My body left the floor, slamming into the ceiling.

"Owwweee!" I said under my breath as quietly as I could. I pushed against the ceiling that I was now lying firmly against. Now to focus on getting down. I closed my eyes and saw myself coming down, and immediately fell to the floor with a loud thud.

"Claire? Are you ok?" My mom rapped on my door.

"I'm fine mom! I...I just knocked my chair over."

I rolled over on the ground rubbing my bottom that was throbbing from its impact to the floor.

"Ok. You need to get to bed soon."

"Five more minutes, please."

I heard her walk down the hall towards her bedroom. I had to try again. It didn't seem so scary that time. Focus on flying. Tightening of the chest. On the ceiling. Focus on the landing. Back on the floor. I soon realized this whole flying thing was something I could control with my mind!

After brushing my teeth and saying good night to my mom, I turned on my lamp so she couldn't tell I was still awake. I must have practiced leaving the ground and returning at least 50 times. The more I did it, the more control I had. Before I went to bed, I was able to fly to the ceiling and return with only a slight impact. On one of the tries, I hovered above the ground for a good five seconds. I was slowly getting more control of my body and my abilities to control the lack of gravity on it.

Maybe this flying thing wasn't so bad after all.

Friday I returned to school. More confident that I wasn't going to fly away, I was able to focus on catching up on all my missed work. I sat with Lexi and Alicia at lunch listening to all I had missed at school that week, and life in general. I tried to be into the conversation, but in my mind all I could think about was flying.

"So anyways, tonight Lexi and I are going on a double date with Shawn and Tater." Alicia said.

"Tater?" I laughed.

"Yep," said Lexi. "He's buddies with Johnny and Shawn. He's from Texas, that's why they call him Tater."

"Hmmm..." I smiled.

" We would have invited you and Johnny," Alicia chimed in, "but Shawn said Johnny hasn't heard from you all week Claire."

I fidgeted with my uneaten salad. "I know. It's just that I was so sick. I mean, I didn't even text you until Wednesday Alicia."

"Which is weird," she said throwing her hands up. "Do you realize that a day hasn't gone by since we were in grade school that we haven't talked or at least texted? You had me so worried!"

"I know," I sighed, looking guilty and biting my lip. "I'm so sorry."

"So have you talked to Johnny?" Lexi asked.

"No, we were supposed to go out tonight, but I

haven't talked to him so I don't think that's going to happen."

Alicia and Lexi stared at me. I knew they thought I was crazy, but I had this weird feeling about being around Johnny right now. This flying thing had me so freaked out and rightfully so. The stuff that did this to me came from where he worked, and it somehow made me tie it to him. I know that isn't fair or makes any sense, but that was how I was feeling and I couldn't shake it. I had no desire to see him right now, and besides that, I was afraid he would figure out something was wrong with me and report it back to his commanding officers. We would both be in big trouble then. I feared Johnny would get in trouble for allowing me around such secretive government stuff. The Army was his life, and being a pilot was his dream, and I didn't want to ruin it for him.

"But anyways, I hope you guys have so much fun on your date." I tried to change the subject. "I want all the details tomorrow Lexi."

"Oh trust me Claire. You will be the first to know," she smiled.

After school Kass and I stopped at the store and bought stuff to make tacos with. Friday nights I liked to make dinner as much as I could because I knew my mom would be tired from her long week. While I was cooking dinner, Kass cleaned up the house so she would come home and have nothing to do but relax.

Mom was so grateful, and after dinner she immediately fell asleep on the couch. Kass and Kyle went to a late movie, and I found myself in my room alone looking up gravitational studies again. My text dinged and my tummy jumped wondering if it was Johnny. It was Lexi. She sent me a selfie of herself and Tater. I looked at her beaming face and Tater, who was a tall, dark haired, blue eyed cowboy. Good grief! Did Johnny have any unattractive friends? I could tell she was having a blast and I texted back my approval of Tater. What a hottie!

I smiled at the next selfie they sent me, of all four of them playing putt putt. I did miss Johnny. The last time I had heard from him was through a text on Thursday that simply said, *"Please call me when you're feeling better."* I picked up my phone tempted to text him, but unsure of what to say now.

My eyes again turned to my laptop, but I had exhausted all ideas of what to search for online. Nothing but weird alien sites were coming up now.

A late summer breeze blew in warmly from my open window making my sheer curtain fly to the ceiling then flow lightly to the ground. It reminded me of how I had been practicing flying in my room throughout the week. I had become a pro at controlling myself, and my lack of gravity. I got up and looked outside into the perfect moonlit night. My chest tightened again, and suddenly I had an overwhelming desire to fly. I had been wanting to test myself outside, and now seemed like the perfect time.

Tip toeing past my sleeping mom and out of the French doors in the kitchen, I stepped out into the hot night, onto my backyard patio. Our backyard bordered a small forest that eventually led down to the Cumberland River. Tall trees swayed slightly, and I could see the highest branches of the oak trees a few feet into the dark woods. That would be my target.

Closing my eyes, I took a deep breath and let my mind take over. I shot into the air with lightning speed, and felt the adrenaline rush shoot through my body. I went a little quicker and higher than I had hoped, and for a moment the panic I had been feeling all week set in. I started feeling a little out of control. My arms and legs were all over the place, and I had trouble catching my breath. I looked down at my wrist where the Saturn rings displayed their usual in flight, bright pink glow.

"Claire, calm down. Focus," I reassured myself. "Hold yourself at this altitude."

My flight steadied to a stop, and I looked down setting my sights on the top of the tallest Oak tree. I hung in the air for a moment, taking in the breathtaking scenery below. The houses looked like little glowing boxes, and to the south I could see a barge floating down the river. Beyond that I could see the sparkling lights of the city. I took another deep breath, leaned my head down, and slowly descended toward the tree.

"Slowly Claire. Focus." I whispered to myself.

Approaching the tree, my arms reached out to move the smaller branches and leaves, as I entered the top of the elderly Oak. I immediately regretted wearing my jammie shorts and tee. The branches scraped up my legs and arms, but at least I hit my target. Luckily, I wore my chucks instead of my flip flops.

I stood on the large branch at the top of the tall oak tree, hanging onto other limbs to steady myself.

"Claire, you did it!" I congratulated myself. Tears welled up in my eyes and flowed down my cheeks, as all the anxiety from the week came flooding out. I knew that as far as my safety goes, this flying thing was going to be ok.

SEVEN

BY SATURDAY NIGHT, I was a different girl. I couldn't believe I could fly. I was no superhero, but my confidence level had grown to a superhero size. That night at work I tried to focus on mundane tasks, but all I could think about was getting off work and flying again.

Alicia and I had so much fun, before I knew it the night was over. We sat at the table in the back room counting our tips and listening coincidently, to Frank Sinatra's "Come Fly With Me." I sang it just a little louder this time than usual.

"So how did you do tonight?" I asked her.

"Hmmmm…" she counted the last few dimes. "I'm just at $78.00. How about you?"

"$105.00," I smiled shrugging my shoulders.

"Darn you, Claire! You beat me almost every weekend."

"Oh, come on Mony. You know it's only because I skate faster."

She sighed. "I guess that's true. If tips were based on looks and personality, I would definitely have you beat."

I threw a wadded up napkin at her. "You're such a brat," I laughed.

"So what are you doing the rest of the night?" she asked.

"Just goin home. How about you? Are you going to see Shawn?"

Alicia's smile faded. "No, he has guard duty. But we're going to hang out tomorrow. Do you and Johnny want to do something?"

I just shrugged my shoulders.

"Did you ever call him?"

"Not exactly."

"Claire, what is up with you lately? You've been acting so weird this week. First that tattoo. Then your Michael Jordan stunt, and then practically ignoring me because you're sick this week." She quotationed the word sick with her fingers, so I knew she didn't fall for my flu excuse either.

"Alicia, I said I'm sorry. I can't explain it. It's just been a rough week."

"Well, what about Johnny? Are you going to keep blowing him off? You at least owe him an explanation."

As if on cue, Mr. Arnold appeared in the door. "Claire? You have a young man here looking for you."

I looked at Alicia who's eyes grew wide as she cocked her head sideways and gave me an "I told you so" look.

"Ok, Mr. Arnold. I'll be right there. Thank you."

Alicia grabbed my hand. "Let him down easy. He's a sweetheart."

I stood up and grabbed my stuff. "I will. I'll text you later."

"Ok. Love you, Clairey."

"Love you too, Mony."

I walked into the parking lot and found Johnny's truck parked in his usual space. He stood at the back of the truck and stared at me stone face as I approached him. I had no idea how to start this conversation, so I hoped he would be the first to speak up. But he didn't. He waited for me. I leaned beside him against the back of the truck, unsure of what to say.

"Hi Johnny." That's all I had in the moment.

"Hi Claire."

I looked over at him and swallowed hard. "I've had a really rough week.." I started to explain.

"Everyone has rough weeks Claire." His eyes were kind, but I could tell he was agitated at me.

"Look, I love being with you, but blowing me off is not the way to handle this. If you're not ready for us, just let me know. I'll try to get over it, but not knowing what is going on is too hard to deal with."

He was right and that was very fair, but he could not even begin to imagine the nightmare I had been through this week. I wanted to tell him more than I wanted to tell Kass or Alicia, but I was too afraid. I felt so alone in all of this, and I needed to feel safe. Johnny always made me feel safe, but I couldn't tell him.

I felt like I knew Johnny the person so well, but I didn't know the soldier in him well enough. What if he told his Sergeant out of obligation or duty, or whatever you would call it?I was worried about becoming some kind of governmental science experiment and like I mentioned before, Johnny losing his shot at becoming a pilot. But most of all I worried about mom and Kass, and how it would affect them. So I made up my mind that I would never tell him, which would be such a betrayal if we stayed together. I have always been honest with him. All I could do was end this. End one of the best things that has happened to me in a long time. My heart was breaking, and I didn't want to do it.

He stared down at me with his perfect green eyes. I would miss them.

"Johnny, I just….it's like you said, I don't think I'm ready for this. Everything is happening fast and I'm just not ready."

"I can slow it down. I thought maybe I was going too slow for you. I had no idea things were going too fast."

Oh wow. He seemed genuinely sad. His tone was

almost pleading. This was so hard. *"Think about his career, Claire."* I reminded myself.

"No Johnny. I promise. You are so perfect and so good to me. It has nothing to do with you. I just...I have too much going on." I saw Johnny look down at my shirt that I was nervously twisting. He knew that was my sign for being uncomfortable and like the gentleman he is, politely backed away.

Johnny took my hand lightly squeezing it. "Ok, Claire. If this is what you want. But if you ever need me for anything, you know I'm always here for you." I saw his eyes watering, but I knew he would not let me see him cry.

He leaned over and kissed my cheek. In return I hugged him as tightly as I could. I didn't want to let go.

As could be expected, none of my friends or family could understand why I ended everything with

Johnny. I did my best to explain myself, but of course, nothing made sense. They were all annoyed with me and I couldn't blame them. From their perspective, I was being stupid and letting a great guy go. Alicia told me all she ever heard was me whining because I didn't have a boyfriend and now that I had an amazing one, I was throwing him away. I snot cried when she told me that, because she was right and I was missing him like crazy.

The next week dragged without talking to Johnny everyday. I felt like there was a hole in me that could not be filled. He had very quickly not only become my boyfriend, but one of my best friends. He would text me everyday in the morning, when he had lunch break, and all evening if we didn't get to see each other that day. I found myself at those particular times checking my phone, and if I did get a text, hoping it was him. From what Shawn told Alicia, Johnny was having a hard time too. As mean as it sounds, that made me feel a little better. At least I knew he was still thinking about me.

EIGHT

THURSDAY I SAT in science class listening to my teacher, Mr. Franklin, explain to us the space program and how far it had come in the last six decades. We watched a short film, where astronaut Neil Armstrong bounced around on the moon, and my stomach butterflied with excitement. I paid more attention to Mr. Franklin now than I ever have and when the bell rang, I made a beeline to him.

"Excuse me, Mr. Franklin?"

"Ah, Claire. How can I help you young lady?"

"I have a question...I know it may sound weird," I lowered my voice, "but, have you ever heard of anyone being able to fly?"

He stared at me for a moment, unsure of what I was asking. "Fly as in, space flight?"

I shook my head. "No, I mean a person actually flying. Like... losing gravity...umm... Superman?"

He smirked at me. "Claire, that's physically impossible."

I pressed in more. "Well, have you ever heard of anyone trying to make it happen? Maybe a scientist that was experimenting with it?"

"No, a true scientist would know better than to waste their time on such foolishness. I went over loss of gravity earlier this week. Did you pay attention in class? I explained the term 'zero gravity' and the misconceptions of it."

"Yes Sir." I looked down at the ground, regretting having asked him. "It's just that Lexi and I had a discussion about it this week and I was just curious."

He smiled at me. "Well, I appreciate you asking and your interest in my class."

I smiled back. "Thanks anyways, Mr. Franklin."

I picked up my backpack and headed to the door. "Hey, Claire!" He called after me. I walked back to him.

"Now that I think about it, I did hear of one scientist experimenting with it, but it was a long time ago. He was an officer at Ft. Campbell."

"Oh. That's interesting," I said trying not to sound too overanxious. I was almost certain he was the same one Johnny had told me about. "Do you know who he was?"

"Well, no. I can't recall, but I'm sure I read it in some article. I used to teach part time at the high school out there. Listen, if you're really interested, you can probably find it at the Ft. Campbell library."

"Ft. Campbell has a library?"

"Yes. Go through Gate four and it's about a mile down the main road on the right."

"Great! Thanks again, Mr. Franklin," I said reaching out to shake his hand.

"No problem Claire. I love to see my students so interested in science."

I walked down the hallway thrilled with the information he had given me. I had never thought to check for a public library. I knew I needed to get as much information as I could about what was going on with my body and the effect flying could have on me. Not knowing what that pink stuff contained, scared me. It was inside of my body and I had to find out all I could about it.

"What assignment are you working on?" Alicia asked, as we stretched out at basketball practice Friday after school.

"Science. It's kind of like an extra point assignment I can add to my science grade. Mr. Franklin told me about it."

"Claire, you're in science honors class. I don't think you need any extra points. Besides, it's Friday night. Can't you do it next week?"

"No, I'm so sorry Mony, but it has to be tonight. Maybe I can meet you and Lexi after the movie and we can get something to eat or something?"

Alicia rolled her eyes and stretched her leg behind her. "Ok, I guess that's better than nothing."

Coach Alexander blew his whistle. "Alright, girls! Lay ups!"

"Let's go Air Jordan," Alicia teased as we partnered up with each other. I had tried my best to keep my flying under control, especially since that disastrous first practice, and I had gotten pretty good at it. But my lack of gravity was definitely a bonus to my basketball skills. I was making almost every shot, and for some reason I was a lot faster. I had to focus to stay on the ground, or I found myself floating to the basket with ease.

After practice, Alicia and I walked outside together.

"I'm surprised you and Lexi aren't hanging out with the guys tonight," I said.

"Well, we would be, but their company is in the field this week."

"What's that mean?"

"It means, they basically go out and camp out in the woods and do field training. No cell phones, no way to reach them. It's only been four days and I'm missing Shawn like crazy."

"So Johnny's probably with them?"

"I'm sure he is Clairey." She put her arm around my shoulder as we walked through the parking lot. "I don't care what you say, I know you're missing him."

"Maybe a little," I confessed.

"Well, I'm hoping you'll get past this little thing you're going through, before you lose him for good."

I paused for a moment as we approached my car. "Mony, if I'm supposed to be with him, everything will work out. Even this 'little' thing I'm going through. I trust that."

Alicia smiled sympathetically at me. "Claire, I know I've been agitated with your decision, but I just want you to know I'm here for you. I will always be here for you. No matter what, you have to do what you feel in your heart is right and no one else can know that but you....and I'm sorry if I haven't been more supportive of you."

"It's ok. I know I'm being difficult, but I'll move past it."

I hugged my best friend and promised to meet her and Lexi at The Coffee Beaner after the movie, then jumped in my car and headed home to change for my library date at Ft. Campbell.

NINE

AT 6 PM EXACTLY, I pulled into the library parking lot. It wasn't as big as our public library, but walking in I could tell I'd have my work cut out for me. I found the archive section in the basement that was full of large bound books, containing old newspaper clippings, and smelled of antique weathered paper. I settled in at a quiet computer in the corner of the room and began my investigation.

"Hmmmm...Gulf War, 1992," I whispered to myself as I typed in the year in their computerized catalog system. From there I looked up Major Kearney, 101st Lab Technician, the only information I had from Johnny.

Several articles popped up including the first one that welcomed Major Kearney to Ft. Campbell, and recognized him for his work in aeronautics in Houston. He was hosting a lecture here, and that's pretty much all that it said.

I looked for whatever I could find from Johnny's company, thinking maybe Major Kearney was assigned to the same one, since the crate was stored at the hangar. When I entered his company name, a list of soldiers that had died in the war came up. I looked at the young faces staring back at me and my heart melted. They were so young. What a huge sacrifice.

Before I knew it two hours had passed, and I had nothing to show for my efforts. A librarians pinched nose voice echoing over the loudspeaker, snapped me out of my search.

"Attention patrons, the library will be closing in 10 minutes. Please bring your final selection to the service desk."

I looked at my phone. Ten minutes till eight. I scanned the screen one last time looking for any information I could find before I had to leave. Suddenly his name was there, headlining an obituary.

"Major Brian Kearney of Houston, Texas. Deceased May 24th, 2016," I read aloud. I looked for more information on his death, but strangely enough, that's all that was there. My heart sank, and I sat back in my seat stunned. I felt so sad and hopeless. Sad for his death, and hopeless that I had nowhere to go for answers. Was I going to be like this forever? I had no way of knowing the long term effects, and how long I would even be able to fly.

I grabbed my keys, and headed out into the damp night. It was still warm, but a light foggy mist was settling in the area. I started my car, but just sat there feeling frustrated and defeated. I needed more answers.

I've made a lot of dumb choices in my life, but that night I made a desperate choice. No, a STUPID desperate choice. I had to know if there was more information in that closet. Maybe if I got my hands on some more of that pink stuff, I could get it tested and figure out what it was made of. My superhero ego took over, and I decided to break into the hangar. Like I said, so stupid.

I turned my car toward the airfield, all the while telling myself what a dumb idea this was. There was a quiet neighborhood just outside the airfield, and I parked at the end of a cul de sac surrounded by woods. This would be a good place to take off where no one could see me.

Walking into the thick brush, I looked behind me scanning the neighborhood to make sure no one was around. It was so still and quiet, except a dog barking in the distance. I took a deep breath, looked to the sky, and shot through a small clearing in the trees.

I had become so good at flying, my aim was spot on. I didn't even look like I was drowning in the air anymore. I almost flew like Superman, but not quite. I crossed my legs and balled my fists together. When I wanted to go faster I pushed my arms out in front of me, and when I wanted to slow down, I flew vertical into the air, and curled myself into a ball. It was mainly a concentration thing, though. I had to focus hard, especially on things like fitting into narrow spaces and hovering.

The trees provided the perfect cover as I flew over, finally coming to a stop at the edge of the woods. Lights glowed from three long runways in front of me, and I could see the hangar on the other side of the air traffic control tower. There was movement in the tower, so I knew this would be tricky. I weighed my options and decided the best thing to do was go on foot from the trees to the hangar, so I could avoid the air tower. Flying by that thing wouldn't be such a good idea.

I set myself on the ground between the trees, and headed across a large grassy field. By accident I had dressed in all black right down to my leggings and chucks, so I looked like the dumb criminal I was. At least I blended in. By the time I made it behind the hangar, my feet were soaked from the grass. The outside of the hangar was well lit, so I carefully hid behind the Cougar truck Johnny had showed me. Johnny. I missed him so much.

Each side of the building was lined with seven or eight windows that were two stories off the ground. The overhang from the roof provided some shade in the bright lights, so maybe I could get through one of them. I squatted down and ran over to the building. Leaning my back against the wall, I slid up the side. The window was locked, but I could see the one beside it cracked open. I flew over, slid it open with ease, and crawled inside to a small office that was completely dark, except the glow of a computer. I crept to the door and listened with my head pressed up against it for a minute. Nothing.

The door creaked lightly as I opened it, and walked into a dark hallway. I crept down the hall to some stairs that led down and out into the hangar. So far, so good. I knew where the closet was from here.

The closet door was unlocked thankfully, and my heart jumped with the thought of finding another crate or even better, the magical pink liquid. I softly shut the closet door behind me, and turned on my phone flashlight to begin my search. Lots of old filing tubs filled with helicopter instruction manuals and flying hours logged, filled the wall. My eyes scanned the shelves looking for some kind of crate or something with Major Kearney's name on it. I searched and searched and couldn't find anything. I looked at my phone. It was 8:50 by this time. I had already been there for 20 minutes, and didn't want to overstay my welcome.

I sighed and had bent down to check the bottom row one more time, when I heard voices outside in the hall.

"Johnson, check these last two rooms, just to make sure. I got the closet."

The door handle started to turn and I flew to the top shelf just as it opened. I quietly rolled to the back of the shelf as the closet filled with light. The sound of footsteps walking around had me frozen up against the wall, and I prayed the soldier would not look up here.

"*Stay still Claire. Breath slowly.*" I thought to myself. I listened as he walked around, moving boxes and whistling to himself.

After three very long minutes, he left leaving the closet in darkness. I let out a big sigh of relief and stayed there a couple of more minutes just to be sure. In my back pocket, my phone started buzzing. I opened it to see Lexi calling me. Crap. I forgot about meeting them.

I flew down off the shelf and tiptoed to the door. It was quiet outside, and my hand shook in fear as I opened the door. I cracked it slowly and peeked into the hallway. All clear. I decided to try and go out the back door instead of the window I came in. I'm pretty sure I left it open, and that's why they were checking the hangar anyway.

The exit light glowed above a door at the end of the hallway, and I crept as fast as I could toward it, and opened the door quietly. I was scuttling as close to the ground as I possibly could across the gravel parking lot, when I heard one of the soldiers yell to the other.

"There's someone there!"

A bright flashlight shined from the building, across the parking lot and on me. I pulled my hood up, and ran as fast as I could toward the field.

"Dude! It's a girl!" the other soldier yelled.

I looked quickly back at them, and they both started chasing me.

"Hey! Stop! Now!"

"Get on the Ground! GET ON THE GROUND!"

"No way!" I gasped quietly. I just had to get to the trees. Once there I could fly out without them noticing me. I ran with everything I had in me, thankful for all the time I had spent out jogging. I didn't tire too easily. My Saturn rings started glowing in anticipation of me flying. "Not yet!" I told myself. "Keep running!" I ducked into the trees just as they were getting closer, and looked for an opening. The moon cast a bright beam onto the forest floor before me, signaling where I could make my exit out of the thick branches. I followed the light and shot up in the trees. Branches whizzed past me and I looked down to make sure neither of the soldiers had seen me. That's where I made my mistake. A thick branch seemed to come from nowhere, and I collided with it. I hit it hard, and pain shot through the back of my head, sending me falling back down into the tree bouncing off branches. I managed to grab one at the last minute, and held on for my life.

"Where did she go?" one of them yelled.

"I heard something over here," said the other.

I hung there as quietly as possible, not moving while they searched below. Something warm ran down my face, and I realized my forehead was split open as blood dripped on my shirt. There was nothing I could do, but let it drip. If I moved an inch, they would see me.

The flashlight shined several times in my direction, but at last they gave up. When they were at a safe distance, I swung myself far off the branch, and flew into the open sky. Not bothering to land in the trees as a cover, I flew right up to my car, jumped in, and drove home as fast as I could.

Stupid idea. I was a lucky girl.

TEN

BY THE TIME I made the 20 minute drive home from Ft. Campbell, I knew exactly what I was going to tell my mom.

"Good grief, Claire! What happened to you?" My poor mom. I saw the concern in her eyes, and I didn't blame her. The amount of blood all over my face made it look like I got jumped by a gang.

"Mom, it's not as bad as it looks," I said underneath my black sweatshirt, that I was using to control the bleeding.

"What happened to you?" she asked again pulling the sweatshirt away from my head and gasped.

"It was so stupid. I ran into a tree branch." That wasn't a lie.

"At the library?"

"Yes. I ran into it hard."

"Well, I guess so!"

She took me into the bathroom with the first aid kit, and started to clean me up.

"I don't know Claire," she said leaning down to look more closely. "This might need stitches."

"No mom," I argued pulling my hair from my face. "It's fine really."

"What is this?!" Mom gasped grabbing my wrist looking down at my saturn rings.

Oh crap.

"When did you..? Claire! This is a tattoo!"

"I know mom," I stared down at it with her. "I'm sorry."

"When did you do this?" I could tell she was hurt more than anything.

The front door opened and Kass called us from the living room. "Mom! Claire! I'm home!"

"A couple of weeks ago," I answered. Her eyebrows arched in surprise. "I know. I should have told you, but it was kind of a last minute thing."

Kassie poked her head into the bathroom. "Hey!" She stopped when she saw mom's face. "What's going on?"

"Claire had an accident," Mom explained.

"Is that a tattoo?!"

"Yes Kass," I murmured.

"Oooo. It's so cool. When did you get that?" Kass asked excited.

"A couple of weeks ago," I smiled slightly.

Mom looked sternly at me, and my smile faded fast. "Claire, you should not be making any life decisions like this without consulting me first. You're only 17."

"I'm so sorry, mom." I was genuinely sorry, but I reminded myself that I did not make this choice. It was made for me.

Mom shrugged her shoulders. "Well, there's nothing we can do about it now. I hope you're ok with having Saturn rings stamped on your wrist for the rest of your life. And Kass, don't you get any ideas. This kind of stuff we need to talk about first."

"Yes, Ma'am," said Kass smirking at me while mom bandaged my head.

I shook my head at her. At least the tat took the focus off my head. I tried not to laugh despite everything. Was this really my life?

Saturday night at work I convinced Alicia the reason I didn't show up to meet her and Lexi was because of my head. She forgave me because... what else could she do? I did have a huge bandage on my forehead.

"Can I see it Claire?" she asked lifting up my bandage a little.

"Oww Mony," I cringed. "Hold on. What is it with you and goriness?"

I slowly lifted the bandage so she could see my gash.

"Eeewww! That is a good one."

"I told you so."

"Well, I'm sorry, but I had to make sure there

wasn't another tattoo under there. Maybe a half moon or something."

I rolled my eyes at her. "I saw Shawn outside waiting for you. He had some other guy with him."

"That's Tater," she laughed. "We are going to watch movies at Lexi's. Want to come?"

"No thanks. I don't feel like being a fifth wheel."

"Come on Claire," she smiled. "I'll introduce you to Tater."

We walked outside where the guys were waiting. My stomach turned when I saw them standing there without Johnny.

"Hey sweetness," Shawn said giving Alicia a big hug. "I've been missing you like crazy."

I walked over to Tater and shook his hand. "Hi Tater. I'm Claire."

"Claire, I've heard a lot of nice things about you. It's nice to finally meet you," Tater said in his thick Texas accent. Funny that he hit it off so well with our California bred Lexi.

I wondered if all the nice things he had heard about me came from Johnny. I wondered if Johnny had gone in the field with them that week.

"So how was field training this week?" I asked, trying to find out.

Shawn held Alicia closer. "Well, we survived, but Johnson here got out of it. He was guarding the hangar from girl ghosts."

"Oh man, don't start that again. I saw what I saw," Tater said.

"What are you guys talking about?" Alicia asked.

"Apparently there is a girl ghost haunting the hangar," Shawn explained. "Tater and Reynolds claim they saw one last night."

My mouth dropped open as I slowly began to realize they were talking about me. Tater's last name was Johnson, the name I heard one of the guys yell right before they chased me.

"I DID see her Shawn. Reynolds saw her too."

My hand immediately started fidgeting with the bottom of my shirt and I told myself to stop it in my head. "So what exactly happened?" I asked in a half croak/half normal voice.

"Well, I found one of the offices open and the window open, I swear it was closed when I checked earlier in day, but anyways we decided to check the hangar just to be safe. Everything checked clear, but then I'm outside and see this small figure sneaking across the parking lot. I know it was a girl, because I got a glimpse of her before she pulled up her hoodie."

I looked down, scared Tater would remember me, while Shawn started snickering at Tater's story.

Tater continued unphased. "So we chase her into the woods and this girl just disappears."

Alicia looked enthralled. "You mean she just disappeared right in front of you?"

"Well, no. But we were right behind her. We lost sight for no more than three seconds and she was just gone."

Shawn interrupted him. "Tater, that can't be

possible man. That airfield is surrounded by two story high fences with barb wire on top. She would have had to climb that fence to get out of there."

"Maybe she was a ghost," Alicia offered.

Shawn laughed harder, and Alicia playfully hit him in the arm. "Don't make fun."

"I know it doesn't make sense," Tater explained. "Reynolds and I went back to the hangar completely creeped out. We were so glad to get out of there at midnight."

"So, are you going to tell Silva on Monday?" Shawn asked.

"Monday? We told him this morning. I'm not waiting around and getting called into his office like the other guys."

"What other guys?" I asked before I could even think about it.

Shawn looked at me like he didn't want to bring up Johnny's name in front of me. "Well Claire, Johnny and some of the other guys who worked a couple of weeks ago all got called in for stuff going missing in one of the storage closets."

My heart sank at the thought of Johnny getting in trouble. "What kind of stuff?" I asked again.

"Just some boxes of rations and stuff. Don't worry Claire. Johnny isn't in trouble. He can do no wrong in Silva's eyes."

"See? I think this girl has something to do with that," Tater theorized. "Maybe she's stealing the stuff from the closet."

"Yep, she's risking jail time to break into a government facility and steal packaged peanut butter and jelly," Shawn laughed again.

Tater shook his head smiling. "Maybe she was hungry."

"Alright, enough of this," Alicia said walking over and hugging me. "Claire are you sure you don't want to come with us? I feel like I haven't seen you in forever."

I smiled and hugged her tightly back. "Fifth wheel," I whispered in her ear.

"I'll text you tomorrow," she said and walked to Shawn's car with Tater.

Shawn came over and put his arm around me. "So Claire, I'm not trying to bring up anything to hurt you, but just so you know, Johnny really misses you. When we were in the field, he talked about you alot."

My heart leapt inside of me, knowing that he missed me. My mixed up girl feelings knew that I couldn't be with him, but the other side of me wanted him to ignore all of that, and pursue me anyway.

I was starting to think he was getting over me, so it was nice to hear that he still cared.

"Thanks Shawn. I really miss him too," I shrugged my shoulders. " Maybe someday everything will work out."

Shawn squeezed me and then headed to the car. I felt tears well up in my eyes. This was so hard. What I wouldn't do to be with Johnny tonight.

ELEVEN

THURSDAY WAS MY mom's 47th birthday. Kass and I took her to her favorite Chinese food buffet. Kass bought her a new set of pearls, her favorite. Of course they were not even close to real, but from her reaction, you would have thought they were just plucked from the ocean. I got her a gift card to her favorite clothing store and promised I would go shopping with her soon.

"So Claire, are you going to the game tomorrow night?" Kass asked dipping her sushi in some brown sauce. Gross. Sushi is so gross.

"I think so."

"What do you mean you think so? This is only the biggest game of the year!"

"Sooorryy," I laughed. "Of course I'll be there."

"Who are you guys playing?" Mom asked.

"East Central," answered Kass. "the biggest rival

game of the year. We are dressing up in our usual redneck garb."

Mom and Kass started talking about Kyle and the game. I tried to follow along with their conversation but my thoughts turned again to my talk last weekend with Shawn and Tater, and my little excursion at the hangar. I still couldn't believe I had been so dumb. My mom had told me in the past I was a 'shoot from the hips' kind of girl. (I'm pretty sure that means I'm impatient, and I make rash decisions.) But anyway, I decided to try and not fly this week, out of fear of someone seeing me and it getting back to any one of Johnny's higher ups. I had asked Lexi earlier this week if Tater had said anything about seeing Maj. Silva and she said no. She did mention that Tater was creeped out by the experience all week and that's all he would talk about. I felt bad for what I did. Well, kind of.

We were on our way home with my mom when my text dinged. I assumed it was Alicia or Lexi seeing if we could meet up after dinner. It was Lexi, but not because she was wanting to meet up.

"Claire, please call me ASAP."

My thoughts immediately went back to my conversation with Tater last weekend. I worried about what I did last Friday, and the effects it would have on Johnny. I even had a nightmare that Johnny and his Major were standing by watching me get arrested for trespassing.

Kyle was waiting for Kass when we got home. He was so busy with football, they were only able to see each other after practice and when Kyle finished his homework.

"Mom, I'm going to get ice cream with Kyle for a few!" Kass yelled from the front porch.

"Ok! You have an hour," Mom said.

I looked at the clock. It was already 8.

"Claire, I'm going to get in the shower. Thank you so much for my birthday dinner." Mom squeezed me so tight.

"You're welcome, Mom."

I went to my room eager to call Lexi. I hit call on her name and listened as the phone rang.

"Claire?"

"Lexi! Is everything ok?"

"Yes. I'm sorry. I didn't mean to scare you."

"It's ok. What's up?" I asked trying to sound nonchalant.

"Well, I know it's none of my business, but Tater told me something that I thought you should know."

"Ok."

"It's about Johnny."

My tummy flipped. "Is he ok?" I asked, my voice quivering with concern.

"Yeah, he's fine. It's just that....," She paused for way too long.

"Lexi?" I coaxed her. "It's ok. You can tell me." I just knew for sure she was going to tell me he was in trouble. I was so wrong.

"Claire, Tater said Johnny is talking to some girl in another company. She's been coming around him a lot, and they have been hanging out."

"Oh," I whispered, relieved that he wasn't in trouble, but hurt that he was able to move on so quickly.

"Are you ok? Do you want me to come over?"

"No, Lexi. I'm..I'm okay," I stammered, feeling like someone had punched me in the gut. " I can't expect him not to date anyone. He's a great guy."

"I'm sorry Claire Bear. I struggled telling you, but I know if it were me in your shoes, I would want to know."

"Lex, you know me very well. You did the right thing. I'm glad you told me."

"Are you sure you don't want me to come over?" Lexi was such a sweet friend.

"No Lex. I promise I'm fine. I'll see you at school tomorrow."

We hung up and I sat on my bed staring at the phone. My eyes filled with tears. I knew he would eventually start seeing someone else, but just not this soon.

I wiped my eyes, and knew I had to get out of the house at least for a few minutes. I knocked on the bathroom door and let my mom know I was going out but would be right back. I threw on my chucks and went out the patio door. Jumping on the porch rail, I bent my knees and shot up into the early fall sky. The stars were so bright tonight. I felt the warm air hit my face, and left the smell of trees and earthly vegetation below. Soon nothing but fresh air enveloped me.

Higher and higher I climbed until I felt safe enough to not be seen. I lifted my arms and took a deep breath, lost in the pure bliss of flying. What I thought was a curse was now filling my life with happiness. I was falling in love with flying more and more, and couldn't imagine my life without it. Everything else seemed so ordinary and dull in comparison.

Pausing in the sky, and not sure of which direction to go, I did a 360 looking at the beautiful city lights of Clarksville below me. Across the river in the distance, something caught my eye. The 100 year old courthouse clocktower shined white against the black sky and looked so inviting. I set my sights on the top of the clock, clasped my hands together in my best Supergirl pose, and rocketed across the sky. Had I been in my car, it would have been at least a 20 minute drive through town. I reached the clock tower in three short minutes and scanned the area double checking for people on the ground. When I felt it was safe, I perched myself just inside the shadow ledge on top of the tower and pulled out my phone. Frank Sinatra was always at the top of my list and "Fly Me to the Moon" had been my favorite lately.

The City of Clarksville was so beautiful at night. Century old buildings surrounded the courthouse in the older part of town, and just beyond those, the newer buildings stood in architectural contrast. Two blocks over at the old Roxy Theatre a play was letting out.

I looked north toward Ft. Campbell and thought

again of Johnny.

"How can you already be dating someone else?" I said as though Johnny was sitting right beside me. "How did you move on so quickly from us?" I leaned back against the old tower steeple and inhaled in the fall air.

A scuffling sound, along with a guy's voice shouting, ripped me from my self loathing. I looked down to see where the noise was coming from. Two men ran from a convenience store just outside the city square and jumped in a black pick up truck speeding off.

"What the heck?" I said to myself.

Another man soon exited the store. "Somebody call the police! I've been robbed!"

The black truck was out of sight of the store keeper, but I could see it in the distance speeding up the hill and out of the downtown area.

Without thinking I shot into the air and took off after the truck. I had no trouble catching up to it, while keeping my height at a safe distance. My phone was in my back pocket and I pulled it out and dialed 911.

"Clarksville 911, what's the location of your emergency?"

I looked down trying to recognize any landmarks or buildings that would help me recognize a road.

"Ummm...just give me a minute. I'm following a truck that just robbed a convenience store by the courthouse."

"Ok, ma'am do you see any street signs so you can give me your location?"

"Well... not just yet."

"What kind of .."

"Oh! Oh!" I interrupted her, recognizing Clarence's Thrift Store. "They just drove by Clarence's Thrift Store! They're headed west on that road!"

"Ok Ma'am. What kind of vehicle are they in?"

"A black truck."

"And what kind of vehicle are you in?"

"Ummm... well, about that."

"What color is your vehicle?" she tried again.

I looked down at my red shirt. "Red. My vehicle is red."

"And your location now?"

"Ok, they're turning onto Riverside Drive, heading towards Taco Bell."

"Got it. And Ma'am, what's your name?"

"Can I remain anonymous please?"

"Sure."

I looked to the south and saw two police squads headed in the direction of the pick up. Their streets were going to meet!

This is where I got stupid. "Ok, Ma'am, I see two police cars heading toward the truck. They are coming from the south and are going to meet at the intersection in about one minute."

"Ok..." The dispatcher sounded confused. "Are you saying you can see the officers coming, but you're behind the truck still?"

I slowed to a stop way above the intersection, not knowing how to answer that one.

"Hello?" she asked.

Panicking, I hung up the phone. I watched as the pick up made a quick turn into a parking lot and hid behind a building. Crap. The two squad cars slowed at the intersection and circled the area, while the occupants of the pick up remained inside. I had to call back.

"Clarksville 911."

"Hi, I was just calling to let you guys know the black pick up that was involved in the convenience store robbery is parked behind the building that shares a parking lot with McDonalds. The occupants are still in the truck so please tell the officers to be careful."

I hung up the phone and watched as the two squad cars reapproached the area. They drove around the corner of the building and got out of their cars with their weapons drawn. Oh wow. This was so cool. I felt like I was living an episode of Live PD. Squad lights shone brightly on the truck and each suspect exited the vehicle with their arms up.

I clapped my hands and smiled. "Nice job Claire," I said congratulating myself, when my phone rang. It was mom. I had already been gone an hour.

"Claire, where are you? It's already 9:30?"

"Three minutes away mom," I said and hung up, shooting across the sky toward home.

TWELVE

FRIDAY NIGHT, KASS and I walked through the gate to the football stadium decked out in our redneck garb. I wore my trucker cap with my hair in two braids, my favorite plaid flannel, denim shorts, and as always my chucks. Kass looked the same, except she proudly donned Kyle's practice jersey instead of the flannel. She had to draw freckles on her cheeks, while I displayed mine all natural.

We squeezed through the crowd and over to the student section, where Alicia and Lexi were waiting for us. The bleachers were already packed with still another half hour until game time.

"Claire! Kass!" Alicia yelled down from the third row. We walked past a large group of seniors standing at the bottom of the bleachers, and took our place on the bottom three rows where all the seniors were. The juniors were behind us, followed by the sophomores, and freshmen at the top. I loved my school. My classmates got behind our teams and really supported them, which was especially important this game. We were playing our cross town rivals. We had been playing them for the last 80 years, and so far have beat them every year of my high school career.

"Kass, there's Kyle," Lexi pointed out.

Our attention turned to number 7 on the field, where Kyle was warming up throwing the ball.

"Wow. He looks so hot," Kass said staring at him.

We all laughed and I squeezed my little sister close. "He is so adorable Kass. I'm so happy for you."

"Thanks Claire," she smiled hugging me back. "He definitely makes my life more happy."

The game was soon underway, and we led immediately with a 74 yard kickoff return touchdown. Kyle was spot on with his passing, and by half time we led 21 to 7. We went to the concession stand to get a drink and get out of the stuffy bleachers. It was a humid night.

"So Lex, did Tater tell you about the girl ghost he saw last Friday night?" Alicia asked laughing.

"What ghost?" asked Kass intrigued.

"Yes," Lexi sighed rolling her eyes. "That's all I've heard about this week."

"What ghost?" asked Kass again as I stood quietly by, trying not to look as guilty as I felt.

Lexi turned her attention to Kass. "Tater and his buddy chased some girl off the airfield, and into the woods last weekend. They said she was creeping around the hangar."

"Shawn thinks she was a ghost," Alicia laughed.

"I know," Lexi smiled, but then her face turned serious. "But Tater is convinced it was a person. He described her to me and everything."

My eyebrows shot up in curiosity. "What did he say she looked like?"

"He said she had long dark hair and was very pale," Lexi almost whispered, as if she were telling a ghost story.

"She sounds like a witch!" Kass exclaimed.

I looked at her almost insulted, then down at my skin. I wasn't that pale. I had got a pretty decent tan over the summer.

Alicia interrupted with a big sigh. "Lexi, he barely got a good look at her. He said she pulled her hoodie up before he could even see her."

I snooped for more information. "Lex, what happened when Tater told the Major?"

"Well, Tater said the Major seemed very concerned and now the whole airfield is on alert. They are adding more guards, because this is the second time in the last two months that there has been a breach of security there."

"Wow. That sounds pretty serious," I said, my eyes wide. So much for me trying to break in again for more information.

"It just doesn't make any sense," Alicia added. "Have you seen that airfield? It's surrounded by tall fences and barbed wire. Shawn showed me around, and there is no way anyone could sneak their way in."

"And why would a girl want to?" Kass asked bewildered.

The two minute warning for the game sounded, and we headed back to the bleachers. We had so much fun cheering for our team and when we won, the whole school ran onto the field to congratulate the team. I could tell already with Kyle leading the way, our team was going to have an amazing season.

Saturday night after work I headed home exhausted. We had an extra busy night. It seemed like the whole school turned out to celebrate our big win the night before. It was after 11 when I pulled into the driveway. As usual my mom was waiting for me on the couch sleeping. She would never go to bed until she knew we were home and safe. I woke her up to let her know I was home.

"Mom, I'm home," I said gently shaking her shoulder.

"Oh, hi honey," she replied with a big yawn.

"You can go to bed now," I said kissing her forehead. "Is Kass home yet?"

Mom rubbed her eyes. "No, she's spending the night with Tracy." Tracy and Kass had been friends as long as Alicia and I.

Mom sat up on the couch. "How was work tonight?"

"It was ok. Super busy. I'm going to put my tips in the can, ok?"

The can was a metal mug we had hidden in the back of the cabinet behind the cups. Only mom, Kass, and I knew it was there. We took money from it when we had extra costs or an emergency. The last I checked I had over $500 from the summer saved in there, which was pretty good considering I had to take my car payment and insurance out on top of everything else.

"Thank you Claire, but why don't you take that and buy yourself something. You've been working so hard, and you deserve it."

I sat down by my mom and hugged her tight. "I'm fine mom. I have everything I need and then some. Maybe we can keep saving and take a trip to the beach next year." We hadn't had a family vacation since my dad died 9 years ago.

"Ok. Maybe we can look into that," she said. But I knew she was just saying that to appease my idea. Mom hadn't wanted to do anything like that since dad died. I think it reminds her of him, and his death is still very raw all these years later.

I made sure all the doors were locked before retreating to my room. I was in the bathroom brushing my teeth when I heard my text ding from my bedroom. I figured it was Alicia wanting to compare tip amounts.

I finished brushing my teeth, changed into some jeans and a tee, then sat on my bed and opened my phone.

"Hi Claire. It's Johnny. I hope this text doesn't wake you if you're sleeping. You don't have to respond, but I just want you to know that I can't stop thinking about you. I miss my Claire Bear."

I caught my breath as I read the text, so unbelievably happy and relieved to hear from him, but also bewildered that he missed me. Lexi said he was seeing someone else now and the thought of that had hung over all week like a storm cloud, dripping huge drops of depression on me. It was all I had thought about. Imagining him with her at the hangar, going out to dinner, and to the movies. All the things we had done together.

Now what do I say to him? I wanted to be back with him so much, but again reminded myself of what he could lose being with me.

I walked over to my window, and looked up into the bright darkness. The light from the moon reflected off the clouds and looked so inviting. My Saturn rings were faintly glowing, enticing me to the sky.

My thoughts turned again to Johnny and what I should say to him, or if I should say anything at all. The "fly by the seat of my pants," side kicked in and took over as usual. I was just going to be honest with him. I picked up my phone.

"Hi Johnny. I miss you too. So much it hurts."

I stared at my phone waiting for his reply. Five minutes passed and nothing, while my rings glowed a brighter pink. I shoved my phone into my back pocket and tiptoed past mom's room, stopping to listen. Her deep breathing, assured me she was fast asleep.

Once outside on the back deck, I found my usual launching spot, threw my hair into a bun, and took off cutting through the black sky. I had no idea where I was going except up. I flew to about 300 feet finally coming to a stop, and decided to hang out for a while there. Lying on my back, I looked at the stars as clouds passed over between the moon and I. A shooting star came from the north making a bright streak above me. I couldn't believe this was my life and how lucky I was.

My text dinged and vibrated from my back pocket. I sat up in a chair position, my feet dangling in the air, and grabbed my phone. It was Johnny.

"I'm so sorry you're hurting Claire, but I can't tell you how happy I am to hear that. I'm hurting too. I want to see you again so bad. Do you think we can meet this week just to talk?"

I paused for a moment. "Well, it couldn't hurt anything," I said trying to talk myself into it, and it didn't take much to do that.

"Ok Johnny. I would love that."

A loud engine noise caught my attention and I looked down to see a truck barrelling through my quiet neighborhood. The driver slammed on his brakes in the middle of the street, coming to a stop in front of a house two blocks from my own. The person got out of the truck, grabbed something from the back, and proceeded to pour it all over a car sitting in the driveway.

I immediately dropped from the sky, landing in the backyard of the home next door. I crouched down and followed the fence that divided the two houses, peeking through the bushes that butted up against the fence.

"I should be minding my own business," I quietly preached to myself.

The potent smell of gasoline filled the driveway, confirming my suspicion. The car was drenched in it.

A tall white man in a camouflaged jacket returned from his pickup truck. I watched as he grabbed a newspaper and lit it on fire. He then proceeded to throw it on the car, but the newspaper burnt out before it could ignite.

Oh Crap. I grabbed my phone from my back pocket and dialed 911, careful to block my number again, before I dialed.

"Clarksville 911," answered a male operator.

I covered my mouth on the phone trying to be as quiet as possible, as the man returned to his truck.

"Hi, I'm on Ridgeway Drive, and there is a guy parked in the middle of the street trying to catch a car on fire."

"He's trying to what?" the dispatcher asked as if he didn't believe me. (At least it wasn't the same girl as last time.)

"He's trying to set a vehicle on fire. He's in a green pick up truck and a camouflaged jacket. He's a white male, approximately 6'00."

"Ok ma'am. What's the address?"

"Sir, I don't know the exact address. I'm in the yard next door." I watched as the man returned to the car. " Oh my God. He's coming back with the gas can.... and he's pouring gas in the passenger car seat."

The man paused for a moment as if he heard something and looked in my direction. I ducked behind the bushes trying to remain as still and quiet as possible. Once again he lit a newspaper and a large flame burst in the car. He then ran back to his truck and jumped in.

"Ma'am? Are you there?" asked the dispatcher.

I flew to the roof of the house next door and hid behind the chimney.

"I'm here. The car's on fire, and the guy is leaving."

"And what's his direction of travel?"

"He's driving…" It took a moment for me to figure out which direction he was going. "Ok, he's going north out of the neighborhood towards Ft. Campbell Boulevard."

Soon the pickup was out of my view from the roof. I looked over at the car that was now a bright ball of orange and white fire. The smell of burnt rubber and leather filled the air. The windows burst and the alarm on the car activated, screeching through the calm night.

I shot up in the air trying to keep my eye on the pick up and the car at the same time. Much to my relief, the neighbors of the house I had been standing on came out. A male,in his bare feet and shorts, ran to the house where the car was parked, and began banging on the door to warn the occupants. I turned my attention to the pickup truck, trying to figure out where it had gone.

"Ma'am we have police and fire enroute to your location. Can you still see the truck?"

I looked to the east and saw police coming in with lights and sirens, followed a couple of miles behind by the firetrucks and ambulance. I scanned the area trying to spot the truck to no avail.

"No Sir. I've lost sight of the truck."

"Ok, well can I get your name and number?"

"I'd rather remain anonymous please."

"Ma'am it would help the officers if you would leave your name since you witnessed the crime."

"I'm sorry Sir, I can't." And with that I hung up the phone, so bummed I didn't follow the truck.

The next morning I texted Johnny back, telling him I fell asleep before we could make a plan, which was pretty much true. Flying wore me out, and when I came back from the arsonist fiasco, I was exhausted and crashed on the couch.

I was sitting in church with Alicia Sunday morning when my phone vibrated. I looked down and my heart leapt in my chest when I realized it was Johnny.

"Hey Claire Bear."

"Hey Johnny."

"Don't worry about last night. I'm sure you were tired from work and I got tied up in a game before I could text you back."

"It's ok. I was pretty exhausted."

"Do you think we could meet up sometime this week?"

"Who are you texting?" Alicia whispered to me during the sermon.

I smiled a guilty smile at her.

"Seriously?!" she exclaimed almost too loudly.

"Shhh!" I hissed.

"How did that happen?"

"I'll tell you later." I went back to texting Johnny.

"Ok, Johnny. When and where?"

"Can I pick you up on Thursday night and take you to dinner?"

I hesitated about doing a dinner. If he was seeing someone else, I didn't want to sit through a whole dinner with him.

"Maybe you can come over Thursday night. I have basketball practice that night and a test on Friday. We can sit on the porch swing and talk."

"That sounds perfect. Thanks Claire."

"No problem Mr. Perfect."

I looked over at Alicia who was staring at me intently, begging for any information I could give her.

"He's coming over to talk Thursday night," I whispered. "But that's it. Nothing more."

"Well, it's a start!" she said, her eyes wide with excitement for me. Alicia really liked Johnny and had made her disapproval well known to me, when I ended it with him.

I sat through church trying to pay attention to the sermon, but all I could think about was Johnny, and the problems I could cause him on his journey to be a pilot. Who was I to mess up his dream? I loved flying and I couldn't imagine my life without it, but I loved Johnny even more. I would give it all back just so I could be with him.

I closed my eyes as the Pastor prayed a final prayer, and slipped one in for myself. I needed a lot of guidance on this one. I didn't want to be selfish, but I just couldn't imagine life without my Johnny.

THIRTEEN

MY WEEK LEADING up to my talk with Johnny was full of school, basketball, flying, and a little crime fighting. I know I should have just stuck to flying minus the crime fighting thing, but I couldn't help myself. First of all I felt an obligation, since I had intervened in the first two crimes, to help people. I couldn't stand to think there were people out there in trouble, and I could have done something to help and didn't. I found myself checking the paper every morning to see what I had missed, and always thinking of what I could have done to make a difference. And second, plainly put, I was just nosey.

By the time Thursday afternoon rolled around, I had helped the Clarksville Police catch three more bad guys. Two robberies, and a hit and run.

I also knew the dispatchers were catching onto me. When I called about the hit and run, I heard the dispatcher who had answered say to another, "It's her again." They kept asking me how I could possibly have the information I was giving to them and the only answer I could come up with was, "I just know." I know how that sounds so stupid, but that's all I had.

Thursday night after dinner, Kass and I hung out in her hippie decorated room. I was laying on her peace sign comforter, when I heard Johnny pull into the driveway.

"So what did you decide Claire? Are you going to get back together with him?" Kass asked from

her overstuffed bean bag chair. Between her and Alicia, all I had heard about was Johnny and getting back with him. Even Kyle was asking when they could hang out again.

I got up from the bed, and walked over to her tie dyed framed full length mirror. I wasn't particularly dressed up. I had thrown on some comfy sweats and the black 101st Airborne tee Johnny had given me. It was my favorite. It fit me perfectly, and had a Chinook etched in the background behind the lettering. Johnny had never seen me in it, so I thought tonight would be the perfect night to throw it on.

"I don't know Kass. I'll just see how it goes," I replied spraying on her Angel Kiss body mist. The smell of lavender and a crisp sweet honey fragrance filled the air. I was adding a little leave in conditioner in my curls when mom appeared in the door.

"Claire, Johnny's here."

"Thanks Mom," I said smiling slightly. I was so

nervous. I turned to Kass. "Wish me luck."

"Good luck," she smiled crossing her fingers.

I walked down the hall to the living room where Johnny stood by the door waiting for me. We locked eyes and I couldn't stop staring at him. It had been a month since I had seen him. I know a month doesn't sound like a long time, but it is when you have to go without seeing or talking to someone you care so much about. I was so happy to see him again, I felt tears brimming the bottom of my eyes. He looked incredible and smiled nervously at me.

"Hey, Claire Bear."

"Hi, Johnny Angel."

"You look better in that than I do," he said pointing out my tee and breaking the tension.

"It's my favorite," I giggled, then looked up at him. "Want to go out on the porch swing?"

"Sure."

We walked out into the dark night. The smell of fresh cut grass and sweet honeysuckle enveloped us, as I turned the porch light on dim to keep the bugs at bay. We sat on our white wicker porch swing, that had been my favorite place to be up until the accident. I used to come out here and sit forever, but now my life was full of flying. Any extra time I had was spent off the ground.

We rocked in silence for a moment and I waited for Johnny to say something. I liked waiting for Johnny to take the lead. I don't know if it was from my lack of having a father in my life or what, but he made me feel secure and I trusted him to lead our relationship. Yes, I know, woman power, blah..blah..blah. I am all about feeling empowered as a woman. But sometimes a girl just needs a guy to make her feel safe, and that's what Johnny did for me.

"So what's up with you getting a tattoo?" he smirked.

I looked down at the ground smiling and shaking my head. Thanks Alicia.

"Let me see it."

I looked over at him. "Johnny..."

"Come on. Let me see it," he laughed.

I took a deep breath and let it out. I slowly turned my wrist over and showed him my saturn rings that were glowing slightly.

Johnny lightly grabbed my wrist and pulled it closer to his face trying to see it better. "What is that Claire?" He laughed harder. "Glow in the dark planet rings? What the heck, girl?"

"Don't make fun!" I said pulling my wrist away and slapping him lightly on the arm, but I was laughing just as hard as he was.

"Did Alicia talk you into that?" he covered his mouth trying to hide his laughter. I loved seeing him laugh, even at my expense. We laughed a lot together.

"Nooo…" I said through my giggling, "it was a last minute thing."

This made him laugh even more. "Oh Claire," he tried to compose himself. "What am I going to do with you?" He looked over at me and slightly rubbed his hand over my tattoo. "My little rebel girl."

Chills ran over my body at his touch. He smiled at me noticing my body shaking.

"So when are we going to end this stupid separation thing, Claire? I miss you, and I know you miss me too."

I stared back at him. I was pretty sure sitting here on this swing, with this most perfect guy, I

was the luckiest girl in the world. A million girls would love to be in my shoes right now, but I was the one. The one he picked. The one he chose to jump out in front of, doing his cute little pivot dance. How could I let him go? If I did, he was going to find another girl and I would be regretting this big time. Oh yeah...by the way. What about that girl?

"But Johnny, I heard you were seeing someone else already," I emphasized the "already" part.

"What? Claire, what are you talking about?"

"I heard you were seeing some girl that works by you." I turned my body toward him looking him in the eyes.

"I have no idea what you're talking about." He paused for a moment thinking. "Are you talking about Frazier?"

"Her name is Frazier?" I cringed.

"That's her last name. Claire, she's just a friend. She's going for the rank of Specialist just like I am. That's it," he said firmly. "Nothing more."

I nodded my head silently, to let him know I believed him. Johnny leaned in closer, and put his arm around me.

"Claire, you are the one I care about. I haven't even thought about dating anyone." His tone was almost pleading. "I was waiting to see if I could get back with you. There is no way I would jeopardize that with someone else."

Oh wow, that was so sweet. I put my head on his shoulder. "Johnny, I believe you. It's ok."

Johnny looked at me relieved. I could tell he really cared about me. Flying superpower or not, I couldn't let him go. Somewhere deep inside me I just felt that somehow this would all work out. Besides that, I couldn't imagine not having him around. I felt like a big part of me was missing when I didn't talk to him daily. Not only was I missing my boyfriend, but now one of my very best friends.

I grabbed his hand and pulled it close to me. "Johnny, all I know is I've been miserable without you. I can't be away from you anymore. I just have to trust that everything else is going to work out."

He smiled and pulled me closer to him. I wrapped my arms around his broad shoulders and warm neck and held him tight. I could smell his familiar cologne, a mixture of a sweet and spicy- woods scent. I finally let go slightly, and felt his hand gently against my cheek. He leaned down and kissed me softly on my forehead, then down to my lips for a long moment. I slid my hand up his arm to the back of his neck and pulled his lips back to mine. I had dreamed of kissing him again for the last three weeks, and I was not ready to be done yet. I could tell he felt the same way. He returned my kiss, and when we finally let go, my heart was racing. Johnny leaned back gently on the swing pulling me underneath his arm. I laid my head on his chest.

"Man, Claire. I missed you so much," he whispered. "Don't ever do this to me again."

Friday morning I woke to the sun streaming through my window, and a big smile on my face. I had Johnny back in my life and that made me so happy. I threw on my jammie shorts and went to meet mom in the kitchen, for our morning chat over breakfast, before she left for work. The rich aroma of coffee and bacon filled the air, and mom looked up from the Leaf Chronicle, our city newspaper.

"Well, you look chipper this morning," she said her eyes twinkling. "Happier than I've seen you in a while."

"Johnny and I had a good talk last night," I smiled sitting down and buttering my wheat toast.

"Well, that's good to hear. I could tell you missed him, sweetie."

"I did mom. We're going to start dating again," I said biting my toast.

Mom looked down at her paper as though she was reading, but was still talking to me. "That's wonderful, if it makes you happy," she said cautiously.

I chewed on my toast trying to figure out exactly

what she meant by that. I could tell she was worried about me. When I broke up with Johnny she was the only one who didn't give me a hard time. She always supports my decisions and is my biggest cheerleader.

"I'm happy mom. I thought about it alot and I know I made the right decision." I nodded at the paper. "Anything good in there this morning?" I asked wanting to change the subject.

"Well, there was a car fire, just a few blocks from here, actually," mom said reading through her glasses. "Hmm...It looks like someone set a car on fire in our neighborhood. The police are thinking it was this lady's ex-husband, but they're not sure."

I set my toast down and grabbed the paper from her.

"I heard about that," I said looking at the paper closely. "I didn't know it was her ex-husband though. What a jerk!"

Mom laughed. "Claire, why this sudden interest in crime?" She stood up and stacked the dishes to put in the sink. I was so engrossed in the article I didn't even hear her question.

"It says here, someone called in to report it and officers are requesting that witness come into the station to make a statement." I put the paper down. I was that witness.

"Well, hopefully that witness will come forward, so they can put whoever did this away for a while. I can't imagine what that poor lady is feeling. She must be terrified."

I stood up and walked over to the sink by mom. "Mom, what happens if that witness doesn't come forward?"

Mom paused from rinsing the dishes. "Well, I suppose they need the witness to identify the man. It will help their case against him."

"Oh," I said biting on my nail. Just great. There was no way I could come forward. There was too much of a risk of being caught and tied to the other cases.

All morning at school I thought about the arsonist case, and how I could be a witness without revealing my identity. How could I not? If this guy was crazy enough to set her car on fire, who knows what else he could do? I worried for the victim and felt an obligation to help her out, so the arsonist could get as much punishment as possible.

At lunch I decided to bring it up to my girls and see what they thought.

"So, I have to ask you guys something, kind of a dilemma thing," I said to Lexi, Alicia, and Tina, who played the forward position on the team.

"Ok, shoot," Alicia said intrigued.

"So, what would you do if you witnessed a crime and you were the only witness? The cops are asking for the witness to come forward, but you don't want to reveal your identity?"

"Did you witness a crime Claire?" Lexi gasped.

"No, Lex. It's a question for Criminal History."

The table was silent for a moment as everyone pondered my dilemma. Finally Tina spoke up.

"Well, you could write the police a letter, tell them the name of the suspect, and describe what he looked like."

"Or, even better," Alicia interrupted, "you could somehow get a pic of the suspect, identify him, and turn it in with a letter signed anonymous. But I think that's the best one could do."

Wow, that was actually a really great idea.

"That's a really great idea," I said.

"Do you have to write a paper on it?" Lexi asked. I love Lexi, but she is all of 115 pounds and at least half of that is nosiness.

"Not exactly. Just something to ponder," I smiled and then tried to change the subject. "Hey, how are you guys feeling about our scrimmage next month?"

Alicia sat up straight in her chair, excited for any kind of basketball talk. "I think we might have a shot this year, especially with the way you've been playing Clairey."

I smiled as Alicia's remarks opened a floodgate of memories from the last few weeks of practice. Alicia was right. I had been playing like a young female version of MJ. It was not easy finding balance in my flying when it came to basketball, and I found myself soaring to the basket with ease. And it wasn't just the lack of gravity issue either. Flying gave me a self confidence like I had never experienced before, and it showed on the court.

"I hope so," chimed in Tina. "East Central has beat us every year since 8th grade. It would be nice to beat them our Senior year."

Lexi's eyes perked up and she looked at me. "So Claire is the basketball star here?" she asked.

"She is this year," Alicia answered patting me on the back.

"What do you mean this year?" Lexi prodded even more. "Were you not as good last year?"

I shrugged my shoulders not knowing exactly how to answer that one.

"Seriously, Claire. It's like you ate some superpower basketball pill," laughed Tina. "Lexi, last year Claire was lucky to score ten points a game."

"Zip it Tina," I laughed throwing my dirty napkin at her. "Lex, I wasn't THAT bad."

"Oh, come on, Claire. You know we suck!" Alicia exclaimed, and we all started laughing.

"Ok, I am definitely coming to your games now," said Lexi. "This I gotta see."

FOURTEEN

FRIDAY AFTERNOON BEFORE the football game, I took a jog through my neighborhood to see if I could get a name or address from the mailbox of the arson victim. I couldn't think of any other way to find this guy and at least a last name was a start. I slowed my pace to a walk as I neared the home. I glanced in the yard of the house beside it and saw an elderly black woman kneeling down pulling weeds from a beautiful garden of tulips. The detective in me surfaced, and I began my investigation.

"Those tulips are so beautiful," I smiled. "Your garden is amazing."

"Oh, thank you," the woman returned my smile. "Tulips are very resilient and easy to grow."

"I don't believe I've ever seen a red one with pink trim. How in the world did you do that?"

"Well, I've had a lot of years to practice," she

answered with mischievous grin. "Would you like to come in the gate and get a closer look?"

"Sure!" I said.

A mixture smell of sweet tulips and antique furniture awaited me, as I opened the adorable white gate and walked down the cobblestone path to her home. I was a plant lover and tulips were my favorite, so this was a real treat for me.

I spent the next 30 minutes with my new friend, Lillian. She, and her husband Nute, had lived in this neighborhood for over 40 years, and was one of the coolest people I had met in a long time. We talked tulips, family, and last of all the neighborhood.

"You know Claire, when we first moved here, all these businesses were not around. It was just a brand new subdivision in the middle of corn fields."

"I'm sure that's been a big adjustment for you," I said, "and the crime rate going up."

"Well, that too," she smiled, her wrinkled hands slightly shaking as she placed new soil around a freshly planted tulip. "That car fire that happened last week, wouldn't have happened here 40 years ago. People used to respect each other's belongings, and not allow rage to guide their thought process."

"Yeah, I heard about that," I said casually. "Do you know if they caught who did it?"

"Not that I'm sure of, but there is talk that it was her ex-husband. She's not here anymore, you know. She and her little girl went to stay with her parents. She's terrified."

"I don't blame her," I said staring over at the empty house. "I wouldn't want to stay by myself after that either."

Lillian picked up her garden hose and started watering the flowers. "Well, I knew Luke was not a good character from the moment I met him. You know how you meet someone and something just doesn't sit right?" I nodded. "That's how it was when I met Luke."

"Luke is her husband?" I asked. Lilian nodded her head. "Too bad no one saw it happen," I further probed.

"Someone saw it happen. A female called it in. The police questioned me, but I didn't see or hear anything. Nute and I go to bed with the sun. We didn't even hear the fire trucks respond."

"Lillian, what kind of vehicle does Luke drive?" I asked hoping not to be to obvious.

"Ummm...just in case I see him around the neighborhood."

"A truck. A green truck. But I doubt he'll come around here anymore."

My text dinged from Johnny. OMG, I forgot about Johnny. It was already 5:40 and he was picking me up for the football game at 6:15.

"Lillian, I'm sorry, but I have to go. It was so nice to meet you."

"Well honey, it was certainly a pleasure to meet you. You make sure you come back around and see me again."

"Yes Ma'am, I will." I promised.

I left towards the arsonist's house and looked for a name on the mailbox. The last name Trent stood out in bright gold letters against the black mailbox. As I passed the familiar driveway I looked for any signs of the fire, but the only remnants I could see was black burn marks left on the driveway. The burned out car was gone and the driveway was completely empty.

"Alright Luke Trent," I said to myself as I jogged away. "I am going to find you."

Later that night after the football game, Shawn and Alicia, Tater and Lexi, Kyle and Kass, and Johnny and I, squeezed in a round booth at our favorite restaurant, Pizza House, to celebrate the fifth win of the season for Kyle. So far we remained undefeated.

"Claire, did you let mom know we would be home a little late?" Kass asked as we waited for our pizzas to arrive.

"Yes, of course," I said.

"Claire forget something?" Lexi teased me. "I've never met someone as OCD as Claire. I can't imagine her forgetting anything."

"Seriously," laughed Kass. "Have you guys ever seen her room?"

"No, what's up with her room?" Shawn asked smiling sideways at me. "Is it freaky or something?"

"Really Shawn?" Alicia asked playfully hitting him

on his bulging bicep, as everyone laughed. Good grief. That guy must work out all day.

Kass continued into a descriptive rundown of my room. "It's just too perfect," she laughed. "Everything is white, except the hardwood floor. All of her stuff is either alphabetized or organized by color."

Lexi chimed in. "And don't dare wrinkle her sheets or her comforter. She will kick you out of the room for that nonsense."

Everyone laughed again and Johnny squeezed my leg under the table, almost as if to ask if I was ok with everyone picking on me. I looked at him and rolled my eyes, laughing to let him know I was fine.

"Well, my little Miss Perfect does have a bit of a wild side," Johnny said still looking at me, but clearly talking to everyone else.

"What are you talking about?" I laughed.

"This," he said gently taking my left arm and putting my wrist up on the table.

"We're all shocked about that one," Alicia teased. "Claire is the one less likely to get a tat out of all of us."

"What are those? Saturn rings?" Tater asked leaning in for a closer look.

"Yes, because she loves the sky," Alicia said rolling her eyes and laughing.

"Zip it Alicia," I laughed. "Seriously you guys? Did I miss the pick on Claire memo?"

"Saturn rings must be really popular right now," Shawn said. "I've seen those somewhere before."

I looked over at Shawn intrigued. "Oh really? Where is that?"

The waitress interrupted my question placing three large pizzas in front of us. The salty smell of melted cheese, onions, and sausage filled the air, as everyone began to dig in, picking their favorite. I chose the supreme and let my question sit on hold while we ate.

"So anymore girl ghost sightings Tater?" Alicia asked.

"None that I know of, but I haven't pulled guard lately," Tater replied trying to keep his pizza filled mouth closed. "Johnny might know. Silva's had him out there a lot the past month, because the higher ups are freaking out right now."

Everyone looked at Johnny wide eyed including me, waiting for his response.

"It's all good," Johnny replied after taking a drink. "There's so much security out there now, I can barely get in the gate."

"I think it's pretty cool that a girl could break into such a high secure facility," Kass grinned mischievously.

I smiled at her in appreciation for the compliment, she had no idea she was giving me.

Shawn leaned back in his seat putting his arm around Alicia. "I don't understand what a girl would be doing out there anyway. It's almost like there's some secret spy Hollywood movie stuff going down."

"Well," Johnny said, "Silva did tell me they sent some K9's out, and they followed the scent from the office to the woods. Then it was just gone."

"Wow. Maybe it was a ghost then!" Lexi exclaimed.

"A ghost with a scent Lex?" Kyle laughed.

"Yes," Lexi said emphatically. "A ghost can have whatever it wants to have, Kyle. It's a ghost."

We all laughed at Lexi's assertiveness.

When everyone was pretty much done and Johnny went to the bathroom, I leaned over and asked Shawn again while everyone else was talking to each other.

"Shawn, did you say you've seen these rings before?"

"Yeah Claire, I was actually just thinking about that," he said wiping his mouth. "There is a couple of small boxes in the hangar at work. I saw them painted on there. They look almost identical to yours."

"Oh...that's an interesting coincidence," I said trying to not sound as flabbergasted as I was. "When did you see that?"

"I see them all the time. They are in the medical closet out at the hangar."

I stared at Shawn for a moment, my mouth slightly gaping open. I tried to hide my shock, but I failed miserably. There were more boxes. I knew there had to be more of that stuff somewhere. The wheels in my head started turning and I started plotting. I had to get my hands on it.

"Claire are you ok?" Alicia asked nudging my side. She had been talking to Lexi, and had missed our whole conversation.

"Yes, I'm good," I said snapping out of it. "I'm just

tired."

Johnny returned to the table and gathered our bill. "Are you ready to go beautiful?" he asked extending his hand down for me to take. I grabbed it and he lifted me gently out of the booth.

Johnny and I were quiet for the first few minutes on the drive home. I was so tired from the long week and I knew he was too. I squeezed in as close as I could to him with my seatbelt on, and laid my head on his shoulder. Johnny placed his hand on my knee.

"Hey Claire?" he asked softly.

"Yes?" My response was barely audible. I was so relaxed.

"I hope it was ok that I showed everyone your tattoo tonight. I know I tease you about it alot, but I actually like your Saturn rings."

I giggled at his sensitivity. "Johnny, it's fine. Really. They were all going to see it sooner or later, anyway."

Johnny laughed. "Well, you're a good sport. You took a lot of teasing tonight. I just don't ever want you to feel hurt or uncomfortable. Plus from one OCD person to the next, I can definitely relate."

I snuggled up closer to his arm. "It's so nice to be with someone as perfect minded as myself," I teased and he chuckled. I could have stayed where I was for the next year without moving an inch, and been totally fine. I was so happy.

I spent Saturday morning searching the web for any information I could find on Luke Trent. So far I had not been able to find any kind of social media information. All I needed was an address so I could get a pic and mail it in to the Police, but I could only find him listed at the address on Ridgeway.

"Great," I said to myself blowing a loose curl out of my face. "The only way I'm going to get a pic of this guy is by luck."

Little did I know a little bit of luck was going to fall right into my lap that very night.

Saturday night, I rolled my way through 70 orders at work. We were so busy, it was all Alicia and I could do to keep up with the west side of the parking lot. Cars honked, and 50's music blared from the loudspeakers.

"Claire, pick up! Alicia, pick up!" Mr. Arnold bellowed from the window.

Alicia rolled up beside me, coming to an almost perfect stop in front of the window.

"Mony! You have really got your stopping technique down!" I complimented her as I picked up a large tray.

"Thanks Clairey! I can almost keep up with you now."

Off we went dodging customers and cars, to the far west side of the front parking lot. I had just circled a black convertible full of kids from school, and started to cross the drive when a truck flew off the main highway and into the parking lot. I skidded to a stop barely missing the front bumper, almost losing my tray. The driver stopped, and looked down at me not saying a word. My heart skipped a beat as I caught my breath.

"Hey, man! Slow it down!" Caleb Taylor, one of the lineman from our football team, yelled out from the hood of the convertible. He jumped down and walked over to me. "Claire, are you ok?"

I looked back at the truck, the green truck, as it pulled away heading to the other side of the parking lot. "Luke Trent," I said loud enough for Caleb to hear me.

"You know him Claire?" Caleb asked.

"Old neighbor," I replied. "Thanks for checking on me Caleb. I'm ok."

I dropped off the order and skated to the east side of the building, peeking around the corner to see where the green truck was parked. Luke Trent had parked in the back corner as far away from everyone as he possibly could. Alex, one of our newer waitresses, skated over to greet him. I had to figure out a way to get his picture, knowing this could be my last chance.

"Claire! Pick up!" I skated back to the window and delivered a few more orders, all the while keeping my eye on the truck.

"Think, Claire. Think," I said to myself.

"Alex! Pick up!" I turned to find Alex and saw her

at the black convertible talking to Caleb and his buddies. She glanced at the window and I saw her saying bye to everyone. Without thinking I went to the window, grabbed her order, and read the ticket. Slot 47. This was Luke's order.

"I will be delivering this one," I said to myself as I took my phone out of my apron pocket and placed it on the tray. Now the difficult task of getting a pic unnoticed.

"Ok, sir. That will be $7.80," I said as I approached the truck.

Luke Trent stared at me for a short moment before digging in his pockets. I picked up my phone with his bag trying to balance both of them in the same hand, and quickly set my phone to camera mode. This was going to be tricky.

Luke handed me almost the exact amount needed. I owed him a dime. I dug into my apron with one hand trying to distract him. He looked at my apron and I pushed the multi picture on my phone, letting it go to work, hopeful I could get at least one good shot.

I gave him his change, and he quickly pulled away. Of course there was no tip. Why would he?

What a loser.

Alex skated over to me. "Claire, I'm sorry about that. I didn't get to the window quick enough, I guess."

"Oh no, Alex," I reassured her. "I took it thinking it was mine. I should have paid more attention. But anyway, here is the tip he left you." I handed her

$5.00.

"That's yours, Claire."

"No, Alex," I said shoving the money in her apron. "It's not your fault I grabbed your order. Please take it."

Alex smiled and thanked me. I gave her a wink, patted her on the back, and then skated to the storage room eager to look at my phone. I pulled up the pictures and was thrilled to find there were quite a few I could use.

"Well, that was worth almost getting ran over for. Way to go Claire!" I smiled.

Sometimes it's good to be your biggest fan.

First thing Monday morning I placed a manilla envelope in the mail addressed to Detective Lee of the Clarksville Police Department. Detective Lee was handling the arsonist case, and was the one who requested for the "anonymous female witness" to come forward. I hoped this was going to be good enough. Inside I had included five pictures of Luke and his truck, and a descriptive letter of what I had seen on the night of the fire.

Despite the fire fiasco, I still had an overwhelming desire to help people. I spent as much time as I possibly could in the air. I had become so addicted to flying and couldn't wait until the sun set, so I could take off into the dark night. I spent a lot of time online researching how high I could go safely, and so far the highest I had been was 1000 feet.

One sleepless, cloudy night I flew as high as I could go without being detected. I passed a big fluffy cloud to my right, then flew above it. I looked down on one of the most beautiful sights I had ever seen. The earth's surface was gone and nothing but a fluffy white layer stretched beneath me. The moon shone it's brilliant light across the surface of the cloud illuminating it. I layed on my tummy and watched as it rolled off to the east below me.

I was pretty fast too. Once I set my mind to it, I could jet. I was flying at speeds that felt at least 100 miles an hour. I didn't have anything that could measure height or speed, but I was sure I was pretty close to accurate.

By the middle of October, I had added nine more assists to the Police. The dispatchers had given me a nickname, "Miss Sky Walker", because they said I could see everything at once. I knew this to be true, because the last time I had called in, Operator 132 (the guy dispatcher), called it out to the other dispatchers he worked with, "I got Miss Sky Walker on the phone!" So now, I sort of had a name. I still refused to give out any of my information, despite the dispatcher's constant urging of me to.

FIFTEEN

I WALKED INTO the kitchen before school to eat breakfast with my mom on a foggy Thursday morning, anticipating the long day I had ahead. First school, then grabbing dinner, and finally our big game against East Central. I was so nervous, mainly because I knew Johnny and Shawn would be there watching.

"Good morning sweetie," Mom said, sipping her coffee and smiling. "I saved the crime section for you." She pushed the morning paper toward me. She found my interest in the city of Clarksville's crime amusing.

"Thanks Mom," I said looking down at the front page. "I can't believe it's already the middle of October."

"I know!" She agreed. "Basketball season is here. Are you excited about the game tonight?"

I sipped on my orange juice. "Honestly Mom, I'm

so nervous."

"Nervous about what?" Kass asked as she came into the kitchen. "The scrimmage?"

"Of course, the scrimmage," I laughed. "We're going to get our butts kicked, just like we do every year."

My mom frowned at me. "Claire, if that's the attitude you go into the game with, then you won't have much of a chance. You need to be more positive."

Kass and I looked at each other smirking at the all too familiar lecture. We knew that one was coming.

"I know Mom, but East Central is the best team in our conference. I'm just being realistic."

"Not so fast, Claire," Kass said sitting down with us. "Mom, all the girls are talking about what a great player Claire is, and how she is going to carry the team this year."

Mom looked over at me, her eyes raised in excitement. "Oh really? I'm not surprised. I can't wait to watch you tonight, Claire!"

"Thanks Mom," I blushed. "But don't get your hopes up."

I peeked outside the locker room door before the game that night. 30 minutes until tip off. The stands were half full which was a good start to the season. Besides our families and a few close friends, not many people came to our games, and I couldn't blame them. As painful as it was to play so terribly, I was sure it was even more so to watch. I scanned the home section and spotted my mom sitting with Kass on one side of her, and Johnny on the other. Kyle sat next to Kass and Shawn, Lexi, and Tater sat beside Johnny. My sweet little mom looked so content squished in between all of them.

"Is Shawn here?" Alicia asked looking over my shoulder.

"Yeah. He's sitting with Johnny and my mom."

I took a deep breath and turned to look at Alicia. We faced each other and clasped hands, silent for a moment. She looked back at me, her face mirrored with the same worried look I gave her.

"We'll be ok Claire," she said finally.

"You don't sound too confident, Mony."

"That's because I'm not," she sighed.

I tried to lighten the mood. "Johnny and Shawn are going to leave third quarter, ashamed that they even know us." This set us on a giggling frenzy, and I felt the tension and worry start to melt away.

Sometimes my dull sense of humor worked.

"Alicia! Claire!" Coach yelled from the locker room. "Let's get this show on the road!"

Before I knew it, it was game time. East Central looked as polished and as good, as I remembered. Although they had only two returning Seniors, they played as if they had twelve. Tina won tip off for us, sending the ball to me. I took it down and yelled out our first play. This called for a shot from our center, but she missed and I was on my way to the basket for the rebound. The lack of gravity on my body helped me out jump, out shoot, and out run everyone. I made that first rebound shot and never looked back. By the end of the game we were ahead, 56 to 47, and I was actually the lead scorer with 30 points! I had even scored five three points shots, the last one swooshing silently in the net as the final buzzer sounded. The East Central team stood on the court looking as puzzled and surprised as our fan section did. I high fived my teammates and ran off the court to the sound of Johnny yelling "That's my girlfriend!" as loud as he could. I smiled and waved at him and my mom, then glanced down at my tattoo rings that were glowing on my wrist. I kissed them lightly, and ran to the locker room to the unfamiliar sound of thunderous applause and whistles from our fans.

We had won our first game against East Central in ten years.

Friday night after the football game I came home to an empty house. My mom was at a women's conference in Nashville, and Kass went out with Kyle after the game. Johnny and his platoon had left that morning for training in the field, and I wouldn't be able to see him until Sunday night.

Normally, I would have been nervous coming

home late by myself, but tonight I was actually pretty excited. I had this superhero boldness that had come with flying, and being home alone also meant more flying time. It wasn't easy finding time to fly when mom and Kass were home. I had at least an hour until 11, Kass' curfew, and she would be home.

I put my hair up in my "flying bun" and threw on a light jacket, because the air was a little more damp than usual. Now, where to go. I could go sit on the clock tower for awhile, or just spend some time up in the air hanging out. I decided to just fly up and see where the breeze took me, but no crime fighting tonight. Just fun.

I turned the back porch light on so I could see where to land when I got home. The last time I went up I forgot to, and scraped my leg on the patio chair coming down.

The door slid closed behind me and I ran off the patio, launching myself into the open night sky. It was extra dark out, as the high clouds covered the moon. As I rose into the air I felt my body shift in the strong breeze. I could smell and taste the salt water in the clouds, no doubt picked up from the Gulf of Mexico, and now rolling into our skyspace above middle Tennessee.

I flew across the sky looking down at the flickering lights of the city and turned my body, doing barrel rolls and flips. I liked to shoot as high as I safely could, and then drop free fall at a heart stopping pace. I never realized until now, what a dare devil I was.

Before I knew it, the alloted 30 minute time I had given myself was gone, and I had to rush to try and beat Kass home. I would have a hard time explaining to her my absence with my car parked in the driveway, and every light in the house on.

I approached my neighborhood, careful not to descend too quickly, out of fear of someone seeing me. I hovered over my house, did my routine check of the area, and then dropped quietly into my backyard. I walked up to the back patio looking down at my glowing tattoo rings and up to the back door. I looked up to grab the door handle and found myself face to face with Kass.

OMG. I hope she didn't see me.

Kass stood in the kitchen, her mouth slightly open, and her eyes wide in terror, shaking her head no. She saw me. I froze unsure of what to do. I calmly walked to the slider and opened it. Kass backed slowly away, still shaking her head, feeling her way behind her with her hands, while keeping her eyes on me.

"Kass..." I began.

"Claire?" her voice cracked as she almost fell over the kitchen chair. "No...what did I just see Claire?" she asked, her eyes wide in disbelief. Then screamed it at me one more time. "WHAT DID I JUST SEE CLAIRE?!!"

"Kass….please." I put both of my hands up as a sign of surrender, hoping that would let her know I was safe. She looked like she was scared I was going to hurt her. "Just...just let me talk to you for a second."

"What are you Claire?" she scowled at me.

I looked at her in disbelief. "What..what do you mean, what am I? I'm Claire. I'm your sister," I said pointing at myself.

"No, you're not! You have to be some kind of an alien or something," she yelled at me. " Or a witch!"

"Kass... no! I'm not. I..I promise. Please just listen to me," I begged. "I can explain."

Kass backed slowly towards the living room finally reaching the front door and putting her hand on the handle. I knew I had to do something and fast. If she got to her cell phone or out the door, I was going to be in serious trouble. I inched my way to the other side of the living room, as far away from her as I could, and knelt on the floor.

"Kass, please look at me," I swallowed hard. "I'm going to sit here and I promise you, I won't get up off this floor until you feel safe with me. Please."

Kass stared at me for a moment, as if she were trying to see inside of me. She finally spoke, her voice shaking. "Did I see you fall out of the sky, Claire? Did I see you fall into our yard, and not get hurt?"

I took a deep breath. "Kass, you did see me come from the sky." I took another deep breath. "But I didn't fall from the sky. I...I flew down from the sky. I can fly, Kass."

Kass caught her breath putting both hands over her mouth in disbelief.

I looked at my frightened baby sister, feeling so bad for her. I couldn't imagine how she was feeling in this moment. I would be freaked out if I was her too.

"Trust me," I said talking fast to keep her from freaking out more. "I'm just as confused and as scared as you are. I don't understand what's going on with my body. I have no answers for it, but I'm working on figuring it out. There are some answers I can give you, if you want to sit and listen to me."

I watched as Kass' eyes slightly turned from a scowl to a touch of sympathy.

"What happened you to Claire?" she almost whispered.

I breathed a sigh of relief. She was going to let me explain. I started from the very beginning with her. I covered everything from the hangar accident, to my flight over the trees away from the scruffy guys, and my attempted break in to the hangar.

An hour later we sat face to face on my bed, staring down at my wrist, looking at my tat that was slightly glowing.

"You mean you're the ghost girl? The ghost girl from the hangar?" she asked in wonder.

"Yeah, that was me," I replied bashfully, but with a bit of pride.

"And this just appeared from nowhere?" Kass said rubbing her finger lightly over it.

"Yes," I said. "This is where the cut was. The next day it was a tattoo." I shrugged my shoulders in bewilderment.

"This just doesn't seem real. It's almost like some kind of a movie or something," she gasped.

"You're telling me," I agreed.

"Does anyone else know?"

"No. I haven't even told Alicia yet, but I'm going to. She will be so hurt to know I've kept such a big secret from her. I wasn't for sure if I was going to tell anyone, but I'm actually glad you found out. If something happens to me, at least you'll have an idea."

Kass sat up straight on the bed. "Happens as in YOU DIE?" she asked the worry returning to her face.

"Kass, I don't think I'm going to die, but I don't know what's going to happen to me. That stuff got into my bloodstream and I have no idea what it is. That's why I have to get back into that hangar and

find it, so I can get it tested or something."

"Why don't you just ask Johnny for it?"

"No!" I said sternly. "And you better not tell anyone. If I get found out, I want Johnny to be able to say he had nothing to do with it. I don't want to mess up his career."

"So, you can just go outside and fly right now if you wanted to?" she asked.

"Mmmhmm."

"Can I see you?"

I sighed. "Kass, I don't think that would be such a good idea. You're a little too freaked out right now."

"No, Claire. I promise. I won't freak out. Please!" she begged. "I just need to see it for myself."

"You saw me already and you freaked out," I laughed. " I don't think a second time will be any better."

"That's because I thought you were a witch or something. I know you're just you now."

I stared at her for a moment.

"Please Claire."

"Kass…"

"Please," she pleaded.

I thought for a moment and then finally agreed. "Ok, come on," I said standing up and throwing on a sweatshirt.

Kass jumped off the bed and followed me outside to the patio porch.

"Ok, stand over there." I pointed to the other side of the patio, and walked to the edge of the deck. I turned and gave her a little wink, bent my knees, and then shot into the air. I looked down and saw her staring straight up at me, her eyes as big as saucers. I paused at about 200 feet, turned in the air like a helicopter with my arms out, and then dropped effortlessly back down to the patio. Kass smiled big and was breathing heavily. I could tell she was so overwhelmed.

"How can this be real?" she asked her eyes filling with tears. She came over and touched my arm, almost as if she didn't believe I was real.

I held up my glowing tattoo and stared down at it. "I know. I ask myself that everyday, but it's definitely real."

Kass wrapped her arms around me and I hugged her back.

Mom's car pulling in the driveway interrupted our conversation, and we scurried to get back in the house. We were just locking the slider when she walked into the kitchen. Kass and I stood at the table side by side, trying not look as suspicious as we felt.

Mom put her purse on the table and looked at us skeptically, almost as if she knew what we had been up to. We smiled innocently.

"What have you girls been up to?' she asked arching one eyebrow at us.

"Nothing," we said at the same time.

She stared at us for another moment and then relaxed her skeptical face. "I'm so sorry I'm late girls. I didn't intend on it going that long."

"It's fine mom. We've just been hanging out," I assured her.

Kass and I looked at each other and breathed a sigh of relief.

SIXTEEN

SUNDAY AFTER LUNCH, I decided to take a quick jog to my antique neighborhood before Johnny came over. Kyle was coming too, and we were all going to order pizza and watch a movie. I was so excited to see him. It had been three long days, but in Johnny time that felt like forever.

I grabbed a ceramic bunny that I had bought for Miss Lillian's tulip garden and decided to stop by there on my way and drop it off. Miss Lillian seemed genuinely happy to see me again, and her eyes lit up when I gave her the bunny. I even got to meet her husband Nute, who looked a close second to Santa Claus, and was such a sweetheart.

"Claire, I'm so glad you stopped by. We have some good news for you. The police arrested Luke," she smiled big. "I thought you would like to know since you seemed so interested in the case."

I gasped with excitement. "That's so good to hear Miss Lillian! Have you heard anything about what led to the arrest?"

"Well, the paper just said the Police got a break in the case," Nute said in his raspy voice. "It's definitely put our minds at ease 'round here."

I looked over at the still empty house next door. "What about his wife? Is she coming back?"

"Doubt it," Nute answered. "And I don't blame her for not coming back. That guy was nothin' short of crazy."

I thanked them both and headed out on my run, feeling like I had a ten pound weight lifted off my chest. I was unsure if my pics had anything to do with the arrests, but I didn't care. I was just happy he was caught.

I ran toward the downtown district and felt the warm sun, but lightly cool breeze against my skin. The leaves on the trees were starting to turn rich shades of gold, orange, and red. I loved fall. It was my favorite time of year, and lucky for me Tennessee had long falls full of warm days and cool evenings.

The air smelled of fried food from Jackies Burgers and filled the air as I passed, then the smell of oil and gas as I reached the tiny gas station on the corner. I slowed my pace and approached the busy intersection, waiting patiently for the light to change, after pressing the pedestrian button. The sound of a service bell caught my attention, and I turned to see where it was coming from. The garage door at the gas station was wide open and I noticed two men in service coveralls staring at me, whispering back and forth between themselves. They glared at me with a nervous look in their eyes. For a moment I couldn't remember where I had seen them before, and then suddenly it all came back. My heart skipped a beat and my mind took me back to the gravel road. I stared at them harder. The scruffy men. The only two people, other than Kass, who knew my secret. They saw me fly.

"So this is where you guys came from," I said to myself. They must have followed me home from the service station.

Anger filled every crevice of my face and I glared at them while they stared back, then slowly backed into the garage. I vowed to myself to get them back, someway, somehow.

An hour later I jogged slowly up the stairs to my porch and Kass greeted me at the door.

"Claire, where have you been?" she asked and then lowered her voice. "Were you flying?"

I rolled my eyes. "No silly. I went for a jog, remember? And watch what you say!" I said looking over her shoulder for mom.

"Well, you better get in the shower. The guys are going to be here in 30 minutes."

"Ok. I'm going now." I walked in the house. "What are we watching?"

Kass held up two movies. "Well, I was thinking one of these two."

I looked at her choices. "The Little Mermaid or

Enchanted? Right Kass," I said shaking my head and smiling at her.

"What? Neither of the guys have seen these."

"They are not going to watch those. You have to find something with fighting or zombies."

An hour later, Johnny and I sat on the love seat, and Kass and Kyle on the couch watching Enchanted. I looked at the guys who had their eyes glued to the screen, and we were only ten minutes in to the movie. What the heck?

The doorbell rang. "Pizza's here!" I said jumping off the loveseat. I opened the door and to my delight saw Alicia and Shawn standing there, with a case of pop and a bag of chips.

"We got done at the mall early, so we thought we'd stop by," Alicia said hugging me and then walking in.

"Yay!" I said hugging her and then Shawn. "Come on in!"

Shawn walked in and looked at the TV. "Oooo! Enchanted! I love this movie!"

I looked over at Kass who gave me an "I told you so" smirk. I shrugged my shoulders in disbelief.

We had so much fun watching the movie. The best part was listening to Shawn sing- a- long, which made me wonder how many times he had seen this movie. He, of course blamed his expertise of it on his little sister.

"Yeah, sure baby," Alicia teased him.

After it ended we melted into the couches for an hour and talked about everything from football to helicopters.

"Hey, Claire, did they ever catch that arsonist?" Alicia asked.

Kass looked at me as if she was warning me to be cautious. I had told her everything about my crime fighting spree, including the arsonist. She had hung onto my every word, and had spent the last two days staring at me like I was a rock star.

"Actually, I just found out today that they arrested him this week," I said.

"That's such a weird thing to happen around here," Alicia said. "This is normally such a quiet neighborhood."

"Usually," I said standing up, stretching, and clearing the paper plates off the coffee table, "but lately it's been kind of crazy around here."

"Like what?" Kyle asked. "What kind of crazy stuff?"

I started to explain myself, but Kass beat me to it. "Well, Claire got followed home by two guys a couple of months ago. They chased her all the way home." I glared at Kass, who I could tell, immediately regretted her reply.

"What happened Claire?" Johnny asked looking at me with a worry in his eyes.

"They didn't follow me all the way home. I lost them at the fence," I explained.

Johnny stood up and walked over to me gently grabbing my hand.

"It was nothing Johnny," I said trying to shrug it

off.

"That's not nothing, Claire. Did you call the police?"

"No," I said as my chest tightened at the memory of being lifted off the ground. "I didn't need to. I got away."

"I didn't know about this either," Alicia said looking at me with hurt in her eyes. I knew what she was thinking. I always told her everything. Her stare made me feel so guilty. I hated it when she looked at me like that.

Shawn grabbed Alicia's hand. "Claire, you really should have reported that. They could very easily do it to some other girl, and she might not be as lucky as you."

At this point everyone was staring at me with worried expressions, except Kass who looked at the ground knowing she opened up a big can of worms for me.

I looked at Alicia. "I'm sorry," I apologized to everyone, but kept my eyes on her. "I guess I was just trying to forget about it."

If they only knew the real reason I didn't report it. I could just imagine myself trying to explain to the officer why I was soaking wet, smelling like chlorine, and how I ended up four blocks away from the fence. But most of all, I didn't want to worry my mom.

Johnny squeezed me close to him and kissed my forehead. "Well, at least you're alright." I could tell he was trying to lighten the mood in the room, but most of all make me feel better about it. I loved how he protected me, even from the cold stares of my best friend. Chills shot through my body. I'd never seen Alicia look at me that way before.

After everyone left, I walked with Johnny to his truck. I let him hold me close as he leaned up against the passenger door, and smelled the sweetness of his skin. Johnny has this natural smell that I can't describe. It's not a cologne or a soap smell or any other kind of artificial scent. It's a fresh, light aroma. Almost like something you would expect to find on a tropical island. It's such a unique smell, and I can't get enough of it. I'm not an obsessed crazy person, but I asked him to bring me one of his shirts every weekend when I see him. I send the old shirt back with him, and keep the new one under my pillow so I can smell him anytime I want. I was relieved when I asked him, that it didn't scare him away. Instead, he seemed flattered and made sure he always brought one with him.

"So when can I see you this week?" he asked as he squeezed me close. "Did you want to check out that movie this weekend?"

"Definitely!" I said without thinking, then I remembered my Friday and Saturday night were busy. "Oh crap, Johnny. I have to be at the high school Saturday for Track or Treat."

"What is Track or Treat?" he asked laughing.

"It's basically like trick or treating, but all over the high school. Kids come and each organization dresses up as something for their booth. My basketball team is doing The Wizard of Oz."

"Ohhh," said Johnny smiling. "And you're Dorothy?"

I smiled sheepishly. "No, the Witch."

"The good one?" he asked.

I laughed. "The bad one."

"I've got to see this, Claire."

"Kass and I always dress up for Halloween when we pass out candy. Want to come over? I'll be wearing it," I said with a little too much excitement.

Johnny smiled. "Heck yeah. Any chance I can be with my Claire Bear, I'm taking it."

Oh man, he was so sweet to me. Johnny lightly touched my cheek with his finger, then traced my face down to my chin. He gently lifted my face toward him, and lightly lowered his lips to mine. I felt an amazing jolt of electricity shoot through my lips all the way down my body. I had never felt anything like I felt when Johnny was kissing me, and every time I kissed him it felt like the first time. I pulled him closer as I always did, not wanting him to stop yet. I was sure he thought I was some pathetic desperate girl having never kissed a guy and never able to get enough of him. But he didn't seem to mind. When at last I let him go, he gave me one last hug.

"I can't wait to see you again," he said climbing in his truck.

"I can't wait to see you again too," I smiled back at him. "Buckle that seat belt, Sir."

I'm not a person that dreams a lot, but that night I had a pretty bad one. I dreamed I was out flying, but not here in Clarksville. I was in a huge city. Everywhere I looked there were skyscrapers. I flew around them in circles, watching myself in the mirrored glass windows. Another crazy thing, it was light outside. Everyone could see me and I didn't care. I looked down and saw hundreds of people staring and pointing up at me. One of them was Alicia. She just looked at me and then pointed at the sky above me. Suddenly, I felt gravity rush over my body. It clutched me with the same sensation that I had felt when I first started flying, and I plummeted to the ground. It felt so real, and I woke up in night sweats worried about what a dream like this could mean.

All week at school Alicia practically ignored me. She spoke to me only when necessary, but even then it was very cold. Practice was especially difficult. We always worked together, but she paired up with Tina. This was so hard for me to process. Alicia and I had never been mad at each other, and we definitely never went out of our way to not speak to each other. In fact, I could not remember one argument we had ever had.

As soon as practice was over on Thursday, I grabbed my stuff from the locker room hoping to catch Alicia in the parking lot. I leaned against my car waiting until she finally walked from the gym entrance.

"Alicia!" I yelled waving her over. She paused and looked at me, before reluctantly walking to my car looking at the ground the whole time.

"Hey Mony," I said quietly. "Please don't be mad at me anymore."

Alicia shifted on her feet, still staring at the ground. I could tell she was thinking before she spoke. Unlike me, Alicia was more patient and thought through her words. That was one of her many character traits I admired. I was not as disciplined, and pretty much called things as I saw them.

At last she spoke, a ton of frustration pouring out of her. "Claire, I'm really trying not to be, but I don't understand why you're cutting me out of your life. I mean, Sunday night, finding out about those guys chasing you was the last straw. You know, I don't know what is going on with you, but you haven't been yourself in the last two months." She sighed, putting both hands up in frustration. " I just can't figure it out. I feel like I don't even know you anymore."

She was so right. "I know," I said agreeing with her. "I'm so sorry. I don't mean to cut you out….it's just..." I couldn't finish my sentence. I didn't know what to tell her.

Alicia didn't answer me, but instead stared down at

the ground again. I felt like such a jerk. I knew I had to tell her what was going on with me.

"Mony, we need to talk about something. But I can't talk about it here. Can we meet sometime this week?"

This caused Alicia to look up from the ground at me. A worried expression consumed her face. "Are you ok Claire?" she asked.

"Yes," I answered quickly reassuring her. "I just need to talk to you about something really important."

"You're scaring me." She was so frustrated. "We're talking tonight."

"Tonight?" I asked meekly.

"Yes, tonight," she answered sternly.

I looked at my phone. "Ok, go home and change, and Kass and I will pick you up at 6."

Alicia looked at me skeptically. "You're bringing Kass? Claire, do you really think that's a good idea? Why don't you just come over?"

"No, Mony. Trust me. It's a good thing."

"Fine," she said annoyed swinging her backpack over her shoulder. "Why do you have to always be so dramatic?"

I watched her turn and walk away. This was going to be a long night.

SEVENTEEN

"YOU WANT ME to do what?!" Kass asked after dinner as we stood out on the back patio. "I DO NOT want to be there when you tell Alicia you can fly, Claire."

"Keep your voice down, Kass!" I said covering her mouth with my hand. "Why do you have to be so loud?!"

"I'm sorry, but I don't want to go through all that drama again. Besides, Kyle is coming over after practice and we're going to get ice cream."

"Seriously?" I asked. "You're going to put ice cream above your own sister?"

She sighed, rolling her eyes. "Fine Claire. This is just too insane."

"Really Kass? You think I don't know that?" I grabbed her hand and pulled her back in the house. "Come on. I have to pick her up at 6."

15 minutes later we were on our way to Alicia's,

and Kass was still going on about how "insane" this was going to be. Insane seemed to be her favorite word since she found out I could fly.

"How do you think she's going to take this, Claire?"

My face frowned as I thought about how hard it was going to be telling my best friend something as crazy as this. "I don't know, but remember what I told you. Just reassure her everything is ok while I'm up there. Try to not make it a big deal."

"What if she faints? When I saw you drop down, I started to black out and almost fainted."

"You did?" I asked surprised.

"Yeah. I felt so light headed."

I shook my head, rubbing my eyes as a slight tension headache started. "This is going to suck."

"Where are we going to take her?" she asked as we pulled into Alicia's driveway. "And what are you going to say?"

I quickly honked the horn. "We're going to grandma's farm, to the back pasture over the hill. That way no one can see me since it's still daylight."

Alicia approached the car, and I leaned over and whispered to Kass as she opened the door. "And I have no idea what I'm going to say."

Alicia jumped in the back seat. "Hey girls," she said a little more chipper than this afternoon. "Where are we headed?"

"We're going to my grandma's farm. Is that ok?" I asked turning around.

"Ummm...sure?" she replied hesitantly.

I changed the subject to the Friday night football game, and soon Alicia relaxed in the back seat. Thirty minutes later, we pulled down the gravel road that would take us to the back 10 of my grandma's farm. I knew I would be completely safe flying there. The fields were almost empty, now that my Uncle had cut down the last of the tobacco crops for the season. We pulled up to my favorite tree that boasted a huge tire swing we had played on since we were little girls, and jumped out of the car. The sun was just setting, and the sky glowed in brilliant hues of purple and orange. Just above the purple clouds, the evening star shined against a navy blue background.

"It's so beautiful tonight," Kass sighed as she looked up at the sky.

Alicia stared at us both, pushing away anymore distractions that we threw at her. "Ok, girls. What's this all about."

I looked over at Kass who nodded for me to go ahead. "Alicia, (she knew I used her name when I was serious) I've got to talk to you about something, and I need you to listen and not freak out, ok?"

Alicia nodded nervously as she heard the concern in my voice.

I took a deep breath. "Do you remember when I told you I cut myself at the hangar, and the next day this tat was there in place of my cut?"

"Yes," she stared down at my tattoo, and then up at me.

"Well," I paused trying to find the right words to say, " the truth is, I did cut myself. I cut myself bad, but the next day I woke up and this was there in place of the cut."

Alicia didn't say a word. She arched her eyebrows and looked at me like I was crazy.

I continued on. "Everything I told you that happened at the hangar was true, though. And remember that pink stuff that I told you got in my skin and burned?"

Alicia nodded.

"Well, it did something weird to me."

Everything was silent, except the bubbling sound of our little creek down the hill. A black crow appeared from nowhere, flying over us squawking, and making everything even more uncomfortable than it already was. Alicia looked over at Kass and then back at me. This was harder than I thought it was going to be.

"What did it do to you, Claire?" she whispered at last.

I clasped my hands behind my head. My headache was getting worse now, and I was starting to change my mind about telling her. I didn't want her to think I was a freak failed scientist experiment.

"Claire, it's ok. Tell her," Kass said

Alicia walked over to me, and grabbed my hands in hers. "It's ok, Claire. It's just me. You can tell me anything."

"I know I can, Mony," I said smiling at her. Here goes nothing. "So, that pink stuff….it gave me a super power." I felt her hands slowly let go of mine, while not taking her eyes off me. "I know you're not going to believe this but….I can fly."

Alicia's mouth dropped open, and she took a step away from me shaking her head. "Seriously Claire?" she asked calmly. "You seriously want me to believe that? You are seriously wanting me to believe you can fly?"

"It's true Mony!" I said.

"Are you guys on drugs or something?!" She pointed at Kass and me. "You know what? No! I've had it, Claire! Don't ever talk to me again!"

Alicia stomped past my car and headed for the main road. Kass and I looked at each other.

"Alicia!" Kass yelled running after her. "Alicia wait! She's telling you the truth!" Kass caught up to her and grabbed her arm.

"Ok Claire," I said to myself while Alicia was yelling at Kass to let go, "do what you got to do."

Alicia broke free from Kass' grasp, and stomped down the gravel road that led out of the field we had parked beside. I launched myself into the air and flew over Kass who looked up at me with big sparkling eyes and a smile. She loved to watch me fly, and since she had found out last week, she made me go out every night just so she could watch me rocket into the sky.

I positioned myself over Alicia, and then dropped effortlessly to the ground in front of her. Alicia jumped when she saw me, screamed, and took off running to the car.

"Get away from me Claire!" she yelled

Ok, so maybe that was a little dramatic just dropping in front of her. I guess I would have been freaked out too. I had been living in this world of flying so long, it was so normal to me now. I was reminded when Kass found out last week, of how crazy all of this was.

"Alicia!" I yelled. "Wait! Kass grab her!"

Kass grabbed Alicia as she ran by, and held on for dear life. They tumbled onto the black soil field. I ran over to them too scared to fly in front of Alicia again. I jumped on top of them, and we tried to settle her down. If someone would have come by in this moment, I swear they would have thought we were murdering her.

"Mony, please!" I begged as I held down her arms straddling her stomach. Kass had her legs pinned down. "Look at me! I'm still me."

Alicia looked up reluctantly at me. I had never seen her face so full of terror. She was shaking all over and close to tears.

"Claire, you're scaring me," she panted. "Please get off of me."

"I will. But first you have to promise to stop freaking out!" I almost yelled at her. "What? You don't think I'm scared too? I'm not some kind of monster, Mony! I'm still Claire! I'm still your friend, and I need your friendship now more than ever."

I watched her eyes soften just as Kass' had, and she

stared at me for a long moment. "Fine," she panted. "Just get off me!"

I slowly got up, my legs dirty from the dried up black soil. I reached my hand down to help Alicia up, and to my relief she took it and stood up to dust off. Kass and I stood in silence waiting to see what she would do next. Much to my surprise she calmly turned and walked toward the car.

I looked at Kass who shrugged at me. "Well, it could have gone way worse," she said rolling her eyes. "Come on, Supergirl." Kass slipped her arm around my shoulder and we followed a few feet behind Alicia.

"Mony, are you ok?" I asked as we reached the car.

Alicia turned and leaned up against my car looking exhausted. "Well, besides the fact that everything I was ever taught about anatomy, science, and gravity, has just been thrown out the window, I'm just fine." She paused a moment and then looked at me. "You can fly Claire?" she asked, as if she still didn't believe what she saw.

"Yes," I replied almost inaudibly. "I'm so sorry to scare you like this. You're my best friend, and it's been so hard to keep it from you."

We all stood there quiet for a short moment.

"Show me again," she said at last.

"You sound just like me when I found out," Kass said. "And yes Claire, she really wants to see or she wouldn't have asked you."

I moaned inwardly and didn't say anything, but instead walked towards an open area in the grass.

"Hold on," Alicia said holding up her hands and backing up to the other side of the car, almost as if she were scared of me. Talk about making a girl feel like a freak.

"Mony, I'm not going to kill you or spread flying cooties on you," I laughed nervously.

Kass shooed me further away. "Claire, do what makes her feel comfortable."

I nodded and walked a little further away. I reached what I thought would be a good distance from Alicia and listened for any vehicles approaching. When it felt safe, I bent my knees and shot myself into the air. I hit about 50 feet, did a couple of tricks in hopes that it would make her feel more comfortable, and lighten the situation. First I did few flips, followed by a barrel roll, and then landed softly back on the ground. I looked over at Alicia who still hid behind the car.

"How is that possible Claire?" she asked holding both hands to her cheeks. "How can you just fly off the ground like that?!"

I shrugged. "I honestly don't know, but it's something I have to figure out and quick. Come on, it's getting late. I'll explain everything on the way home."

I let Kass drive home and sat in the passenger seat so Alicia could have her space in the back. I packed the 30 minute drive back home with as much information as I could.

"Well, that explains the whole basketball thing," Alicia said.

"Yeah," I agreed. "There is no way I could play that well all by myself. And I've actually thought about quitting, because I don't know if it's ethically correct for me to keep playing with a super power."

"No!" Kass and Alicia yelled at the same time, which made us burst into laughter.

"No Claire!" Alicia reiterated. "We have lost for far too long. We deserve to win however we can get it."

I somewhat agreed with that.

By the time we got to Alicia's we had made a plan for her to spend the night Saturday after Track or Treat. She still had a lot of questions, plus we hadn't spent time together in so long. I felt so much happiness knowing I had Alicia back in my life, and there were no hidden secrets. Two of the people I trusted most in the whole world knew my secret, and I was totally ok with that.

EIGHTEEN

SATURDAY NIGHT I entered the gym at school dressed head to toe in my witch's costume, all the way down to my green skin. I had to admit, I looked pretty convincing. Kass had done an amazing job with my make up and I had opted out of the black wig since my long dark curly hair fit well with my costume. Mom had found an old straw broom at Clarence's Thrift shop, and Johnny had burned down the straw off the end so it looked almost identical to the one in the movie.

"How appropriate," Alicia said with a wink as I approached her.

"I'll get you my pretty, and your little dog too!" I said in my best witch's voice, pointing my green finger at her laughing. Alicia definitely pulled off Dorothy in her plaid blue dress, braids, and red slippers.

"You should have come dressed as Supergirl,"

Alicia said hugging me. I squeezed her back making sure I didn't smear my green make up all over her white shirt.

I laughed. "Actually, Kass said she wanted to buy me a Supergirl costume, with all the crime mess I've been getting into."

Alicia's eyebrows arched and she looked at me surprised. "Crime mess?" she asked.

"Oh, I didn't tell you that part." I patted her on the back. "We have a lot to talk about, Mony."

We had so much fun with the kids at Track or Treat. Of course our booth consisted of a pint sized basketball game. Alicia and I passed out candy to avoid chasing all the rebounds bouncing off the basket.

Lexi kept popping over from the volleyball team. She looked so adorable in her Chicken Little costume, trying to waddle across the gym floor in her duck feet.

"I kind of feel bad about not inviting Lex over to spend the night," I said to Alicia as we walked to my car after it was over.

"I do too," Alicia said putting my broomstick and her basket in the trunk, "but I really want to talk to you about all of this, and I know you're not going to tell Lex."

"You're right. I'm not. Especially with all the drama you and Kass gave me," I said removing my witches hat.

"What drama?" Kass asked walking up to the car.

"You know what drama," I replied, winking at her.

"Well, what did you expect?" Alicia asked as we all got into my car. "Good grief, Claire. You can fly!"

"I know," I said driving out of the parking lot. "I just still can't believe it."

We headed towards home. It was already 10 pm, but still very busy on this warm Saturday night.

"Are you guys hungry?" Kass asked as we drove into the older part of town. "All I had to eat today was breakfast."

"We can go through a drive thru if that's ok. I don't feel much like going into public in this," I laughed.

"Ok, can we hit Jackies? I'm in the mood for a burger," Kass said. "I'll go in and pick it up."

We parked in the busy parking lot of Jackies, and Alicia and I sat in the car waiting for Kass to come out with our food. After breathing in that restaurant smell, Alicia and I changed our minds about eating, and ordered burgers too.

"I know I'm going to regret this in the morning," Alicia sighed as we sat in the car. "This is going straight to our thighs, Claire."

"We'll run it off next week, Mony," I shrugged.

Movement from the alley across the street, that separated the corner service station from the hair salon next door, caught my attention. A light shone down from the side of the service station and I saw two men who looked very familiar emerge from the back door.

It was the scruffy guys. My mouth dropped open, and I squinted my eyes to get a better view.

"Claire, what is it?" Alicia asked following my gaze

across the street.

"Remember the scruffy guys I told you about?" I asked almost in a whisper.

"Yes…"

I pointed across the street. "That's them."

Alicia and I continued to watch as they lit cigarettes and hung outside of a beat up car parked in the ally. Kass came out to the car with a white bag full of fries and burgers.

"I got mom one too, just in case she's still awake," she said climbing in the back seat.

Alicia and I didn't say a word, but continued to watch the two guys.

"What are you guys looking at?" Kass asked, as she leaned up between the two seats following our stare across the street.

"Alicia, I have an idea," I said to her. "Trade me places and drive, ok?" I jumped out of the car and went around to the trunk to grab my broomstick.

"Claire, what are you doing?" she asked getting out and walking around to the driver's side.

"Just trust me," I smiled.

"What's going on, you guys?" Kass asked sticking her head out of the back window.

"Kass, shhhh! They are going to hear you," Alicia said to her.

"Who's going to hear me?"

Alicia turned and looked at her. "It's the scruffy guys, Kass."

I instructed Alicia to drive around to the back of

the buildings adjacent to the service station. I got out of the car and put my black witches hat on, grabbed my broomstick, and walked to the front of the car. Alicia and Claire watched wide eyed as I jumped on my broomstick and lifted off the ground floating just above the hood of the car with the headlights shining on me. I adjusted my long black skirt so it hung down on either side and wondered if I looked as intimidating as I felt. The look of awe in Kass and Alicia's eyes assured me I did.

"Hold on! I want to get a pic!" Kass yelled fumbling through her purse.

Kass found her phone and began to click away as I posed as mean looking as I could, and in the last one throwing out a peace sign. When she was done, I flew over to the driver's side window.

"Ok, if I'm not back in 10 minutes call the Police. But, I'll be right back girls." I winked and flew off on my broom above the buildings, skimming the top of them to lessen the risk of being seen.

I landed on the roof of the beauty shop building and peeked over at the two scruffy guys below. They were still there drinking beer, talking loudly, and laughing. What jerks. I listened in on their conversation.

"I told her I didn't care what she thinks," the shorter one said, his words slurred. "I'll come home whenever I want to."

"Dumb broad," laughed the taller one. "It's like they say, women are only good for one thing."

My face flushed in anger. I looked down towards the end of the alley that led to the back of the building. It was dark, except for one tiny light that shined from the beauty shop. That would work perfect. I climbedon my broomstick and flew around to the back of the alley.

"Claire, you are so crazy," I whispered as I prepared myself mentally. I have to admit, I was pretty scared, but my anger towards them far outweighed any fear I had. I took a breath and flew around the corner hovering in the middle at the end of the alley. I stared at them both, talking myself out of flying over, and whacking them in the head with my broom.

The scruffy men continued to talk for a moment. Finally the taller one stopped mid sentence and stared at me, his face frozen in fear. The second soon followed and he squinted at me almost as if he were trying to figure out if what he was seeing was actually there. I must have looked pretty scary, because both of them started breathing heavily and shaking uncontrollably. I slowly flew to the top of the salon building, following the wall and inched closer to them. I narrowed my eyes and gave them the most evil glare I could.

"It's...it's the flying girl," the short one gasped.

"Good evening," I hissed in the most intimidating witch voice that I could. "You big guys enjoy intimidating women and putting them into frightening situations?"

Neither said anything, but shook their heads no,

trying to catch their breaths.

I flew to the other side of them, and started backing them down to the darkside of the alley. The short scruffy, backed into a garbage can falling backwards, making the contents of the can spill greasy garbage all over him. It was all I could do to keep a straight face as I watched him struggle to get up and catch up with his friend, who didn't bother to stop and help.

I thought I was going to have an issue figuring out what to say to them, but before I knew it the words came falling out. "I'm going to tell you this one time, and one time only. If I ever hear of you scaring or harming another woman, or anyone for that matter, myself and my coven will reign a full scale assault on you. We will cast spells on you, and everything that touches your being, and you will curse the day you were born. Do you understand me?"

Wow! Where did that come from? My coven? That was pretty good.

Both of the scruffy men backed up to the side of the building, shaking in fear. This is great, I thought to myself. I know revenge isn't always the answer, but this felt oh so right.

"I asked if you both understand me?" I said with more anger and flying closer to them.

"We understand," the taller one said out of breath. "We promise we won't."

"See that you don't." I backed off them and slowly flew backwards to the end of alley. "We're watching you," I warned as I flew around the side and out of sight.

NINETEEN

I FLEW BACK to the car as quickly as I could, just in case they got bold enough to follow me. I landed beside the car, threw my hat and broom in the trunk, and jumped in the back since Kass had moved to the front.

"Let's go!" I said to Alicia, eager to get out of there.

Alicia flipped a U-turn, and gunned it out of the alley. I turned and looked behind me, but there was no sign of the scruffies anywhere.

"What happened, Claire?" Kass asked excitedly. "You look like a happy girl...ummm witch."

I smiled and leaned back in the seat so exhausted from flying. "That was the best, you guys!" I practically yelled, throwing my arms into the air. "You should have seen their faces! They were so scared! To see the the look of terror in their eyes made me so happy."

"Yeah!" Alicia said. "Now they know what it's like

to make someone else feel that way. Good job Claire."

We pulled in our driveway and I saw the familiar lamp on in the living room window. My tummy tingled in happiness. Either my mom was up reading and waiting for us, or she had fallen asleep on the couch in an attempt to. We entered the house quiet at first, just in case she was sleeping. To my delight she was still awake, reading her book and drinking coffee.

"Hello girls!" She smiled.

"Hey Mom! Hi Mrs. Haley!" We all greeted her.

"Alicia, we are so glad to have you over tonight. You just make yourself at home."

"Thank you, Mrs. Haley," Alicia said.

Kass kissed mom on the head, and plopped the cheeseburger in her lap. "Mom, we bought you a cheeseburger from Jackie's."

"Oh girls, you didn't have to do that. Thank you. I really appreciate it."

"You're welcome." I gave her a squeeze. "I'm going to get a shower. This green make- up is itching my skin."

"Your mom is so sweet," Alicia sighed as we headed to my bedroom.

"Thanks Mony." (She says that every time she talks to my mom.)

An hour later, after mom had gone to bed, Alicia, Kass, and I sat on my white shag rug, freshly showered, and eating our burgers and fries.

"I can't believe you're letting us eat on your rug, Claire," Kass giggled.

"Only because there are towels," Alicia teased.

"Ha. Ha," I replied dryly.

Alicia leaned back against my bed. "So tell us everything that happened tonight, because let me tell you, you made a very convincing witch."

"Really?" I asked, my eyes wide.

"Definitely!" Kass giggled picking up her phone. She opened her pictures and handed it to me.

I looked at the picture, a front shot of me hanging in the air above the car, looking down straight faced into the eye of the camera. My black dress flowed perfectly around my legs, and I leaned forward, both hands grasping the broom handle. This was pretty much the coolest pic I had ever seen. It could have been on the cover of a magazine or novel, and it was of me! I flipped through the next ten shots, each one more intimidating than the last, with the final one of me in the air, right before I flew over the building. I sat there in awe of what I was seeing. I had never seen myself flying before, and it was pretty overwhelming.

"Claire, are you ok?" Kass asked.

"Yeah, it's just…it's just that I've never seen myself flying before. I still can't believe it."

"Kass, you have to send me these," Alicia said taking the phone from me.

"Mony, are you crazy?" I gasped. "Kass is going to send them to me, and then she's erasing them forever! Can you imagine if they get in the hands of the wrong person?"

Alicia's shoulders dropped. "Oh, I guess I didn't

think about that."

I grabbed Alicia's hand to let her know I didn't mean for my statement to come across as brash as it sounded. "I'm sorry. It's just that I've thought about it. A lot. And it scares me."

Kass looked at me, her smiling eyes now filled with concern. "What do you think would happen Claire? I mean, if someone found out."

I shrugged my shoulders. "I don't know. I'm pretty sure they would lock me up in some science research hospital, evaluate me, and study me like some mutant alien."

Everyone was quiet for a moment as they both stared at me.

"Well, that's incredibly morbid," Alicia said at last.

My voice was softer now. "I know. I'm sorry, but it's true. And that's not the worse part even. The worst part is Johnny. He will lose his rank, and with that his dream of becoming a pilot."

Kass looked at me skeptically. "Come on Claire. Do you really think all that will happen? It was an accident."

"Kass, yes, of course," I stressed. "especially after the whole hangar break-in debacle."

Alicia sat up, almost startled. "Wait a second. You're the ghost girl, Claire? The mystery girl all the guys have been talking about the last two months?!"

I shrugged my shoulders up, looking like a child who just got busted doing something they shouldn't. "Um...guilty," I said with a slight squeak in my voice.

"What could possibly make you do something so stupid, Claire?" Alicia asked, sounding more like a mother than a friend.

"Because Mony, I had to!" I argued. "I have no clue, as to what is going on with my body or how it's going to affect me in the long run. That pink goo is in my bloodstream now, and I have no idea what it is. I need to get a sample, so I can have it tested."

"Well, can't you find out who invented it and ask them?" Alicia reasoned.

I looked her in the eyes. "He's dead, Mony." Again, silence.

Alicia breathed in and promptly let out a deep sigh of frustration. "Where exactly is this pink goo stuff?"

"Well, the flask bottle I landed on is gone. Johnny cleaned it up and threw it out. And when I broke in that night, I didn't see any more. But Shawn said he saw..."

Alicia interrupted me finishing my sentence, "The box with your Saturn rings on them in the medical closet! I remember him telling me that!" She facepalmed herself. "How could I not put that together?"

Kass and I laughed at her excitement.

"Right!" Kass said. "Which is why we have to get Claire back in that hangar to find it." She looked at me. "I don't want to risk anything happening to you, Claire. I'll do whatever I need to do, to help."

Alicia scooted over to me, wrapping her arm around my waist. "Me too. We've got to figure a way to get you back in that hangar."

"So this is what I was thinking," said Kass scooting closer to Alicia and I, making our circle smaller, "we need to try and get you in there on a day when one of the guys is pulling guard duty."

"Kass, they aren't allowed to have any visitors at the hangar since I broke in," I reminded her.

"I know," she said. "but what I meant is, if you get caught and Shawn, Tater, or Johnny are there, they are going to let you go, and ask questions later."

"That's true," Alicia agreed.

"I don't know you guys," I said. "I would rather none of them be there, so they can say they are clueless, and have no idea what's going on. I know I've said this a thousand times, but if I do anything to jeopardize Johnny's job, I will never forgive myself."

"Well, if you're going back, you're not going alone Claire," Alicia said. "Kass and I will go with you, and at least drive the getaway car."

"Thank you, guys," I smiled at them, so grateful that I didn't feel so alone in all of this anymore.

"We'll make a plan," Kass said. "So anyway, tell Alicia about the crime stuff you've been wrapped up in."

"Yeah!" Alicia agreed. "Tell me EVERYTHING, Claire."

We stayed up late into the night while I told Alicia everything, starting with the accident. Alicia and Kass sat wide eyed listening to my account of the last two months. Kass asked as many questions as Alicia, as if she had never heard me tell it before.

"So Claire, I have a question for you," Alicia asked cautiously. "Have you thought about this being a thing in your life that is only temporary? I mean, what if you're up there at 2,000 feet, and it just wears off or something? You were so incredibly lucky to land in a pool that first night."

I looked down at the ground biting my lip. I wish Alicia hadn't brought this up in front of Kass. I knew she would worry herself sick about it.

"Of course I have," I answered trying to sound like it wasn't a big deal, "but it's highly unlikely.

That's why I need to get that stuff. I think it could answer a lot of questions for me."

Kass jumped up and ran to her room, returning quickly with a sketching pad.

"Ok, girls," she said laying out the pad in front of us. "We need a plan to get Claire back in there to get that pink goo. Claire, sketch out the airfield for us. Maybe we can figure out something together."

I took the pencil from her and began to draw out everything, including the woods, and the neighborhood I had parked in during the first attempt.

By the time we went to sleep, we had devised a plan for me to go back to the hangar, that I felt really confident in. The only thing we didn't have was the date. I knew it had to happen sooner, rather than later, or I could end up in more trouble than I already had coming.

TWENTY

HALLOWEEN WAS THAT Tuesday night. Johnny came over to hang out and help me pass out candy. I was beyond excited to see him and to my delight, he made an effort to dress up too. He looked so adorable as the scarecrow, in a flannel shirt and holey jeans with little patches of hay sticking out. When I told him how cute he looked, he replied, "I decided to be the scarecrow, because I'm pretty sure he was the witch's favorite."

"Didn't the witch set the scarecrow on fire?" I asked confused.

"Exactly," he smiled mischievously.

Yes it was corny, but I loved it. He made me laugh so much.

"Where is Kass and Kyle?" he asked looking around the house.

"Kass ended up going to Kyle's. His parents are going to a party, so he had to watch his younger sister.

I think they might stop by here with her to trick-or-treat, and then they are going to watch the fireworks over Riverwalk."

"And your mom?" he asked.

"She's helping out at the church tonight."

Johnny walked over and pulled me closer, gently lifting my witch's hat brim. "Sooo, you're saying I have a night all alone in the castle with the witch?"

"Yes, Sir," I replied, wickedly squinting my eyes at him and circling his face with my finger, "and I'm going to cast a spell on you."

"Uh-oh," he murmured kissing me, "I'm feeling dizzy already."

I kissed him back breathing in his sweet smell, and thought for the thousandth time how lucky I was to have him in my life. I couldn't ever imagine life without him in it.

Johnny pulled away from me suddenly, and sniffed the air waking me out of my trance.

"Is something burning?" he asked.

"My lasagna!" I gasped.

We both ran towards the kitchen, and I yanked the oven door open. A dark cloud of smoke plummeted from the oven as I grabbed some oven mitts and put the lasagna in the sink, rescuing it from it's fiery demise.

Johnny and I looked down, coughing at the blackened dish that was sizzling against the wet metal.

"Just perfect," I sighed disappointed in myself.

"It doesn't look that bad Claire," he smiled down at

me. "I like fried lasagna."

I giggled at his obvious lie. He would probably eat it just to make me feel better. The sound of the doorbell interrupted our conversation.

"Oooo! Trick or Treaters!" I gasped grabbing his hand, and pulling him towards the door.

"They're not going anywhere Claire!" He laughed.

I grabbed the candy bowl, thankful that I didn't color my skin in that itchy green paint. I thought it might be a little too scary for the little kids, plus I would rub it off from kissing Johnny all night anyway.

I opened the door to a Spiderman and a mini witch looking up at me. I knelt down to greet them.

"Well, hello there!" I said.

"Hey," the little girl pointed at me. "you look like me!"

"Yes I do," I laughed, "but you definitely make a better witch than I do."

"Hey Spiderman!" Johnny said to the little boy, "Look at those muscles! I can tell you've been working out."

The little boy giggled holding up his arm to flex his muscles at Johnny. "Oh yeah! That's what's up buddy!" Johnny slightly squeezed his little arm muscles.

Their parents thanked us and headed back down the sidewalk. I waved, and looked past them to see Alicia and Shawn pulling into the driveway.

"Oh look! Alicia and Shawn!" I smiled.

"Oh yeah," Johnny sounded less enthused than I

did. "Did you invite them?"

"No. I thought they were hanging out with Lexi and Tater tonight."

As if on cue, Lexi and Tater pulled in behind them in Tater's truck.

I looked at Johnny as he let out a deep sigh. "Great," he said smirking at me.

"Johnny," I laughed.

"I'm sorry Claire, but I was looking forward to spending some time alone with you tonight," he laughed through his obvious disappointment.

I shrugged looking up at him. "I know. Me too."

"Hey Claire!" Lexi said as they came up the sidewalk.

"Hey guys!" I said. "What are ya'll up to?"

Shawn gave Johnny a fist bump. "What's up bro? We were just going to see if you guys wanted to hit the Slaughter House with us."

"The Slaughter House?" Johnny laughed.

I looked up at Johnny. "It's one of the oldest haunted houses in Clarksville. It's in the old meat factory in underground stalls. They used to keep the animals there before they were killed."

"Seriously?" Lexi gasped. "That's where we're going?!"

"TMI Claire," Alicia said putting her hand on my shoulder. I had forgotten about Lexi being a vegan.

"Just kidding Lex," I said trying to do a little damage control.

"Come here. I want to show you something." Alicia

grabbed my hand and led me into the house.

"What's that smell?" she asked, waving her hand in front of her nose, as we entered the kitchen.

"Oh, I burnt my lasagna," I sighed.

Alicia laughed and pulled off her crossbody purse, setting it on the table. She dug around in it for a moment before finally pulling out a newspaper, unfolded it, and handed it to me.

"What is this?" I asked.

She pointed at the bottom half of the front page. "Read the headline."

"UFO SPOTTED IN THE SKY ABOVE MADISON STREET- RESTAURANT PATRON CLAIMS TO HAVE SEEN A WITCH"

I looked at the grainy picture someone had obviously taken from the window of the restaurant. In the picture the sky was dark except for a faint glow of light coming from behind one of the buildings. A black silhouette of me was etched against the dim night sky as I hovered over the rooftops. I looked pretty much like a black blob except for my pointed hat, and the front and back of the broomstick. Oh man. This sucked. I had worked so hard at keeping out of the public view. I slowly sat down at the kitchen table staring at the picture trying to figure out if there was anyway I could have been mistaken for something else. I cocked my head sideways. I probably could have if my hat had not been so distinctive.

Alicia sat down slowly beside me and rested her chin in the palm of her hand. "So Clairey, what do you think?"

I shrugged my shoulders, listening to the sound of the doorbell, and Lexi greeting the trick or treaters with oohs and ahhs. "I don't know, Mony. Maybe they'll think it's a camera trick. It's not exactly the clearest pic."

"Maybe," Alicia said. "but I'm just saying the police might put this pic together with all the 911 calls you made and get suspicious."

"Really?" I asked furrowing my eyebrows at her. "Do you actually think the Clarksville Police Department is going to go on record stating that there is a witch on the loose in the city?"

"I don't know," Alicia said sheepishly looking at the ground. "I'm just trying to warn you of what could happen. Maybe you should stay out of the sky for a while."

I looked at Alicia and thought about what she was saying to me. One of her greatest qualities was her ability to see past the present situation and look at the bigger picture. I learned a long time ago to trust her young wisdom over my "jump the gun" assertiveness, but I didn't know if I could give up flying for even one day. Flying had become more than a part of my life. It was a big part of who I am. I couldn't imagine my life going back to the way it was. I just had to get a sample of the pink goo. I was curious if this was a temporary situation or something that I would keep forever. I desperately hoped for the latter.

"Ok," I said finally. "I'll stay on the ground."

Shawn stuck his head inside the kitchen. "Hey sweetness, you ready to go get our creepy, creepy on?"

Alicia and I laughed. "I'm coming," she said getting up from the table. "Claire, are you sure you guys don't want to come?"

"Thanks, but Johnny and I are going to watch a movie. We haven't seen each other much lately. He's so busy with Officer's school now."

"Understandable," she said hugging me.

"Hey, do you mind if I keep this?" I asked holding up the newspaper clipping.

"Not at all," she said. "I thought you might want it for your scrapbook. Something to look back on after we figure out how to get you back to normal."

I smiled acting as though I agreed with her. Little did she know I had no intentions of going back to my old self. As long as I could fly, I was going to, and I would stop anyone who would try and keep me on the ground.

A couple of hours later, I stood on the porch waving to Johnny as he pulled out of my driveway. I was always so sad when he left, but I knew I would be seeing him again in a couple of nights. He was coming to my game on Thursday. I was a lucky girl.

I walked slowly to my room. It was already 9, and mom and Kass were not home yet. I changed out of my costume and into my comfy Titans sweats and tee. Laying on my bed, I picked up my phone to text Johnny and thank him for hanging out with me tonight. I had just finished my text when I heard a loud explosion coming from the south. A bright glow of pink lit up the sky in the southern part of the city.

"Oh yeah, the fireworks," I said to myself. I loved watching fireworks, and was pretty bummed I was missing them. "Hmmm.. I've never seen fireworks from the sky."

I grabbed my sweatshirt and headed for the back porch with my phone and earbuds. I knew I told Alicia I would try and stay out of the sky for a while, but this was maybe my last chance to see fireworks from above. Who knows? This whole phenomenon could wear off, and I could go back to being plain old Claire with no chance of ever seeing anything like this again. And yes, I was afraid of it wearing off, but my passion for flying far outweighed any fear of losing my super power.

I quickly slid the slider shut and walked to the end of the patio, my official launching pad. I stuck my earbuds in and set my playlist to Journey, my go to music lately. "Don't Stop Believin" began pounding out of my ear buds. I placed my phone in my arm strap that I had wised up and bought after almost losing my phone during a flight the previous month. My chest tightened, and I felt the familiar rush of gravity leaving my body, as my tattoo lit up a bright pink. I bent my knees and looked down, watching my favorite white chucks leave the patio with lightning speed. I looked toward the bright star filled sky, as Steve Perry's incredible vocals filled my ears.

"Don't Stop Believing!" I sang as loud as I could as I headed toward the bright colored mushroom cloud of fireworks. Sometimes I could be a real goofball, but I was having so much fun doing it.

I lifted myself a little higher into the air as I approached the fireworks, not so much because I was afraid of getting hit, as I was of being seen. I placed myself directly over the fireworks, and sat Indian style in the air. Leaning over, I watched the orange sparkly tails of the fireworks streak into the air below me. They burst open in the sky in a fiery display. I had never seen anything as beautiful. Watching it from the ground was exciting, but watching them from the air was surreal. The air filled with a smokey burnt smell, that I didn't mind at all. I actually liked that smell, and pretty much the smell of anything burning. (Except lasagna. Burnt lasagna is the worst!)

My eighties music played on, and Kenny Loggins, "Meet Me HalfWay Across the Sky," now filled my ears. This song had become my favorite lately. Kass heard me playing it one morning before school and had come into my room teasing me about it. "Well, isn't that the perfect song," she said winking at me.

Speaking of Kass, I wondered where she was down there. I was well over 500 feet, so the people looked like no more than little dots down below. I decided to text her and see where she was, but of course, I was mainly doing it to show off.

"Hey Sissy, where are you?"

"Hey Clairey, I'm still at the fireworks. Is mom home yet?"

"I'm not sure. I'm not home."

"Where are you? I thought you were there with Johnny?"

"No, he had to leave at nine. He has early training in the morning."

"So where are you?"

I leaned over and snapped a pic of a bright white firework that had just popped below me. It drizzled slowly to the ground, looking like a sparkling, weeping willow tree. I sent it to Kass.

"OMG!! Seriously Claire? I can't believe you are above me."

"I know! It's unreal up here!"

"You are so lucky!"

"Thanks Kass. I wish I could share this with you."

"Me too. Can you at least take some video for me?"

"Of course!"

"Be careful, please."

"Always. I'll see you at home in a few. I love you."

"I love you too, you little witch!"

I laughed at her last comment and continued to watch the fireworks, occasionally looking up at the moon that was just a bright sliver in the sky tonight. I layed on my tummy with my hands tucked under my chin to watch the grand finale. The loud booms shook my body as I scanned the skyline with my phone, recording the incredible display for Kass.

When they were at last done, I tucked my phone back into my armband, but changed my mind, and decided to record my flight home. I thought Kass would like to see that too. I narrated a bit for her as I shot through the sky pointing out different landmarks, occasionally soaring up and free falling, so she could somewhat have a feeling of what I was experiencing. I would do anything to take her up with me.

I approached our neighborhood, and looked down the road to see my mom's car pulling into our subdivision. It was already 10 o'clock.

"Hey Kass, do you recognize that car?" I said laughing into my phone. "I'm going to try and beat mom home."

I flew quickly to the woods behind our house and dropped into the clearing, just to be safe, and ran up to the patio. Mom's car was pulling into the driveway as I entered the slider. I went to my room, threw off my sweatshirt, and layed on my bed. I casually picked up a magazine and skimmed through it.

"Claire? Kass?" I heard my mom call through the house.

"In here, mom!"

Mom opened my door. "Hi sweetheart. Did you have a good night?"

I sat up on my bed. "I did. Johnny came over for a while, and we passed out candy and watched a movie."

"That's wonderful," she said coming over and kissing my forehead. She stopped for a moment, sniffing close to my head. "What is that smell? You smell like a campfire or fireworks," she laughed.

My eyes got big for a moment, and then I remembered the lasagna. "It's burnt lasagna. I burned my lasagna."

"Oh, Claire," she laughed again. "What am I going to do with you girls? Is Kass here?"

"No ma'am. But she's on her way home. She went to the fireworks with Kyle."

"Oh, that's right. Well, I'm going to get in the shower. Text Kass, and let her know she needs to be home in 20 minutes please."

"Yes, ma'am," I said smiling at her.

I didn't need to text Kass, because she walked in the door five minutes later, and made a beeline for my room.

"Ok, let me see the video," she said laying on the bed beside me. We laid on our tummies and watched the video, cautiously peeking at the door in case mom came in. I watched Kass' face as her eyes grew wide, occasionally looking over at me in wonder.

"So unreal," she said when it was finally over.

I smiled big, clapping my hands lightly. "I know," I sighed. "I wish Major Kearney was still alive so could I thank him for the pink goo, and changing my life."

Kass hugged me tightly. "I wish he was still alive too, for more reasons than that. I want you to be ok Claire."

"I'm ok, Kass. I promise." I hoped I sounded convincing enough.

TWENTY-ONE

THURSDAY WAS GAME day, our first game together since I had told Alicia that I could fly. We sat at the lunch table alone waiting for Lexi and Kass to join us. They had got out of class late, and were waiting in the longest line I had ever seen in the cafeteria.

"I can't believe you wore that sailor hat to school, Claire," she teased.

"What? I like it," I said smiling, adjusting it on my head, "and that's all that matters."

Alicia tapped my hat lightly, knocking it sideways again. "You are definitely the only one who likes it," she laughed. "You can fly Claire. You're much too cool for that hat now."

"Shhhh!!" I whispered loudly, trying to control my laughter. "Mony, how many times do I have to tell you? You can't say stuff like that out loud. Especially around here."

We had just begun discussing the game for that night when Alicia put her finger to her mouth, discreetly asking me to be quiet for a moment.

"What?" I asked quietly.

Alicia didn't say anything, but motioned with her eyes to the table behind us, where a group of cheerleaders were talking rather loudly. Tracy, the senior cheerleader, pushed a paper to the center of the round table.

"Yes it is!" she exclaimed, arguing with Amy, another cheerleader. "Can't you see it? There's the hat, and then the broomstick is coming from the front and back of the skirt."

Alicia and I looked at each other wide eyed, knowing they were talking about my newspaper debut.

"Tracy, have you lost your mind?" Amy laughed, while a couple of girls laughed with her. "Someone was obviously either playing a trick or it's just a shadow of something else."

"No way," Tracy sternly replied. "Look at the way she's hovering above the building. You can't camera trick that if you tried."

I smiled at Alicia mischievously, while she muffled a giggle.

"You're enjoying this a little too much, girly," she whispered.

Lexi and Kass approached our table and sat down beside us.

"Hey girls!" Lexi said excitedly.

"Goodness that line took forever!" Kass sighed,

rolling her eyes. "We literally have 10 minutes to eat."

Tracy turned around to Lexi who was sitting directly behind her. "Hey Lex, we need a tiebreaker over here."

"Oookay," Lexi replied with uncertainty in her voice.

Tracy grabbed the newspaper clipping and squeezed on the bench between Lexi and Kass.

"When you look at this pic tell me what you see."

Alicia buried her face in her hands, as if it would make the situation go away, while I eagerly awaited Lexi's response.

Kass and Lex leaned in together and looked at the newspaper clipping. Lexi stared at it hard, while Kass gasped loudly and looked at me in shock. I gave her bugg eyes as if to say, "*Don't be so obvious!*"

"Sooo, what do you think girls?" Tracy asked.

"I know this is a stupid answer, but to me it looks like a witch," Lexi said shrugging.

"I agree…" Tracy began, but Kass interrupted her.

"There's no way that's a witch. I think it's a...ummm...you know what it probably is? It's probably a...a...a balloon!"

"A balloon?" Tracy asked rolling her eyes.

"Yeah, you know," Kass replied, (I could tell she was making it up as she went along.) "someone probably bought a balloon shaped like a witch and then let it go."

Kass looked over at me for my approval, but all I could do was grimace at her poor attempt to cover up for me. Oh well, at least she tried.

"There's no way," Tracy said pointing at the narrative under the picture. "It says right here, that the patron who took the pic saw the witch fly over the buildings."

Alicia sighed. "Tracy, I wouldn't believe everything you read. I'm sure someone sold that to the paper for a lot of money."

Tracy got up from the table. "Well," she shrugged her shoulders, "I'm going to get a few more opinions."

"Great," I sighed as I watched Tracy move to the next table and begin her "tie breaker" speech.

"That was weird," Kass said quietly.

Lexi looked over at Tracy talking to a group of guys. "Yeah, but you have to admit, that looks exactly like a witch."

"Well, maybe," Alicia said. "So are you guys going to make the game tonight?" She was a master at changing the subject.

"Tater and I are coming," Lexi said excitedly. "I'm so excited for you guys! Undefeated this year!"

"Yeah!" Kass exclaimed. "What is that? Your third win?"

"Fourth!" Alicia and I yelled at the same time, and our table burst into laughter.

Thursday night before the game, Alicia and I sat in the locker room, in uniform, wrapping up our wrists and ankles for extra support. I tightened my long curly ponytail and adjusted my headband.

"So how are you feeling about tonight?" Alicia asked wrapping her wrist.

I shrugged. "I'm a little nervous. Anderson is supposedly really good."

Shalay Anderson was a D-1 recruit, and every year since 8th grade she had given Alicia and I a beat down everytime we played her school. We hadn't won against her, even once.

Alicia grabbed my hand looking down at my wrist. "Well, this year, you have something she doesn't."

I laughed. "Thanks Mony, but I don't know if that makes me feel much better. I feel like a big fat cheater."

Tina interrupted our conversation. "Hey Claire," she said with a twinkle in her eye, "someone's here to see you."

I looked at Alicia, my eyes bright. "Johnny!" I gasped, jumping up, and heading to the locker room door. Johnny was waiting for me with a single red rose. I immediately walked over and jumped into his arms. I was so glad to see him.

"Hey my little MJ," he said softly. "I know you said tonight is going to be a tough one, so I just wanted to wish you luck and show you this." Johnny pointed at his tee that had our school mascot, a Knight, with a basketball on the front. He then turned around and showed me the back, that had my number 10, and my last name Haley above it.

"Johnny! Where did you get that?"

"At last week's game. I had your name added onto it, at the cleaners on Ft. Campbell."

"That's so perfect. It means the world to me. Thank you."

Johnny smiled and hugged me tightly. "Don't worry, Claire Bear. You're going to do great."

"Thanks mister," I whispered in his ear. "I have a feeling I'm going to get my butt kicked though."

He leaned down and kissed my forehead. "You'll be awesome."

I gave Johnny one last squeeze, and headed back into the locker room to join my team. Thirty minutes later we were on the gym floor, standing for the National Anthem. I looked around at the crowded gym. The stands were packed. Since we had started winning, more people were showing up for our games. Tonight the bleachers were full, with people standing around the top of the gym like they did for the guys games. I found my mom's usual seat and saw her there smiling at me surrounded by Johnny, Shawn, Kass and Kyle, and Lexi and Tater.

Tina won tip off and tapped it to Alicia, who took it down the court with ease. I crossed over and to the side of Shannon, one of the forwards who boxed out while I shot a wide open three. The roar of the crowd was deafening, but somehow above all the voices I heard Johnny yelling at the top of his lungs, "That's my girlfriend! Way to go Claire Bear!"

The East Side Dragons took the offensive side of

the ball, where Anderson answered my three pointer with a drive to the basket. She did a quick switch of hands at the last minute, into an easy lay up. It was her signature move, and put them on the board with two points.

This game was exactly what we expected, a dog fight till the very end. Alicia stepped up and delivered a lot of points herself. I heard Shawn yelling just as loud as Johnny from the bleachers, and caught them fist bumping and high fiving everytime we scored.

I did my best to play in my normal human abilities, but my power to fly was hard to keep under control. In the third quarter, I found myself with the ball on the end of the court by myself with just Anderson guarding me. I started a long drive to the basket. She stepped in to guard me as soon as I reached the free throw line. I drove around her, but her defense was so strong. I set my sights on the net, and two steps after I passed the free throw line, I was flying in the air towards the basket. I didn't slam dunk it, although I could have, but instead made an easy lay up. The crowd went wild, and I caught Anderson looking at her coach giving a "what the heck just happened" shrug.

With two minutes left in the game, we trailed by only two. Alicia was at the line to shoot two free throws. Coach Alexander had put me in the forward position to rebound and had sent Adrian, our other forward, to the half court line in my place. Alicia made her first shot. Nothing but net. And now the second one was in the air, almost as if in slow motion. I watched as it came towards the basket, bricking. It was clearly not going in. I felt my chest tighten as my knees bent, and my black Adidas left the wood floor. I set my eyes on the rebound, competing with the 5'9" forward from the other team. I was only 5'4", but my hands found the ball first, and of course I had more airtime than her. I felt myself falling lightly toward the ground, with gravity not returning to my body as quickly as I wanted it to. The forward landed underneath me, and the next thing I knew I was on top of her. My body flipped backwards, and I fell toward the floor face up and head first, with my feet in the air. I looked up for a split second before my head hit the floor, the weight of my body, pushing my chin into my chest. I heard a loud gasp, and then there was nothing but darkness.

"Claire? Claire?" My eyes opened slowly. I looked up to find myself surrounded by Coach Alexander, the physical trainer, and his staff.

"Claire. You're ok," Ben, our physical trainer, assured me. "You hit your head pretty hard, and we are sending you to the hospital just to be safe."

My first thought was my mom and Kass. "Could you please tell my mom I'm ok? I don't think I need to go to the hospital." I slowly started to get up, but my head was throbbing.

"Lay down Claire," Coach Alexander said sternly. "We need to make sure you're ok, sweetie."

I layed back down as the ambulance crew approached us. They very gently placed my head into a brace, and lifted me onto a stretcher. I saw my mom leaning over me with a worried expression flooding her face. This is exactly what I didn't want.

"Mom, I'm fine. I promise," I reassured her.

She grabbed my hand and walked beside me. "I know, honey. They are just checking you out to be safe." She tried to sound confident, but failed miserably.

The crowd cheered as they wheeled me out. Wow, this was embarrassing.

Two hours later, I sat in the ER room with my mom and Kass, while Dr. Huntley went over the test results with us. Johnny had been with me, but when the doctor came in, he went into the waiting room with Shawn and Alicia to give us privacy.

"Ok, let's take a look at what we got here," Dr. Huntley said as he placed my X-rays on his light screen. "So, everything looks ok. The spine and your neck are aligned properly, and there is no sign of any trauma, which is what we were concerned about because of the way you fell." He then placed my head x-ray on the screen. "And... now your head. We're not seeing any damage here either, but we do think you suffered a minor concussion, just because of the way your pupils responded to light earlier.

So with that being said, we're going to send you home with proper instructions on how to care for yourself over the next few days, and what to watch for."

My mom breathed a sigh of relief and Kass smiled at me, but Dr. Huntley was not finished.

"Claire, I can see from your blood test results that you are an O positive blood type."

"Yes, Sir."

"Well, I don't want to startle you all, and we don't know exactly what is going on, but when we drew blood from you tonight we found something different about your blood."

Mom, Kass, and I sat in silence for a moment, stunned.

"What do you mean?" Mom asked anxiously after taking a short breath.

"Well, I compared her blood test tonight to the blood test results drawn when she had her tonsils taken out last year, and something is different. She is still an O positive, but there's something in her blood stream that doesn't make sense," Dr. Huntley shrugged his shoulders in bewilderment. "It's almost like a foreign matter of some kind."

Kass and I slid a knowing look at each other, while mom started asking a lot of questions. Dr. Huntley answered as best as he could, but I didn't pay much attention after that. I knew exactly what was going on with myself. The foreign matter in my blood was the pink goo.

"Ms. Haley. I would like to have Claire come back next week to our lab so that we can run some further tests."

I shot mom a "That's never going to happen" look and Dr. Huntley caught me.

"Claire, we are not going to hurt you. We want to help you."

"I'm sorry Dr. Huntley, but I'm not going to be anyone's guinea pig. I'm fine. If I start feeling sick or weird, I will let you know."

"Claire," Mom corrected me sharply, "I will decide when, and if you will be coming back."

I didn't respond and dropped my eyes to the floor, but not before rolling them in aggravation first.

"Dr. Huntley, we will cooperate however we need to. I just want to make sure she's ok."

Dr. Huntley put his hand on my shoulder. "I promise you Claire, these are just simple tests. Not a big deal."

It was almost midnight when they finally discharged me. I walked through the hospital parking lot holding Johnny's hand. I talked my mom into letting him drive me home, since he had waited for me the whole time. She was acting so weird, almost like I was going to die if I left her sight.

"She's just being a normal, protective parent Claire," Johnny scolded me gently while he opened my car door.

"I know, Johnny. I'm just tired I guess," I yawned.

Johnny turned me around and wrapped me in one of his awesome big bear hugs. I rested my cheek against his soft sweatshirt and felt his strong arms tighten around me. I felt so happy and safe with him. I hadn't felt this way since I was a little girl. My dad used to wrap me up the same way when I was upset. I missed him so much.

"Everything is going to be ok, Claire Bear. You're ok and that's all that matters." Johnny kissed my forehead.

I buried myself deeper into his sweatshirt. I wish it was all that simple.

TWENTY-TWO

SATURDAY NIGHT KASS and I hung out, and rented some movies. After Alicia got off work, she came over to spend the night. My mom had me stay home from school on Friday and also work on Saturday, out of fear of me hurting my head again.

I heard Alicia pull in the driveway and my mom welcome her in.

"Hi Alicia!"

"Hi Mrs. Haley."

"Awww...That is so sweet of you. Claire will love that. She is in her room with Kass."

I looked at Kass and then at my door, curious as to what she had that I would love. Alicia walked into my room carrying a flowering plant with a big pink bow on it.

"Hey Clairey! Hey Kass!" She smiled and looked at me. "How are you feeling?"

"I'm ok," I said smiling at the plant.

"Oh, this is from me and Shawn, Lexi and Tater."

I got up and took the plant from her. "Thank you, but I'm not dead," I laughed.

Alicia playfully punched me. "We didn't know what to get."

"I'm just kidding, Mony. That's so sweet of you guys," I said hugging her. "Thanks for coming to hang out. I'm so bored, and my mom is being so ridiculous."

"Well, I don't blame her, Claire. Kass told me about the blood issue."

I looked at my wide open door and went over to shut it for privacy, while Alicia continued talking.

"Claire, I'm worried about you too. Your blood is a fragile thing. That's something you shouldn't be messing with."

"I know Alicia," I sighed. "Trust me. That's all I've been hearing from mom and Kass."

"I'm your sister, so I can bug you about it as much as I want," Kass said sticking her chin in the air with a bit of arrogance in her eyes. I threw my Paris pillow at her, and hit her directly on the nose.

"Man Kass, you have the worst reflexes," I laughed. "What a wimp."

Kass jumped up and tackled me on my bed. She knocked me off balance, and we flew off the bed in a heap on the floor.

"Owww!" I laughed hysterically, while she grabbed my leg and pinned me to the ground.

"Who's the wimp?" she laughed.

"OMG! Get off me, you cow!" I was laughing even harder now. Kass was definitely stronger than me and she knew it.

"Who's a wimp?" she asked, pinning my leg harder to the floor.

"Kass, the loser," I giggled uncontrollably.

"You guys, your mom is going to come in here," Alicia said, but even she was laughing through her warning.

Kass put her free hand at the bottom of my neck where she knew I was insanely ticklish. She barely touched my neck, and I squirmed uncontrollably.

"Kass!" I whispered out loud so mom wouldn't hear me, but I was still laughing. "Stop it!!"

"Who's a wimp?" she asked again calmly.

"Not you!" I said in defeat.

"Ok," she said, but she wasn't done yet. "Who's the best sister in the whole world?"

"Oh, give me a break!" I laughed.

"Say it Claire," she demanded laughing at me and tickling me even harder.

I heard Alicia in the background laughing. "Good grief, Claire! Just say it!"

"Fine!" I said catching my breath. "KASS! Kass is the best sister in the whole world!"

"That's right! And don't you forget it!" she said getting up and helping me off the ground.

I looked over at Alicia who was shaking her head at me. "Wow. Talk about the ultimate in humiliation.

Getting your butt kicked by your little sister."

"Whatever!" I chuckled. "She would kick your butt too."

Alicia shrugged her shoulders and nodded her head, agreeing with me.

"Hey, are you guys hungry?" Kass asked catching her breath and straightening her dirty blond ponytail. "I'm going to pop some popcorn."

We followed her to the kitchen, grabbed a couple of bowls, and threw the popcorn in the microwave.

"So, did you get to see Johnny today?" Alicia asked as we sat at the table.

"No, he has guard tonight, but he came over for dinner last night, and tomorrow we are going to lunch after church. What about Shawn?"

"We went to the game last night, and we are going to a movie tomorrow. I wanted to hang out with him today, but my mom said I have to spend one day of the weekend away from him and with the family."

"They think you're spending too much time with him?" I asked.

"I guess. My mom was really happy when she found out I was coming over here after work instead of hanging out with Shawn."

I gave Alicia my most sympathetic frown. "I'm really glad you came over too, but I know how much you love being with Shawn."

"Well, I definitely wanted to come over," she reassured me.

The microwave beeped and I got the popcorn out,

slamming the door shut. I opened the bag and the kitchen filled with the buttery smell.

"Shhh," Kass said as she came into the kitchen from the living room. " I think mom is asleep."

I looked at the clock. It was already 11 p.m.

We grabbed the popcorn and drinks and headed back to my room, finding our usual spots on my big shaggy rug.

"So when you do you go back to the Doctor?" Alicia asked.

"I'm not going back," I said stubbornly.

"You have to go back Claire," Kass said matter of factly. "Mom said you are."

"You should go," urged Alicia. "Maybe the Doctor can help you with all of this. Maybe they can figure out what is in that pink goo."

"You guys, think about what you are saying." I was trying not to sound too annoyed. "What good is that going to do? They are going to diagnose me wrong, because they have never seen anything like this. That's what Dr. Huntley said. Then, they are going to start trying to even out my blood to its normal type, and that mixed with whatever the pink goo is, will cause a worse effect. I would rather get the pink goo, find out what it is, and go from there." (What I didn't tell them, was I was scared they would do a blood transfusion, and I would lose my power to fly.)

Kass and Alicia stopped eating and stared at me for a moment.

"Seriously you guys, I don't want anyone

experimenting with me," I said quietly. "It's scaring me."

Alicia said scooted over and hugged me. "I'm so sorry, Claire. I didn't know you felt so scared. We will do what you feel is right."

"Thanks Mony," I said.

"Kass, do you still have the notebook with the plan we started last time?" Alicia asked.

"I'll grab it," Kass said jumping up and running to her room. She was back in a flash, and plopped the notebook in the middle of the floor. We all leaned over it looking at the sketched out map.

"Ok, so this is what I was thinking," Alicia said. "Claire, if you're going to go in, I think you should go when one of the guys are on duty. I know you don't want to go when Johnny is pulling guard, so I think you should go when Shawn is there. That way if you get caught, he would let you go."

"You mean tell Shawn she's breaking in?" Kass asked.

"No way!" Alicia said. "I just mean, if she gets caught by Shawn, he would let her go. Only two of them guard the area around the hangar."

"But I don't want to get Shawn in trouble," I reasoned.

"No, you won't. Shawn has no idea what is going on, and he can honestly say that."

I bit my lip nervously and looked at Kass.

"I think that's a good idea, Claire," agreed Kass. "If you're going to do this, it would be better to have

Shawn there."

Alicia continued on. "Shawn has to guard again the Saturday after Thanksgiving. I know because he is staying in town and having Thanksgiving with me and my family. And then also, that Saturday night your mom and my mom will be out of town for the women's retreat. I can spend the night, and we can go without anyone noticing us gone."

Kass picked up her phone and looked at her calendar. "So exactly three weeks from tonight?" she asked looking a little nervous.

"Yep, three weeks from tonight," Alicia reaffirmed.

We all sat in silence again looking over the map.

"Ok," I agreed at last. "Let's do this."

TWENTY-THREE

THE NEXT THREE weeks, I did my best to occupy my mind. I worked keeping myself busy with homework and Johnny the best I could, but all I could think about was "Operation Sky Walker." That's what we named our plan, after the nickname the dispatchers had given me.

I did my best to stay out of the air too, but that was almost impossible. The only thing that kept me grounded was a cold I caught from being in the air too much the weekend after Halloween.

The Saturday before Thanksgiving, Johnny stopped by to see me at work. My job slowed down a lot during the winter, and Saturday nights we usually saw less than half the customers we saw in the warmer months. Lucky for me, Tennessee had been having really mild winters the past few years, and the yummy food at Sonic kept the customers coming back even in the cold months.

"Hey Beautiful!" Johnny smiled as I rolled over to him rocking my fingerless gloves and snow hat. I knew I looked like I was on my way to the Alps.

"Johnny!" I gushed. "I thought I wasn't going to see you until tomorrow." I jumped into his wide open arms.

"Well, I thought I would sneak in a little time with you tonight, since I'm leaving on Monday."

I hugged him tighter. "I'm going to miss you so much, but I'm so excited that you get to spend Thanksgiving with your family."

Johnny ran his fingers through my curls. "I'm so stoked to be with my family, but I'm going to miss you. I wish you were coming with me. My mom said the invitation is still open"

I looked up at his perfect face. "I wish so much I could go, Johnny. If Kass wasn't going to be home alone, I would definitely be going with you."

"I understand," Johnny said leaning down and kissing his favorite spot on my forehead.

I was glad I was at least telling him half of the truth. There is no way my mom would ever let us be home alone all night by ourselves. She seemed relieved when I told her Alicia would be spending the night also.

"Claire! Pick up!" Mr. Arnold yelled from the window.

I smiled and kissed Johnny one more time. "See you tomorrow."

Later that night I sat in my bedroom listening to my playlist, surfing the internet, and as always, looking for any information I could find about losing gravity or Maj. Kearney. I stared at my screen trying to focus on what I was reading, but my mind kept wandering to Operation Sky Walker. Exactly one week from today I would be with Kass and Alicia, and we would be preparing to go. I looked down at my Saturn rings. I couldn't believe how much my life had changed in just 5 short months, and what a scary twist it could take next week if everything went wrong. My mind was going crazy with every possibility and scenario of what could go wrong. I didn't want to lose my power to fly, but most importantly I didn't want to lose Johnny.

I had to get out for a little while. I looked at the clock. It was 11:45, and the house was quiet. My mom was asleep and Kass was spending the night at a friend's. I grabbed my fleece lined sweatshirt, gloves and hat, and threw on my favorite UGGs, all in black, so I could blend with the night sky. I closed the slider as quietly as possible, and went out to my usual launching pad on the deck. It was surprisingly mild tonight for November weather. I checked the temperature on my phone. 52 degrees. Not too bad. I looked over my shoulder to make sure my mom wasn't around, bent my knees, and shot off into the sky. My chest tightened and my face lit up as I looked up at the perfect star drenched sky above. I decided to hit 300 feet instead of my usual 500, knowing the closer I stayed to the ground, the warmer the air temperature. It was extra cloudy tonight, so I knew my risk of being seen was minimal. "Stay out of the sky," I heard Alicia's voice warn me as I looked over the city. I knew I told her that's what I'd do, but I didn't say for how long. Besides, that cold had kept me grounded long enough.

I stopped climbing as I felt the air grow colder. "Now where to?" I asked myself. I looked across the bright lights of my city and gasped at the beauty. "This never grows old," I whispered.

The clock tower downtown rang a hollow chime that echoed across the sky, and caught my attention as it stroked midnight. I decided to go sit on my favorite perch at the top of the tower. Adjusting my hat tighter on my head, I headed off to the southern district section of the city.

I was just approaching the beautiful antique buildings of downtown, when I heard screaming and a lot of voices yelling. To the south of the clock tower a visible cloud of gray smoke was mushrooming from an apartment building roof. People were running from the front door, while others stood below pointing up in the direction of the fire's origin.

I flew to the south of the building, landing in a large oak tree in the back of the parking lot. I watched as flames roared from a fifth floor balcony sliding door, shattering it. The curtains blowing out of the window were gone in an instant, as the flames began to lick the roof.

"Did someone call 911?" I heard a man yell.

"They're on the their way!" yelled another.

"Tell them to hurry!" someone screamed. "There are still people up there!"

Suddenly a woman came running from around the back of the building carrying a baby, and pleading to the other tenants. "Someone help me! I can't find Lucy!"

I jumped down out of the tree and ran toward the woman. "Who are you looking for?" I yelled above the commotion.

"My daughter Lucy!" she said turning to me. I had never witnessed such desperation and panic in someone's eyes before. "Please help me! She's only five!"

"Where was the last place you saw her?"

"She was with me! She was right behind me in the stairwell!"

"What floor?" I yelled trying to get her to focus.

"The third. No, it was the fourth! The fourth! We live on the fourth floor."

I ran to the back of the building, looking around to make sure I was alone, and saw no one. I flew to the third floor, landing on a dark empty balcony. The slider door was locked, and there was nothing available to break the glass with. I looked over at the next balcony, and noticed a large planter sitting by a lounge chair.

"That will work," I said to myself and jumped

across the gap.

The planter was heavier than I thought, but I managed to pick it up and hurl it through the glass door. I ran through the dark apartment and made my way to the hallway. Black smoke was already filling this floor, and I knew it was just a matter of time before the flames would be here. I saw an exit sign gleaming through the dense smoke and found the staircase through the door.

"Lucy!" I yelled. "Lucy where are you?" I ran down the stairs to the second floor and opened the door, looking down the long empty hallway. "Luuuccyyy!" I yelled as loud as I could. "Think Claire. Think like a five year old. If I were a five year old, where would I go?" I looked up the flight of stairs and it hit me. Home. If I was five and lost, I would go home.

I ran back up the stairs and opened the door to the fourth floor. Black thick smoke filled my nose and I dropped immediately, crawling on the floor where the air was clearer. "Lucy!" I yelled while trying to cough out the smoke at the same time. "Lucy!" I crawled down the hallway listening for any sign of her. I banged on a few doors and then I heard her sweet little voice.

"Mommy," she cried. "I want my mommy."

I crawled toward her. She was leaning up against her apartment door, knocking on it. Poor sweet baby.

"Hi Lucy," I said calmly. "My name is Cl...umm, Angel. Your mommy sent me here to help you, ok?"

"Ok," she said, her big blue eyes filled with tears.

"Is this your house?" I asked pointing at the door. Lucy nodded yes. "Ok, we are going to go inside to get away from all the smoke ok?" I opened the door to a room full of fresh air.

I grabbed Lucy's hand, and we got up and entered the apartment. I slammed the door behind us, and we walked quickly to the balcony. I slid the door open, and the sound of fire trucks getting closer filled the air. I looked over the balcony for anyone who might be in the area, and thankfully everyone was on the front side of the building. I picked up Lucy. "Lucy, we can't go back down the stairs, so I'm going to show you a cool trick, ok?" Lucy nodded her head again. "Ok, I want you to wrap your arms around my neck really tight. Can you do that?" Lucy wrapped her arms around me and squeezed. "Good girl. Now, one more thing. I want you to put your head down like this, and close your eyes really tight." I gently laid her little head on my shoulder while she buried her eyes into my sweatshirt. I wrapped one arm around her head and shoulder, and held her underneath with my other. I walked over to the edge of the small balcony and quickly lifted us into the air. I heard Lucy gasp as we took off, and held on tighter as I felt gravity leave my body, but not hers. Instead of flying straight into the air I flew at an angle, getting into the trees as quickly as I could. We flew in the shape of a big rainbow and I gently set us down behind the big oak tree.

"Ok, Lucy. You can open your eyes now." Lucy looked up, startled that we were no longer on the balcony. I smiled at her and set her gently on the ground. "Come on, let's go find mommy."

We walked through the crowd of bystanders, firemen, and police officers. I pulled the hood of my jacket up, in hopes of not being seen. I picked Lucy up as the crowd thickened. After a few minutes of looking, I found her mother talking to a police officer, who was relaying information about Lucy to his other officers, who were searching the building.

"Excuse me," I said interrupting her.

"Oh my god!" she said grabbing Lucy from my arms. "Lucy! Thank you God!" she cried.

The officer gently grabbed her arm. "Mrs. Cardenas, this is your daughter?"

"Yes!" she said looking at him, and kissing Lucy's chubby cheeks.

I took this as my opportunity to escape. I quickly ducked behind two big firefighters who were walking by, and melted into the crowd of people. A sergeant yelled into his radio, ordering his officers out of the building as I quickly headed down the street and into the nearest alley. I had to get home before my mom realized I was gone.

I fell asleep that night feeling like I was on top of the world. I loved helping people. I wanted to do this the rest of my life.

TWENTY-FOUR

"CAN YOU EXPLAIN this please?" Alicia asked me Wednesday afternoon, plopping down a newspaper in front of me on the coffee table of my living room.

Kass and I looked up from the tangled Christmas lights we were working so hard to untangle. Every year my family put our Christmas tree up on Thanksgiving night, and mom had given us clear instructions to pull everything down from the attic and get it ready to go.

"Why do we do this to ourselves every year?" Kass asked, yanking on a strand that was wadded in a perfectly round ball of chaos.

"Kass, you're the one who put the lights away last year. As you can see, the ornaments I put away are arranged neatly and by color," I teased her.

Kass rolled her eyes, while Alicia cleared her throat loudly to get our attention back to the newspaper again. I already knew what it was about. Mom had shown me the paper when it came out Monday morning.

"Hellllooo?" Alicia asked putting her hands on her hips. She was in total mom mode today and getting on my last nerve.

"I know, Mony. I saw it Monday," I sighed.

"Saw what?" Kass asked picking up the paper.

"I thought we agreed you were going to stay out of the air?" she lectured me.

"Seriously?!" Kass exclaimed. "This was you, Claire?"

"Yeah," I said trying not to sound too excited in front of Miss Bossy. "What was I supposed to do, Mony? Just fly by?"

"You weren't supposed to be in the air at all, Claire," Alicia said, emphasizing the "supposed."

Kass began reading the article. "MOTHER CLAIMS AN ANGEL RESCUED HER DAUGHTER"

I looked over at Alicia and Kass who were staring at me, with their hands on their hips, waiting for an explanation.

"Well, it's better than being called a witch," I offered meekly.

Kass looked down at the paper again, and continued reading. "A miracle took place at the Willow Woods Apartments on Saturday night, as flames swept through the fifth floor of the 50 unit building. Over 200 residents have found themselves displaced as a result of the fire. Ashley Cardenas stated her daughter,

Lucianna, 5, was following her and her 7 month old son out of the building when Ashley lost sight of her. 'One minute she was behind me, and the next she was gone. It happened so fast. I had my son in my arms, and I couldn't re-enter the building with him. I didn't know what to do. I just started screaming for help.' Cardenas stated a young teenage girl approached her, and asked who she was looking for. 'I told her my daughter was lost, and where I lost sight of her. The next thing I knew, she was gone and returned with Lucianna about 20 minutes later. When I was talking to Lucianna later that night, she told me the girl had found her. She said the girl had told her that her name was Angel, and that she flew them up in the air to safety from our balcony. She even told me where they landed.' Cardenas further stated that her husband is stationed in Afghanistan, and she was home alone at the time of the fire. She is requesting the mystery girl to please come forward so that she and Lucy can properly thank her. This is the second sighting of an unknown flying person in the city of Clarksville within the last month. In October, citizens claimed to have seen a witch flying over buildings in the northern district."

Kass put the paper down and smiled at me. "Way to go, Claire." Then she looked at Alicia. "But, yeah, you have to be careful, especially with Operation Sky Walker just three days away."

"I know you guys. I'm sorry. I was honestly just planning a clock tower visit, and the next thing I know, I hear people screaming. How could I not help? And who knows what would have happened to Lucy if I didn't find her."

"Ok, fine," said Alicia. "But please, no more. They are going to put two and two together if everything don't go as planned."

We all stopped and looked at each other, frozen by the reality of Alicia's words..

"But...but, everything is going to be fine," she reassured us, her voice a little shaky. "So, why don't we go over everything again, just to make sure we know the plan."

Kass pulled out her notebook and we went over everything, for what seemed like the thousandth time. I knew the plan well. I had played it out in my head continuously, since we put it together. I had also thought of every single thing that could go wrong, and how it would affect my family and my relationship with Johnny.

"So Claire, are you still ok about everything?" Alicia asked.

"Yes," I said as confidently as I could, while nervously twisting the bottom of my shirt. "Of course. I mean, I've done it before. Besides, I have to do it. I have to get that pink stuff... and I'm not scared, so don't think that. I can just fly out of there, no problem." I rambled without thinking, another sign I wasn't as confident as I was trying to sound.

"Claire, everything is going to be ok," Kassie tried to assure me, but I could tell she wasn't so sure herself.

Thursday evening my aunts, uncle, and Kyle, joined us, for a nice low key Thanksgiving meal. When we were done eating, Kass and I cleaned up, put up the Christmas tree, and then watched "Meet Me in St. Louis," our first Christmas movie of the season. We had so much fun, but I was really missing my two older sisters, Danielle and Tessa, and of course Johnny. He had been texting and calling me all week. I could tell he missed me too.

The Sunday before he left we had a serious, but not planned conversation about our relationship.

"So Claire, I really want my family to meet you," he had said as we sat bundled up on my porch swing.

"Really?" I asked, a little surprised.

"Yes," he laughed. "Why do you sound so surprised?"

"I don't know. I mean, I want to meet them too, it just makes me a little nervous."

"Why?"

I shrugged my shoulders. "I'm just scared they won't like me."

Johnny leaned his head back and started laughing. "Seriously Claire? Everybody likes you! That's the craziest thing I've ever heard."

I elbowed him in the side. "I'm serious!" I laughed.

"Come here, silly." Johnny squeezed me closer. "I

know they will love you."

"Oh really? How do you know that?" I teased.

Johnny paused for a moment, then sat back so I could see him. "Because... I love you Claire." My mouth dropped open slightly, and I had to catch my breath. "I really do."

"Oh wow," I whispered. I knew I loved him too. "I love you too, Johnny. I really do. I feel so lucky to have found you."

Johnny traced my chin with his fingers and kissed me softly. "That's a weight off my shoulders," he smiled. "I was so nervous to tell you that for some reason, but I've felt this way for a while now."

I kissed his cheek over and over. "Johnny, you can tell me anything."

"I know. I hope you know you can tell me anything too," he said as he moved a strand of curls from my face. "I mean it. I really want us to work. You are the sweetest, caring, honest, and most trustworthy person I know, and I feel so blessed to have found you too."

Johnny hugged me tight, and I sank back into his arms. His words stung my heart. I wasn't trustworthy, and I wasn't being honest with him either. I was trying to balance one of the biggest secrets I've ever had to carry, with the only guy I have ever loved, and I was failing miserably.

TWENTY-FIVE

SATURDAY CAME BEFORE I knew it. I kissed my mom goodbye, and she was off to the Women's retreat with Alicia's mom, Mrs. Perez.

"Claire, I don't want you guys going out tonight while I'm gone," she instructed me as she headed out the door. "I want you to get some movies, maybe order some pizza, and stay in."

"Ok, mom," I said feeling pangs of guilt, knowing that wasn't going to happen.

"Also, double check and make sure everything is locked up before you go to sleep."

"Got it mom."

Alicia laughed as I slowly shut the front door, while my mom continued to call out instructions to me all the way to Mrs. Perez's car.

"Trust me. I got all the same instructions before I came over here," Alicia smiled.

"Mony, I hate lying to her."

"I know," Alicia said plopping down on the couch, "but we kind of have no choice."

I sat beside her. "What time is it?" I asked.

"It's noon."

"Where are our mom's going anyway?"

"Memphis, about three hours away."

We sat on the couch in silence for a moment, with tonight filling our thoughts.

"You know Clairey, if you want to back out at any time, you can," Alicia said.

"No way, Mony," I replied, determined. "I have to do this."

Kass came in the living room and sat in the recliner. "So, Alicia, did you find out where the medic room is?"

"Yeah. Shawn told me last night. Kass, do you have the map of the hangar?"

Kass leaned over the coffee table, and opened the plan folder. "This one?" she asked handing the hangar map to Alicia.

"Yep." Alicia and I sat on the ground with Kass around the coffee table. "Ok Claire, you know where the closet is you found the liquid in, right?" I nodded my head. "Well, Shawn said the medic room is in the same hallway, across from the closet, three doors down."

"That sounds easy enough," I said, feeling a little more optimistic. "Mony, how did you get this info without sounding so obvious?"

"I just asked a bunch of questions about a medic's role in the military, since I want to be a doctor, and the medic closet came up."

"Clever girl," I winked at her.

After lunch we sat in the living room and watched a movie. Outside a thunderstorm rolled in and before we knew it, we had all fallen asleep.

Four hours later the sound of the house shaking woke me. I sat up on the couch, and ran to the window to catch the tail end of three Chinooks flying over.

"Awww, we missed the Chinooks," I heard Kass mumble without getting up from the recliner.

"What time is it?" Alicia yawned.

"Six thirty," I replied.

"Are you guys hungry?" Kass asked sitting up.

I sat on the edge of the couch. "I don't think I can eat to be honest." My text dinged and I picked up my phone. I smiled when I saw it was Johnny.

"Johnny?" Alicia asked smiling, when she saw my expression.

"Yes," I giggled.

"When does he come back?"

"He's actually on his way back now. He has a layover in Atlanta," I said reading my text from him. "He says….he won't be back until late tonight, and he wants to come over tomorrow."

"Awww!" Alicia and Kass said at the same time.

"You guys know what he told me last Sunday night before he left?" I asked.

"What?" they said in unison again.

"He told me he loves me!" I said excitedly. Kass and Alicia nodded at me unimpressed.

"Did you hear what I said? He finally told me 'I love you'."

Alicia cleared her throat. "That's awesome, Claire. Shawn actually said that to me a couple of months ago."

"Kyle too," echoed Kass.

"Oh," I said. "I guess Johnny's a little slower than most."

"Nothing wrong with that," Alicia laughed, putting her arm around me. "How about we get Kass something to eat before she dies over here."

Kass nodded in agreement.

We decided to order a pizza. I forced a small slice down, but was so focused on Operation Sky Walker, I wasn't very hungry.

At 10:30 I walked into the kitchen all dressed in black. Kass and Alicia looked up at me, as they sat at the kitchen table.

"Goodness Claire, you look like you're fixin' to rob a bank!" Kass exclaimed, looking me up and down.

"Or knock someone into next week," added Alicia.

I looked down at myself. They were right. I had on black everything; under Shirt, sweatshirt, skinny jeans, and combat boots.

"I have to blend into the sky, you guys."

"This is true," said Alicia. "but do you think you really need the football eye black too?"

"Yes, I do," I said matter of factly, "for some reason it makes me feel empowered."

Kass laughed, while Alicia rolled her eyes, and I sat down at the table.

"Ok, so we leave here in one hour," Alicia said, and then began to go over the list. On paper, and in our heads, we had my every move timed down to a T. We had a plan for everything going right and a plan if everything went wrong. I just had to trust Kass and Alicia, and trust myself. And I prayed. I prayed a lot.

At exactly 11:30, we piled into Alicia's car, and headed to Ft. Campbell. Alicia had gotten a pass earlier in the day, so we didn't have to stop at the main gate to get one. I directed her to the cul de sac in the neighborhood I had parked in before. She shut off the lights to the car, but left it running.

Alicia took a deep breath. "So Claire, you can call it quits at anytime. If you feel unsure, or you have a bad feeling about anything, you fly back here immediately."

"I will."

Kass reached up and hugged me from the back seat. "Everything's going to be fine, Claire. Just get in and get out as fast as you can."

I hugged her back, and then hugged Alicia. She gave me a final thumbs up, and Alicia and I got out of the car. She walked me to the edge of the woods.

"Mony, if for some reason I get caught, promise me that you'll stay with Kass. Don't leave her alone for one minute, ok?"

"I promise," Alicia said, the edges of her eyes creased with worry.

I smiled at her, walked a couple of feet away, and shot up over the tall trees. I flew just above the thick woods that guarded the airfield, about a quarter of a mile deep. I found my favorite large oak tree, and perched at the very top.

The airfield was eerily still and quiet. My hope was that everyone's guard was down, because it had been a while since I had broke in. I took my phone out of my arm sleeve, and looked at the time. Ten after midnight. The watchtower appeared to be empty, and I saw no one around the hangar. There was a hallowed silence over the airfield. No one moving about, no engine noises, not even a sound from nature. Nothing. I felt like I was in a soundproof room.

I didn't want to rush myself, but I didn't want to leave Kass and Alicia waiting out for me in the car too long. I had agreed to text them through every point of the plan we made.

"I'm in the tree. Getting ready to head to the hangar," I texted them.

I flew down from the tree, and landed quietly in the waist high grass. I took the same path as I had the previous time leaning down, running through the small field, until I got to the large trucks parked on the side of the hangar. The dark side of the large wheels provided a perfect place to hide, and catch my breath.

When we were planning, we had all agreed that

going back through the window was not an option. Shawn had told Alicia that it was just him and his buddy on guard duty, so we decided that I should go through the front door, and create a distraction for the two.

I texted Alicia, "*Call.*" At exactly 12:15, Alicia called Shawn in hopes of distracting him so that all I had to worry about was getting around the second guard. I inched my way to the front door, down the darkest side of the building, ditching in between the roll of trucks, whenever I felt unsafe. At last I was at the front of the building, and hid behind the bush beside the door. My phone vibrated, and I looked at the text from Kass.

"Alicia says the other guard is walking the perimeter. Shawn is in the office. Go now."

I scanned the area double checking for anyone around. My hands shook with nervousness as I put my phone back in my arm band. This was going to be the most difficult part. The front door was lit up, and even if I got inside, there was a good chance of running into Shawn. I moved quickly from behind the bush, and very softly opened the door to the hangar. I walked into the hallway, and heard Shawn's voice coming from the front office. I crept past the closed door, down the hallway, and out in the giant room where two large Chinooks sat. One had the engine cover off, obviously in repair there. I scooted along the wall to the other hallway, on the west side of the building.

The hallway was somewhat dim, as it was the last

time I was here. I spotted the medics closet immediately, and went into the small room closing the door behind me.

"*Medic Closet,*" I texted Alicia.

I turned on the light, and began to scan the shelf for the Saturn Ring box he had told me about. I looked over all the shelves twice. Nothing. Nothing that even resembled anything like the tat I had on my arm. I began to panic.

"Seriously?" I whispered to myself, my voice trembling as I felt the tears filling my eyes.

"All this planning for nothing?"

I scanned the shelves again, and moved everything around. All I saw were medic gloves, peroxide, and bandages, all the common stuff you would find in a medicine cabinet at home. I shut the door and leaned against the wall, sliding my back down it, until I was in a sitting position.

"No," I said as the tears began to fall. "I can't believe this." All the hope that I had was fading, and I felt like someone had punched me in the stomach. I felt defeated and hopeless. I sobbed silently for a moment, then finally wiped away my tears. I had to get back to the girls. I stood up and looked down, noticing my shoe was untied and bent down to tie it. Out of the corner of my eye, I saw a flash of pink splatter. I looked at a green army blanket that was half covering an object shaped like a box, hidden in the corner of the room. I crawled over and pulled the cover off. To my astonishment there was a crate. The crate appeared to be the same crate I had landed on, but much smaller. I pulled off the dusty top of the crate, and felt my breath leave my body. There wrapped in old, yellowing, bubble paper was a tiny glass vial of the pink goo. I held it in my hand like it was gold. The vial was about the size of my pinky finger and shimmered when the lights from the ceiling hit it. I didn't think to bring something to carry it in that would protect it, so very carefully, I wrapped the vial in a small section of the bubble paper and placed it inside my pants pocket.

"I got the goo! Headed back your way now," I texted the girls, throwing the blanket back over the crate.

I walked to the door and listened for the sound of anyone outside. It was quiet, so I crept into the hallway. I did as we had planned and headed down the hall, out the back exit door. I reached up to push the bar open, and when I did the loudest alarm I had ever heard activated. It screamed in my ears and pounded through my body, sounding like an alarm you would hear in a bomb attack. It echoed all over the airfield, and I bolted out the door toward the grassy field.

"Jackson!" I heard someone yelling close by. "Over here!"

Jackson. Shawn's last name.

I sprinted from the hangar, running as fast as I could. A large spotlight from the Air Tower shined down on the ground, and began scanning the area. I made it to the grassy field and looked back. No one was behind me like the last time. The spotlight swept across the field and I made it to the tree line, just as the spotlight came back around. It caught me, and I jumped into the woods. The spotlight stopped, and slivers of the bright light cut through the woods chasing after me. Now they knew where I had entered. I kept running, dodging bushes, while sticks cracked under my feet. I was just a few feet away from a clearing that I would fly out of, when suddenly I felt arms wrap around the right side of my body, tackling me to the ground. We landed hard, and I grunted as the weight of the soldiers body crushed mine. The soldier grabbed my arms, sitting on me, pinning me to the ground. He pulled back my sweatshirt hood and gasped. "Claire!"

I was looking into the horrified face of Shawn.

TWENTY-SIX

"JACKSON!" I HEARD the other soldier yelling from behind us.

Shawn grabbed my hand and pulled me off the ground. "Oh my God, Claire! What are you doing here?"

I looked into Shawn's eyes. "You don't know me," I said just as the other soldier approached.

"Jackson! Is that her? The ghost girl?" He asked grabbing my arm, and shaking me. "You are in so much trouble Miss!"

"Corporal! It's fine! I got her!" Shawn yelled, grabbing my other arm and pulling me back toward him.

The Corporal turned me around and began cuffing me.

"Corporal, not necessary!" Shawn said, and began pulling me out of the woods toward the hangar office.

The Corporal locked my cuffs tighter, and grabbed my other arm.

We soon reached the edge of the woods where the spotlight was waiting for us. Shawn grabbed his radio. "Tower Command, from 42, get that spotlight off! I can't see anything!"

The Corporal was on his radio now. "Tower Command, get a wagon here. We have one in custody."

Wagon. Custody. I was going to jail.

Shawn led me into the hangar office, and sat me down slowly into a chair. I looked at the floor unable to look him in the eyes.

The Corporal came into the room right after. "What's your name miss, and what are you doing on this airfield in the middle of the night?"

Shawn attempted to pull the Corporal to the side and talk to him, but I could still hear every word of their conversation. "Corporal, maybe we should find out more about her, before we start questioning her. She looks like she's no more than 16. If she's a juvenile, we can't question her without her parent's consent." Shawn knew exactly how old I was.

"Fine," said the Corporal. "Pat her down, and see what she has on her."

Shawn walked over to me, and stood me up under the Corporal's watchful eye. I gave him a "you don't know me look again," and he patted me down, stopping when he got to my pants pocket. He grabbed the vial, that had slid halfway out of my pocket from all the commotion. "What is this, miss?" Shawn asked, holding it in front of my face.

I said nothing, but tears ran down my face. Not the vial. Please don't take the vial.

The Corporal sat me back down, and went outside as a car pulled up to the building. Shawn squatted down in front of me, forcing me to look into his eyes.

"Claire, talk to me. What's going on? What are you doing out in the woods?"

"Shawn, don't lose that vial. Please," I whispered.

"That pink stuff?" He asked confused.

I nodded yes. Shawn looked down at the vial in his hand, and then back up at me confused.

"Does Alicia know you're here?"

I heard the door open again. "Call her," I whispered as the Corporal returned with another soldier. Around the soldier's arm was a band with the big white letters, "MP" on it. "MP" for military police. The Corporal grabbed my arm, yanking me out of the chair.

"Not so rough with her Jason!" Shawn almost yelled. Jason walked me out to the SUV that was waiting, and placed me in the back. I read the side, "Fort Campbell Police."

"We've been looking for you for a long time," Corporal Jason said slamming the door shut, and then went to the other side of the vehicle to talk to the MP. I looked out the window at Shawn, who was standing outside the hangar, and on his phone with Alicia, I presumed. I couldn't hear what he was saying, but I could tell from his body movement, he was extremely aggravated. Whoever was on the other end of the line was definitely getting yelled at. I felt bad for not telling Shawn, but what was I going to say to him? *"I'm sorry Shawn, but I need that vial, because it makes me fly."* If I did that, this MP would be driving me to the mental ward at the hospital, or even worse, the government science lab. We had decided in our plan that if I got caught, to say nothing to no one.

The MP got in the car and we pulled off from the hangar. The last thing I saw was Shawn's stunned face, watching us drive away.

Kass and Alicia sat patiently in the car waiting for my return. The last they had heard, I had the pink goo, and was on my way out.

"I don't know Alicia," Kass said as she looked at my last text biting her nail. "It's been thirty minutes since we've heard from her. She should have been here by now."

"It's ok, Kass," Alicia assured her. "If we haven't heard from her in ten minutes, I'll call Shawn."

Alicia's phone rang, and she picked it up immediately. It was Shawn. "Alicia? Alicia? Where are you? Claire just got arrested! Did you hear me?! ARRESTED!"

"Oh my god," Alicia gasped.

"What?" asked Kass.

Shawn yelled again. "Alicia, Claire told me to call you! What's going on?! What do you know about this?!"

Kass gasped when she heard Shawn through the phone. "Where is Claire?" she asked Alicia, and then yelled it into the phone so Shawn could hear. "Where is Claire, Shawn?!"

Alicia threw her hands up. "Hold on everyone! I can't think with you guys yelling!" Shawn and Kass quietened down, while Alicia pulled herself together. "Shawn, I promise I will try and explain everything to you, but for right now can you please tell us where Claire is?"

"Explain to me, Alicia? Explain what?" Shawn's voice began to rise again. " I don't know if I can trust you, or believe anything you say. Were you a part of this?"

"Well...yeah. Kind of," Alicia stumbled over her words.

"She's being held at the brig on Indiana Avenue." Shawn snapped. "When you're ready to be honest with me, then you can call me back." And with that, Shawn hung up the phone.

Alicia stared down at her phone. "Great," her voice quivered. "What are we gonna do, Kass? If we go to the brig, they are going to arrest us too."

"We have to call our moms Alicia," Kass reasoned.

"That's only as a last resort."

"This IS the last resort!" Kass exclaimed. "I don't think we can get anymore last resort than this! I thought Shawn would let her go! Why didn't he let her go?!"

"I don't know, Kass! I don't know! Please calm down!" She looked around into the darkness of the trees. "Let's get out of here. I don't want to be here when they come searching for more clues."

Kass and Alicia went back to our house and tried to call mom. They weren't able to get in touch with her until early the next morning. I'm not exactly sure what happened when they told her. I try not to think about it too much. She and Mrs. Perez left the women's retreat to come home, and I felt terrible for putting her through this. Have you ever had to do something you knew was necessary, but would hurt someone you love? I knew what I did was necessary, but that made it no easier when it came to my mom. I can't imagine what she was thinking, or the embarrassment she felt in front of Mrs. Perez.

TWENTY-SEVEN

"I CAN'T BELIEVE you, miss," the MP said to me while we drove to the brig. "You could have been killed tonight." I barely acknowledged him, and continued to stare outside with my head leaned against the window. "You know Jackson?" he asked trying his best to get me to talk. I continued to stare in silence. There was no way this guy would get anything from me.

We pulled up to the jail around 1 a.m. The whole block of buildings all looked the same, square, and desert tan. The last one was clearly the jail, surrounded by a high fence, with circles of barbed wire around the top. The gate opened automatically, and the SUV pulled into a large garage. The MP came around, and helped me out.

"Just do as they ask," he said almost as a warning to me. He walked me to the door, and a loud buzz followed by the snap of a bolt unlocking, echoed across the garage. We walked down a long hallway, and through a door labeled "booking." An officer in another MP uniform waited behind a bullet proof glass for us.

My eyes began to burn from the smell of bleach in the room, like someone had poured it all over the floors, and had forgot to clean it up.

"Is this the subject from the hangar?" he asked not even looking up at me.

"Yes Sir."

"Does she have any belongings?"

"Just a cell phone is all they gave me."

The vial. Shawn must have kept it.

He continued filling out some forms, finally looking up at us. He stared at me for a short minute looking over his thick rimmed glasses. "How old are you?" he asked me. I continued looking at the ground in silence. "Well, she can't be no more than 17. We're going to put her in the juvenile cell. What's your name Miss?"

I repeated the same silence as before, reminding myself of the plan I made with Kass and Alicia.

"Well, we'll find out soon enough. I'm sure we will be hearing from her parents," the officer said, coming around to let us through the door. I was placed in a cell by myself, behind the desk of the MP. I sat for what seemed forever, before I finally dozed off in an uncomfortable, nightmarish sleep.

The sound of keys in the metal door woke me from my light slumber. A different MP from the one I met earlier appeared in the door.

"Claire, right?" he asked. How did he know my name? "There's someone here to see you."

I sat up and yawned, my eyes blurry from the lack of sleep. "Come with me, please."

I walked behind the officer, pretty positive I was about to face my mom. He led me into a small room, and there, sitting at the table, was Johnny. I gasped when I saw him.

"Claire!" he said, and jumped up to hug me. I buried my face in his chest for a moment before he pulled me away again. He didn't say anything, but just shrugged at me in frustration, his body language saying "What the heck?"

I didn't know what to say to him. For one thing, I knew this room was a recorded one. I could see the cameras in the corner of the ceiling, and besides that, I just couldn't tell him.

"Johnny, I'm so sorry," was all I could manage.

"Claire? I'm sorry? That's all you have...that's all you can say to me?"

I looked into his eyes, that were now flashing with slight aggravation. "I...Johnny, I want to tell you more, but I can't." I looked sideways at the cameras.

Johnny walked to the other side of the room, pacing, and putting his hands behind his head in frustration. "What do you mean you can't tell me?! You're acting like you're some kind of spy or something. What were you doing at the hangar, Claire?!"

I sat down at the end of the table, burying my head in my hands. My head started to hurt from what I knew to be a lack of sleep, stress, and the overwhelming bleach smell I had breathed in all night. Johnny finally came over and sat beside me.

"Claire," he said putting his head down close to mine, and wrapping his arm around me, "I can't help you, if you're not honest with me."

I looked up at him, my eyes filling with tears again. I had already cried most of the night, and my eyes were swollen and sore. "I want to be honest with you Johnny, always, but it's better for you not to know. I don't want to hinder your chance of becoming a pilot." I wiped my tears away and stood up from the table. "In fact, you should leave. Now."

Johnny's voice was soft, but stern. "Really Claire? Aren't we supposed to be in a relationship here? I'm supposed to trust you, and you should be able to trust me."

I was crying hard now. "I know, Johnny. But I just can't. You don't understand."

Johnny shook his head, in defeat. "Can you tell me just one thing? Are you the ghost girl everyone has been talking about the last two months? Was that you?"

I guess I could tell him that. I slowly shook my head yes. Johnny gasped, his eyes wide in confusion. "I just don't understand, Claire. Is this why you got with me? Some big plan to break into where I work?"

"No Johnny!"

"You were using me?"

"Not at all! I swear!" I cried, almost pleading with him.

Johnny stared hard at me. I could read a mix of emotions all over his face; hurt, of course, anger, a little bit sympathy (because I knew he loved me), and a whole lot of confusion.

"Well," he sighed at last, "then I guess there's not a lot left to say, Claire. I guess we're through. I mean, I don't know what else to do. I don't know you at all, and I can't be in a relationship with someone I can't trust." Johnny's voice shook a little at the end, and I saw him swallow back his tears. He headed toward the door, but turned around one last time. "So they...they will probably take it easy on you. You're a minor." He shook his head, trying to discreetly wipe away a tear. "Bye, Claire."

Johnny walked out of the room, the metal door slamming behind him. I sat at the table, sobbing. My heart was broken, and I felt like someone had punched me in the stomach. I knew I did the right thing, and now it was on video. Proof that Johnny had no idea. But still, it hurt. I don't know that I had ever felt such hurt. I didn't want a life without Johnny, but he was safe, and his career was safe, and that meant more to me than my own selfish desires.

I went back to my cell and fell into a troubled sleep. At ten I was awakened by the sound of keys in the door again. I opened my eyes, and didn't even bother to sit up.

"Claire?" A strong male voice filled my cell. "Come on. Your mom is here."

I slowly stood up and grabbed my sweat shirt. My thoughts echoed loudly in my head. How was I going to face her? I can't bear to see her upset. What was I going to tell her? She would never understand.

The MP walked me down a long hallway, and into a conference room. My mom was waiting there with a very decorated Officer. She came over and hugged me at once.

"Oh Claire, are you ok?" She asked. "What happened? Did you get lost or something?"

"I'm fine, mom," I mumbled.

The decorated officer approached me with his hand out, and greeted me in a thick, southern, Spanish accent. "Claire, I'm Major Silva. I'm the Command Operator for the Airfield here at Ft. Campbell."

Major Silva. I had heard that name a lot. He was Johnny and Shawn's commanding officer. I reluctantly reached my left hand out to shake his. He had a firm, strong hand that completely enveloped mine. I attempted to loosen his grip on my hand, but he was looking down at my wrist. He turned our hand shake with my hand palm up, staring down at my tattoo. We looked at each other for a moment, and I saw the astonishment in his eyes. Something about my tattoo had rendered him speechless.

All was quiet for a moment, and then he finally spoke, snapping back into the moment, and letting go of my hand. "That's an interesting tattoo you have there. Saturn rings. What made you chose that?"

I thought hard for a moment, unsure of what to say. "I….um...I love space," I shrugged.

Major Silva nodded his head, but I could tell he didn't believe me at all. "Well, I'm going to let you both have a moment, and then we are going to talk for a little bit if that's ok."

I looked at the ground, while my mom thanked Major Silva, following him to the door. She came back to me and hugged me again. "Everything's going to be ok, honey. He's just going to ask you a few questions, and then we can go home."

"I don't want to answer questions, mom. I just want to go home."

"You have to talk to him Claire, " Mom said putting both of her hands on my shoulders, and looking me straight in the eyes. "I need to know, and they need to know what you were doing out on that airfield last night."

I put my hands on her arms and spoke to her softly. "Mom, I love you, and this is very hard for me to say, but I'm not talking to anyone."

My mom looked at me, shocked by my defiance. "Claire, you don't have a choice. You could be in a lot of trouble here. You need to tell me what happened, and you need to tell me now."

"Mom, I can't talk about it right now. Please," I pleaded. "I just need some more time." "Claire, it's just a few questions," Mom said moving a long curl out of my face. " Explain to him what happened, and then we can go home."

I rubbed my eyes as my headache from earlier started returning full force. "Mom, please. Not now. Trust me on this. Please."

Mom let out a sigh that I recognized as a sign she was backing down. "Ok Claire, but just for right now. We're going to do exactly what they ask us to do though."

Mom walked over to the door, and went into the hallway where Major Silva was waiting. She started talking to him in a light whisper, but I could still hear almost everything she was saying.

"I think Claire isn't feeling too well right now. I think we'd rather go home, and let her regroup before we talk about everything."

"I understand Ms. Haley, but you do understand this is a government facility, and we need to know what she was doing in a restricted area."

"We definitely know that Major Silva, and we will cooperate. I can promise you that. I appreciate your understanding in all of this."

They came back into the room, and I did my best to act like I didn't hear anything.

"Claire, Major Silva has agreed to meet with us later this week," she said. I could tell by her tone of voice and her cold stare, how mad and disappointed she was with me. "Grab your jacket."

I didn't dare argue with her. Instead I got up quietly and threw on my sweatshirt.

Major Silva walked closer to me. "Claire, I told your mom I'm going to let you go home today, but we will need a statement from you. What you did last night was a crime, and we need to talk about it. You understand?"

I nodded my head yes, not looking at him.

He put his hand on my shoulder. "Claire," he said lowering his voice. "I'm sure talking about everything will not be easy, but I just want you to know, no matter what it is you have to tell me, I will understand. And you can trust me." He looked down at my tattoo again. "I mean it. No matter what it is."

I nodded at him, trying to ignore his obvious stare at my wrist. "Ummm...thank you Major Silva." I grabbed my sweatshirt, and headed to the door. My mom thanked him once again as we walked down the long hall to the exit. He led us to the same desk where I had been processed coming in, only this time the office was full of a lot more soldiers. They all stopped what they were doing to look at me. The soldier who came to get me from my cell unlocked a drawer, and handed me my cell phone and the arm band I used for it during flight.

"Ok Miss, you're clear to go," the soldier said.

Major Silva led us out into the bright sunshine. I covered my eyes that were extra sensitive from the darkness of the jail, plus all the crying I had done.

"So, I'll be waiting for your call this week," he said to mom and me as we walked to our car.

"You will be hearing from us. Thanks again, Major Silva," mom called to him.

It was a long twenty minute drive home. Mom was pretty quiet most of the way. When we got home, I went in and showered immediately, then went to my room and fell asleep.

When I woke, my room was partly dark. I could tell I had slept most of the day away. I got up to go to the bathroom, and could hear mom and Kass in the kitchen talking. The smell of fried chicken filled the house. It smelled amazing, but I was nowhere near hungry, though I hadn't ate in 24 hours. I went back to my room and shut the door. A moment later, I heard a knock.

"Come in."

The door slowly opened and Kass came in. "Hey Claire."

"Hey Kass."

"Are you ok?"

"Yeah, I'm fine."

She came over and sat on my bed. "I'm so sorry. We should have made a better plan for you." She reached over my grabbed my hand.

"No Kass, I should have flew out of there sooner. I waited too long. It's all my fault."

"What happened? Did you tell mom anything?"

"No way," I said. "I didn't say anything to anyone."

I proceeded to tell Kass everything about the night. She listened intently, covering her mouth in surprise when I told her about Shawn catching me, and getting arrested.

"Claire, we did our best not to tell mom, but Shawn said they wouldn't release you without a parent. Alicia and I decided we had no choice."

"I'm not mad at you guys, Kass. I put you in this position." My phone text dinged. I looked at my phone hoping it was Johnny. It was Alicia. In fact, she had already sent five texts I missed while I was sleeping.

"Claire, are you awake yet?"

I looked at Kass. "Alicia," I said.

"Hey Mony. Yes, I'm sorry."

"I would call you, but I'm grounded."

"Oh no! I'm so sorry."

"It's ok."

"Have you heard from Shawn?"

"No, he's not talking to me."

"Oh Mony, I'm so sorry, again. I screwed everything up so bad."

"I'm not stressed about it. He can't go no more than two days without talking to me. I'll hear from him again."

"Well, just so you know, I didn't tell anyone about you and Kass being involved. No one has any idea you guys were even there."

"Thanks Clairey. My mom doesn't know either. I'm grounded because I broke curfew. Have you heard anything from Johnny?"

"Yes, and he broke up with me. I will have to tell you about everything at school."

"I'm so sorry Claire. Everything is going to be ok. I love you."

"I love you too."

"Are you going to school tomorrow?" Kass asked as she stood up.

"Girls! Dinner!" Mom called from the kitchen.

I got up with Kass. "I'm pretty sure I am, but other than that, I doubt I will leave the house in this century again."

TWENTY-EIGHT

MONDAY, ALICIA AND I sat at the lunch table waiting for Kass and Lexi. I was sure by now, word had spread among Johnny and Shawn's friends, that I had been arrested on the airfield. If Lexi didn't know, it was just a matter of time until Tater told her.

"So, are you going to tell Lex?" Alicia asked.

"I kind of have no choice," I said playing with my food. "I know Tater will tell her, and she would be hurt not hearing it from us first."

"I know," Alicia agreed, "but what do we say to her?"

I shrugged my shoulders. "No idea," I said as Lexi and Kass entered the cafeteria.

"Hey guys!" Lexi said, as she and Kass joined us at the table. "We have to hit the mall this weekend. I just talked to Jessica, and she said Pacific Beach is having a huge sale, which is perfect because I haven't even started my Christmas shopping yet."

So, I guess she hadn't heard anything yet. I cleared my throat. "Yeah, definitely Lex."

Lexi looked at me. "So Claire, tell me about this weekend. Are you in a lot of trouble for getting caught in the woods around the airfield?"

My eyes grew wide, and I looked at her in shock.

"Kass told me," she laughed.

Kass looked at me smiling. "You just have to talk to the sergeant or something, right Claire?"

"Oh yeah…" I tried to sound as nonchalant as I possibly could. "They just want to clear some things up...it was all so stupid." I tried to laugh casually. I'm such a bad actor.

"So Lex, how many people do you have to buy for, for Christmas?" Alicia asked.

Lexi went into her long Christmas list, and I looked over at Kass who winked at me. That was so easy. I mouthed "Thank you," to her. I'm pretty sure I have the best little sister in the world.

Kass met me after school, and we drove home together. She talked alot abour the weekend, filling me in on what happened while I was in jail. (That sounds so weird to say, btw.) I tried my hardest to concentrate on what she was saying, but my focus was now on a sleek maroon car that had been following us since we had left the school. Normally, I wouldn't have paid any attention, but I had noticed it as we were leaving for school this morning, only because I had never seen it in the neighborhood before. I thought maybe the Wilkensons down the street had got a new car, because it was parked in front of their house. Then I remembered that Mr. Wilkenson had surgery recently and that was probably not a possibility.

So now this car was following us, and I kept glancing in my rearview mirror watching it mimic our every turn.

"Claire, why do keep looking in the mirror?" Kass asked turning around, looking behind us.

"Kass! Turn around!"

"Is someone following us?"

"I'm not sure. Just keep looking ahead."

We approached a busy intersection, and I watched through my shades as the car turned left away from our neighborhood.

"They turned," I told Kass as we both continued to stare straight ahead. "I'm sorry, Kass. I think I'm just being a little paranoid. Forget that, ok?"

Kass patted my knee. "It's ok, Claire. That's to be expected."

Kass and I went into the house. "Hi girls!" Mom called from the kitchen.

"Hey Mom!" we said in unison. We went to our rooms and put our bags away, then joined her in the kitchen.

"You're home from work early," Kass said kissing mom on the cheek, and getting a drink from the fridge.

"Well, I've been checking on everything that happened over the weekend. Major Silva called and he wants to meet with us on Friday, Claire."

I leaned back in my chair, folded my arms, and nodded. "Ok."

"Claire," Mom leaned closer to me over the table, "I know this weekend has been overwhelming, and I've tried to be considerate of that, but if there is anything you need to tell me, I need to hear it. I want to know by Friday."

"I understand, Mom."

"Ok," she said, looking at me firmly. "If you understand, then tell me what you were doing on that airfield. Major Silva made it sound like you could get in some serious trouble."

Kass came over and slid into a chair at the table with us. I looked up at her, and she stared back at me wide eyed. I knew if she could have said anything to help me, she would have, but as far as mom knew, Kass had nothing to do with this, and I wanted to keep it that way.

Mom continued to stare at me waiting for my reply. A reply I didn't have for her. I had no idea what to say. I finally made an attempt at trying to appease her, at least for now.

"Mom….I know you want an answer and I will tell you. I promise... Can you just give me a couple of days?"

"Claire, that makes no sense," she said, clearly

agitated. "Why would you not tell me now? You've always been honest with me."

"Mom, it's so complicated…" I tried to explain, but Kass interrupted to my relief.

"Mom, maybe we should give Claire a couple of days. I'm sure she will tell us when things settle down."

Mom stared back and forth at us both. I could almost read her mind. She knew something was up, and now I was pretty sure she knew Kass was in on it as well. "Ok girls. I'm going to give you a little more time, because I trust you. But we will be talking to Major Silva this week, and get this whole thing cleared up."

I breathed a silent sigh of relief. "I'm sorry, Mom," I apologized again. "Thank you for being so patient."

Mom got up, and kissed me on the forehead. "This is only because I trust you," she repeated herself again. "We are having baked spaghetti leftovers tonight, girls. I don't want it to go to waste."

I looked over at Kass, who smiled with relief at me. "Thank you," I mouthed to her. She smiled at me.

I got up from the table. "I'm not hungry just yet. Do you mind if I take a quick run before dark?"

"That's fine," Mom said to my surprise, although I think she knows how therapeutic running is to me and how much I need it right now.

I went to my room to change, giving Kass a silent high five on my way out of the kitchen. Kass had been getting me out of a lot of trouble lately. I'm her big sister. That's supposed to be my job.

TWENTY-NINE

I THREW ON my gray running pants and a tee, with a light sweat jacket. I pulled my long curls into a high bun, and wrapped my head and ears in a warm headband. The brisk afternoon sunshine melted on my face, but the temperature was already falling with the sun disappearing in the west. The air smelled of clean pine trees, and somewhere, someone was baking sweet fresh bread. This was my favorite time of year to run. I loved twilight at Christmas time, because it was still light enough to run safely, but dark enough for Christmas lights to be on. I was going to do a quick trip through my favorite antique neighborhood, and check out the lights on the Victorian houses. I loved the colorful Christmas trees that covered the large antique windows. Plus, I needed the alone time to clear my head, and help get my mind off of everything. I was missing Johnny so much and my heart was broken knowing we were done. I found myself choking back tears at school today, while Alicia and Lexi were talking about Shawn and Tater.

I ran toward the main entrance out of the neighborhood, instead of cutting through to the gravel road. Ever since I had to deal with the scruffy guys, I hadn't ran that way. In a last minute decision, I decided to run by Ms. Lilian's house. It had been a couple of weeks since I had seen her, and I wanted to stop and say "Hi". I ran past the main entrance, and down the road that led to hers. About half way down, I approached a large van that was parked on the opposite side of the road. I stared at it. Something about the van was out of place, though it didn't appear to be occupied. My heart pounded a little faster as I got closer and cautiously slowed down. My eyes grew wide as the back of the van came into view. The sleek maroon car that I had seen earlier was parked directly behind it. I glanced over, trying not to stare, but was unable to see in the dark tinted windows. I had to get a closer look, so I crossed the road, trying to casually look straight ahead. I bent down to tie my shoe, and glanced quickly at the license plate that read U.S. Government at the top. The U.S.Government? Was I being followed? I changed my course, choosing not to go to Miss Lilian's. Maybe I was being paranoid, but I didn't want her caught up in any of my craziness. I ran down to the second exit out of the neighborhood, cutting back up the main street towards the Victorian neighborhood. The sun was already almost set. If I was going to get down there and back before dark, I had better move it. Picking up my speed, I passed the old city district that was beautifully decorated in bright white lights, and large green wreaths. The road was busy for a Monday night, with people Christmas shopping in the antique stores, and eating at the bistros and coffee shops. I approached the busy intersection where the scruffy guys gas station was, and quickly crossed the road to avoid running into them, then waited patiently for the crossing signal to light up. A few more people joined me, and very soon I was surrounded by a chatty group of shoppers.

A maroon flash caught my eye at the intersection. I squinted my eyes in disbelief. The maroon car pulled up to the light from the other direction. How did it get in front of me? The light changed, and I crossed in the pedestrian walk, while the maroon car went in the opposite direction. I watched it as inconspicuous as I could. When I couldn't see it anymore, I ducked into a jewelry store and stood by the window, pretending to look at a shelf of bracelets.

"Can I help you ma'am?" a man asked me from behind the counter.

"Ummm, no sir. I'm just looking. Thank you."

He nodded, and I slowly twirled the spinning case of bracelets, while keeping my eyes on the street. A couple of minutes later, the car passed again, slowing down as if the driver was looking for someone. It turn the corner, and immediately returned going in the direction it came. I was positive now. I was being followed.

My feet pounded the pavement as I ran home as fast as I could, taking the backroads and cutting through the dreaded gravel road. I ran into my house out of breath, just as the last gleam of light in the western sky slipped away. I shut the front door, making sure to bolt it locked, then checked every window and door in the house.

"What are you doing?" Kass asked as I entered her bedroom to make sure her window was locked.

"Just doing my nightly double check of all the locks," I said matter of factly.

Kass sat up on her bed and looked at me. "The windows, though?" she laughed. "Claire, you're so crazy."

I playfully popped her on the head, and went to take a shower.

That night, I couldn't sleep. I kept thinking about the government car, and why it was following me. I looked at my clock. It was 11:45. I had been laying in bed for an hour and a half, wondering if the car was still out there. A couple of times I thought I heard something outside and got up to look out of my window and investigate. At last, curiosity got the best of me, and I bundled up in my usual warm flying clothes. I tiptoed down the hall, stopping at mom and Kass' doors to make sure they were sleeping. My mom lightly snored, and I heard nothing from Kass.

Out on my launching spot on the back porch, I secured my phone and shot into the sky. The brisk air cut through my clothes, and I pulled my hoodie up over my head. At 500 feet, I stopped and scanned the neighborhood. There at the end of my block, in full view of my house, was the maroon car. Of course, I couldn't see if it was occupied.

"Alright Claire," I said to myself, sitting Indian style, "you're going to wait this out." I put on my fleeced lined gloves I had cut the pointy finger off of, and pulled out my phone. It had been awhile since I had been on Facebook, and I wanted to read the Clarksville Chat to see if they were still talking about the mystery flying girl.

Sure enough, there was a conversation the day the article came out in the paper about the fire. Many people started to tie the witch sighting, with the angel sighting, and were asking if there could be a mysterious ghost girl flying around Clarksville. One dispatcher in the group had brought up the whole "Sky Walker" phrase, and many people were questioning her about my interaction with them. Oops. I could see why Alicia had told me to stay out of the air. Yet, here I sat.

A text from Kass, snapped me out of my Facebook post.

"Where are you, Claire?"

"Up."

"What are you doing?"

"Just checking something out. Is mom still sleeping?"

"Yes. Like a log."

"Ok, I'll be home soon. Don't worry."

Car lights entering the neighborhood caught my eye. I uncrossed my legs, and dropped down to 300 feet, trying to to get a closer look. The silver car circled the block slowly, then drove down the main road, parking directly behind the maroon one. A man got out of the silver car, looked cautiously around the neighborhood, then approached the maroon one. After tapping on the window, another man emerged from the maroon car. They spoke for a moment, then looked toward my house. The driver of the silver car then got into the maroon car, and they switched places.

Now I knew I was under surveillance.

I had to know for sure where these jerks were coming from, although I had a pretty good idea. I decided to follow the silver car back to where it came from. He turned north, and out of my neighborhood. I followed him all the way down the highway, and up to the back gates of the airfield on the south side of the base. The night guard at the gate slowed the car to halt, and spoke to the driver for a few minutes.

At 300 feet, the wind cut through my body. Any trace of warm air from the day was gone, and now a white cloud formed over my face from the air I exhaled. "Come on, already," I gasped through my chattering teeth, while wiping my runny nose with the sleeve of my sweatshirt.

After a very long five minutes, the car finally left the gate. I followed it through the back woods, and into the barracks area of the base. My heart dropped when I saw it pull up to the offices of Johnny's company.

"No surprise there," I said to myself.

The driver emerged from the car, at the same time I dropped into the tree line on the back side of the building. Tip toeing through the tall landscape, I managed to get close enough to see the face of the mystery driver. He was a tall and muscular soldier, who looked like he'd be right at home on a football field.

A moment later, the office door swung open. I strained my eyes, peering over a bush to see who this guy was. My eyes adjusted to the darkness, and I recognized Major Silva, the officer who attempted to interview me on Sunday. He was also Johnny's superior, and I hoped again in my heart, that I had done enough to protect him from any trouble. Major Silva walked over to the man, swinging his coat around his shoulders and smoking what appeared to be a pipe. They talked seriously for a moment and shook hands. While the buff guy headed over to the barracks area, Major Silva got into his black Humvee and pulled away. I ducked behind a rubber tree plant to dodge his headlights.

I thought about following him home to see where he lived, but I decided not to. I looked at my phone. 1:30 am. I still had school in the morning, and basketball practice afterwards. I texted Kass to let her know I was on my way home, looked around to make sure the area was clear, and shot into the darkness.

THIRTY

"SO YOU THINK someone is following you?" Alicia whispered, Tuesday after basketball practice, as we walked out of the locker room.

"No Mony, I know someone is following me," I said emphatically. "He followed me home yesterday, and last night he was sitting down the road from my house."

"How do you know for sure?" she asked as we headed out of the gym.

I stopped her before we opened the double doors that led into the parking lot. "Mony, we are going out into this parking lot, and I can guarantee you, that a maroon car will be somewhere within sight distance of my car." I didn't dare mention that I had followed the silver car to the base last night.

"Ok," Alicia whispered, looking at me wide eyed. I felt bad for scaring her.

She opened one of the metal doors, and we walked into the almost deserted parking lot. I looked around to my right, and Alicia to her left.

"Do you see it anywhere?" she asked.

"Not yet."

"Claire, do you think it could be someone from the military, after what happened on Saturday?"

I shrugged my shoulders while I continued to look around. "Maybe." We reached our cars, stopping to look around one last time.

Alicia threw her duffle bag in her back seat. "I don't see anything that looks suspicious."

My eyes scanned the parking lot, a little disappointed I couldn't prove it was true, but also relieved. "Maybe, I am being paranoid," I said knowing I wasn't. "Hey Alicia, did Shawn say anything to you about the vial?"

Alicia looked at me sympathetically, and put her arm around me. "Not yet, but I'm going to see him tonight, so I'll ask. I promise. I just wanted to wait and ask him face to face, so I can make it sound as casual as possible."

I looked down at the ground disappointed.

"Don't worry Claire, if he has it, I'll get it. I promise."

I gave Alicia our usual goodbye hug. "Thanks Mony."

"Call me if you need anything, ok?" Alicia said. "Anytime. I don't care if it's three in the morning."

"I will."

We left the parking lot with my car leading. Traffic was crazy, and I swear I hit every stoplight. I had just entered the downtown business district when my phone rang.

"Hello?"

"Claire?"

"Hey Mony. What's up?"

"I'm behind you, about five cars back."

I looked in my rearview mirror unable to see her, because of all of the cars behind me.

"What are you doing?" I laughed. "I thought you were going home."

"Well, I was..," she stammered. "But I think I'm behind the maroon car you were talking about. When we left the school, I got caught at the light, and suddenly this car popped out from the tall bush line, by the big red house. And Claire, it has government car plates."

I was silent for a moment. "I'm not surprised."

"They must be following you because of Saturday."

I looked in my rearview mirror again, barely able to see the maroon car. "Maybe Mony, but I have a feeling this has more to do with me and flying. I think they know something about it."

"Seriously?" she gasped. "How is that possible?"

"Well, Sunday, when Major Silva saw my tat, he looked at me like he had seen a ghost. He also said if I have anything at all I need to tell him, that I can. I don't know, there was just something about the way he said it."

"Well, I definitely believe you," Alicia said. "In fact, I'm going to follow you home, so I know you made it safely."

"No Mony. Thank you, but I will be fine. Kyle is at my house with Kass. I don't want you leaving my neighborhood alone."

"Please Claire, I would feel better knowing you made it home ok."

I appreciated her concern, but I was not about to wrap her up in this any more than I already had. "Alicia, no. I promise I will text you as soon as I'm in. I don't want them following you home. As far as they know, you had nothing to do with this, and I want to keep it that way."

She was quiet for a moment and finally let out a big sigh. "Ok, but text me as soon as you're in."

"I promise."

I turned into my subdivision, and watched as the government car slowed down, and passed by my neighborhood entrance. I made a sharp, quick turn into my driveway, where Kass and Kyle were waiting on the porch, putting up Christmas lights. I had texted, and asked them to wait for me. Kyle walked out to my car and opened the door.

"What's goin' on Claire?" he asked.

I grabbed my basketball bag, and climbed out of the car. "Oh nothing," I shrugged. "Just some troublemakers following me. Thanks Kyle."

Kyle walked down to the end of the driveway and looked around. Kass put her arm around me, leading me inside. "Who was it, Claire?" she whispered.

"Just some troublemakers. It's ok, Kass."

I went to my room and shut the door. I layed on my bed trying to think my way out of this one. I knew I would have to talk to Major Silva on Friday, but I had no idea what to say. I knew what I did was wrong, but how was I going to tell them why I did it? Maybe if I had a one on one with Major Silva before Friday, I could tell him what I knew he already knew. That I could fly.

Wednesday morning I packed my bag for school. I went in the kitchen and threw an apple, and a bottle of water, into a brown paper bag.

"Oh Claire, you look extra nice today," mom said as she came in and kissed my cheek. "Do you have to dress up for some special occasion?" I looked down at my outfit, black skinny jeans, with my black riding boots, and a gray blazer with the whitest tee shirt I had. Quite the contrast to my usual comfy sweats and hoodie. My curly hair was extra shiny, with my curls bouncing. I had even added a little extra make up. I wanted to appear as mature and business like, as I could. I was on my way to pay Major Silva a visit.

An hour later Kass and I pulled up at school. Kass

grabbed her backpack, and reached for the door handle.

"Come on, Claire. We're gonna be late."

"Actually Kass, I'm not going to school today."

"And why not?" she asked, sounding like mom.

"I have to go to Campbell. I need to talk to Major Silva."

Kass' eyes grew wide, and she threw both of her hands into the air. "Claire! Are you out of your mind?! I thought you said you couldn't trust him."

"I have to Kass," I quietly replied, trying to calm her down. "I need to talk to him before I have to talk to everyone else Friday."

"No, on Friday you're just going to tell them it was a dare, and leave it at that. Why would you..."

"He knows Kass," I interrupted. "It's as simple as that. He knows about my tat, and that means he knows what it represents."

Kass sat back in the seat in a huff. "You're going against our plan."

"Well, sometimes life is like that," I reasoned with her. "You can't always follow a plan. Just trust me. I know what I'm doing." Now I sounded like mom.

"Does Alicia know?" she asked.

"Yeah. I talked to her last night. I was going to tell you, but Kyle was over, and I didn't get a chance to."

"What did she say?"

"She said she understood, and for me to text her and let her know I'm ok."

Kass stared at me for a moment. "Will you text me

too, Claire? I'm scared for you."

I leaned over, and hugged my little sister. "Of course I will, and I'll pick you up after school today too."

Kass hugged me tightly, as if she were hugging me for the last time, and slowly got out of the car. "I promise, Kass. I'll pick you up," I reassured her.

Kass smiled anxiously, and waved through the closed car door. I watched her walk to the school, turn, and wave at me again. I took a deep breath and pulled my visor down, looking at my brown eyes. They stared back at me, large and frightened.

"This is stupid. This is so stupid, Claire."

THIRTY-ONE

THE TRAFFIC ENTERING Ft. Campbell was bumper to bumper. I sat patiently waiting for the line to move in between the light changing, thankful for the extra time to think. I prayed once again that I would not run into Johnny. I missed him so much, but at the same time I felt undeserved anger towards him. Alicia told me I should try and see it from his point of view, and I definitely could. In his eyes, I was some crazy, criminal person, and I really couldn't blame him for staying away from me. If roles were reversed, I would probably do the same.

The light changed, and I drove to the visitors building to get a pass. I had never been on the base during a work day. It was so busy. Loud Army trucks roared past, and helicopter blades popped in the sky. Men and women of all ethnicities, shapes and sizes, paraded proudly past in their crisp green uniforms.

I put the visitors pass in my front windshield, and drove towards Johnny's company.

"Claire, it's not too late to change your mind," I whispered out loud, then argued with myself., "No, you have to go. You need to talk to Major Silva alone."

I pulled into the parking lot in front of the companies office. I took a deep breath, and got out of the car, hesitating by my door. "Go Claire."

I followed the small path to the door I had seen him come out of on Monday night, and opened it slowly, not sure of what I'd find inside. A long hallway extended into the distance, and to the right, laughter came from an office. Through the doorway, I found a small office with glossy waxed floors, that smelled of cologne. Helicopter and Air Force Jet posters plastered the wall, along with a giant map of the area. The phone rang just as I entered the door. The young soldier behind the desk looked up at me and smiled, while he gave me the 'just a minute' signal with his finger, and answered the phone. I slid into a chair by the water cooler, waiting for him to finish his conversation.

My palms were sweating as I clutched my phone nervously in my hand. Two voices echoed from another office down the hall.

"I don't care what you tell them Sergeant!" The deeper voice boomed, as they got closer. "I want those itineraries to me by Friday. I should have had them last week!"

I looked out into the hallway from my seat, nervous that the grumpy voice would be coming in the office where I was. Their footsteps echoed closer and closer, and then stopped just outside the door. Great.

"I'm going to go pick them up right away, Major," the other voice answered.

I looked up as Major Silva walked into the office. He froze in his tracks when he saw me. "Claire," he said startled to see me. His scowled face softened, and so did his booming voice. "What are you doing here?"

I don't know what happened in that moment, but a fresh boldness came over me, and I stood up. "Major Silva, I need to speak with you."

"Claire, I can't talk to you about the case without your mom's permission."

"I don't want to talk about Saturday. I want to talk to you about my privacy, and ask you to not have me followed anymore." The office grew quiet, and both soldiers sitting at the desks looked at Major Silva and me, bewildered. I cleared my throat. "Please."

Major Silva looked at me, and shook his head slightly smiling. "Come with me." He paused and ordered the guy behind the desk, "Davidson, hold my calls."

We walked to the end of the hallway to his very large office. I secretly opened my phone and hit record, as he invited me to sit down on the tall leather chair across from his desk. I looked at his book shelf that was full of awards and medals. One of them stood out; a Purple Heart from Operation Desert Storm.

Wow.

He sat at his desk, and we both looked at each other in an awkward glare for a moment. Major Silva looked like he was trying to figure out what to say to me. Finally he spoke.

"Claire, this is sticky territory for me. I can't discuss Saturday with you, or anything that's going on with it, but I can tell you a story." He got up from his seat, and walked over to his shelf of awards. He took down a gold photo frame, and handed it to me. I looked at the picture. It appeared to have been taken overseas, somewhere with a lot of sand. A much younger Major

Silva and a friend smiled back at me, with an arm on each others shoulder. They posed in front of a large tank.

Major Silva sat on the edge of his desk and pointed at the picture. "That's my best buddy. He and I have been best friends since 4th grade. We grew up in Houston together, and played football together in high school."

"Hmmm…" I thought to myself. *"That's where Major Silva got his southern, spanish accent from...Good grief! Focus Claire."* Major Silva drew in my attention again.

"He had a brilliant mind. He was always conducting all these science experiments with his dad, who was also a scientist of Aeronautics at the Houston Space Center. In fact, they are both the reason I'm in the Air Force today. His ultimate goal was to eventually have a job at NASA." I nodded at him, and he stared off somewhere past me. "But he died in 2016. It was a very suspicious death. They found his body in a field, about a half a mile behind his home. The doctors said he had all the classic signs of being hit by a car, but there wasn't a road in sight."

"I'm so sorry Major Silva," I said. I was genuinely sad for him, but I couldn't understand what all this had to do with me.

"Thank you, Claire. It was hard. When they found him, I had to fly to Houston to identify his body. He was an only child, and he had no family left." He stopped and looked at me in silence for a moment. I shrunk in my chair slightly, under his intense gaze. "When I went to identify him, there was a strange symbol on his wrist I had never seen before. It was Saturn rings, identical to yours. Identical to the ones on the crate, in the hangar."

My eyes grew wide, and I gasped silently.

Major Silva sat in the chair beside mine. "May I?" he whispered reaching out his hand toward my left wrist.

I swallowed hard, and slowly extended my hand toward him. He softly pulled back my blazer and looked at my wrist. "Just like Brian's," he said in awe.

"Brian?" I asked surprised. I looked down at the picture again. Clearly marked on Major Silva's uniform was his last name, and on Brian's uniform was the name 'Kearney.' "Brian Kearney?" I asked in disbelief.

"Yes," said Major Silva. "Have you heard of him?"

My voice lowered, and I looked at the ground. "I...I've been trying to get as much information on him as I can."

Major Silva nodded his head slowly. "And why would you do that, Claire?" he asked softly.

I didn't know how to answer that, and it was obvious he already knew, so why was he even asking? I stared back at him. I couldn't bring myself to tell him I could fly, but suddenly other words came tumbling out that I had no control over. Six months of frustration piled up inside of me.

"Major Silva, who leaves something as powerful as that pink potion just laying around where someone else can find it or break it, or even worse have it cut into their body like I did?!" My voice got higher and my intensity grew. I stood up, and began pacing the floor. "Who does that? I would hope the US Government could do a lot better job protecting it's experiments, or whatever that stuff is!! It was in a storage closet for goodness sake! An unlocked storage closet! And don't blame Johnny for this! Johnny had nothing to do with this! I've kept my flying power a secret from him too."

I stopped dead in my tracks in front of his huge bay window. Outside a blustery wind howled across a perfectly trimmed courtyard. Did I just say 'flying power' out loud?

I turned and looked at Major Silva. He stared back at me in silence. I was a little shocked at his lack of surprise. Kass and Alicia had almost lost it when I told them.

"So Claire...you're telling me you can fly?" he asked

calmly.

I closed my eyes, and slowly nodded my head yes. I opened them, and saw him looking at me, still as cool as he could be.

"You don't seem surprised," I said a little irritated.

He shrugged his shoulders. "I'm sorry Claire. I just...I don't know even what to say. I mean, I knew it was a possibility. I've been dealing with this for a year now. How did it happen? Please tell me everything."

I walked closer to him and sat on the edge of his desk. "I promise to tell you everything, if you'll make me one promise." Major Silva nodded. "You have to promise me that Johnny will not get in trouble for this, and that it will have no affect on his career whatsoever."

He nodded his head. "I can promise you that. I mean, I've never had any intentions of Angel being punished for this. He is one of my best soldiers."

I reached my hand out, and Major Silva and I shook on it.

"What? Are you guys a couple or something?" he asked slightly smirking.

"Not anymore," I replied feeling my heart sink.

I sat down by Major Silva and told him my whole story, as detailed as I could. He listened intently, asking questions about flying, and how I controlled myself. I did my best to answer them all.

"So only your sister and your friend know about everything?"

"Yes."

"Why didn't you tell your mom?"

"My dad died a few years ago and she still hasn't gotten over it. I didn't want to add to her worries, plus I didn't know how long this would last anyway."

"Well you know Claire, that's one of the reasons I had you followed. Honestly, I kind of had an idea, and I don't want you to end up like Brian. In the journals, he wrote that he swallowed the potion three months before he died. If this wears off, and you're out flying around, that's it for you. I know now that's what happened to Brian."

"But, I didn't swallow it.."

"Which is why it might be affecting you differently."

"So the guys following me know?" I asked.

"Not exactly. I just told them to keep an eye on you."

Major Silva got up, and went to his desk drawer. He retrieved a key and walked over to a closet. I watched as he bent down, and unlocked the bottom drawer of a file cabinet just inside the closet. He pulled out a small box, and returned to his chair.

"When Brian died, he left me this box." He showed me a faded old cigar case that looked like it was at least 50 years old. " Inside of it was this letter, and a key to a safety deposit box at his bank in Houston, where the potion and journals were kept. I read the letter, and he explained to me the pink potion, he called 'Rocket Juice.' His dad had been working on it since the sixties, and before that his grandfather, who was a scientist for

Air Force during World War II. Like I said, Brian had no family, so he left the potion, and 12 journals full of his families findings to me. I read the journals, and I didn't know what to do with it all." Major Silva paused, and looked down at the floor, thinking for a moment. "I contacted my higher ups. To this day, I don't know if I did the right thing, but I felt like it was information the military should have. When you stumbled on it, the journals and the potion were stored in crates until the government officials could get here to pick them up. We decided it was too risky to mail them."

I looked at the Major inquisitively. "You said crates plural."

"Yes, four crates all together. Three with the potion in it, and one with the journals. The smallest sample potion box went missing about three months ago. My guess is that it got thrown out."

"And the other pink potion, and the journals are gone?"

"Yep. They sent two investigators here after your crate accident. They took them immediately.

I bit my lip, so that I didn't say too much. I couldn't believe he didn't know about the smaller vial yet. Did Shawn still have it? I sighed in frustration. "I'm sorry Major Silva, but why would you store something so important in a crate, in a closet, where anyone could have access to it?"

Major Silva shook his head. "No one's perfect, Claire. It seemed like a good idea at the time."

That was fair enough. Don't even get me started on all the stupid choices I've made.

He paused for a moment. "Do you think you can show me...that you can fly?"

I smiled. "I was wondering when you were going to ask." I walked over to the corner of his office out of view of the door. I popped up in the air, and sat in my favorite Indian style position, shrugging my shoulders. "That's pretty much all there is to it."

Major Silva stared up at me, his face in awe. He walked over and waved his arm under me, as if he were checking for a rope or something. I looked down, smiling at him. "There's no strings attached, Sir," I joked.

Major Silva took a deep breath. "Unreal Claire. I've read his journals, and imagined it in my head, but seeing it...I just can't believe it."

"Miracles still happen, I guess," I said slipping to the ground. I looked down at my tat, the rings slightly glowing pink. "Those journals, did they answer any questions, like how we got the Saturn rings, or...or...how long I will be able to fly?"

"Unfortunately, no Claire. Brian thought maybe the rings were a bruising side effect from the formula, and as far as flying goes, we are going to have to monitor you."

"So, what's going to happen to me Major Silva?" I asked quietly.

Major Silva put his hand on my shoulder. "Claire, I promise you. I'm not going to let anything happen to you. Ever. You're my responsibility, and the US government's responsibility now, and we will protect you."

I looked at Major Silva, whose eyes were full of kindness and concern. For the first time in six months, I felt covered and safe. I breathed a sigh of relief. "Thank you, Major Silva."

"Call me Sebastian, and you're welcome, Claire."

THIRTY-TWO

SEBASTIAN WALKED ME out to my car. I didn't realize how quickly time flew. We had been talking for over two hours.

"Don't worry, Claire. I will talk to Johnny," he assured me.

"Are you going to tell him our secret?" I asked quietly, as two soldiers walked by.

"I'm not sure. I have to present this to my higher ups. They are aware of what's going on, and I have to tell them about you, sweetie." I must have looked terrified, because he added, "Claire, I work with some great guys. I promise, no one will hurt you."

"Ok," was all I could say, not fully convinced.

"You have my number. If you need me, call me. And tell your mom I will be contacting her about our meeting. Until then, don't say anything to anyone."

"Yes Sir. Thank you Major...I mean, Sebastian."

That night after dinner, Kass, Alicia, and I sat at our usual meeting place, the big shaggy carpet on my bedroom floor, listening to the conversation I had recorded with Major Silva.

"So what do you guys think?" I asked when it was over.

Kass sat back on her pillow and folded her arms. "I don't know, Claire. He seems genuinely concerned for you, but who knows?

"Well, do you guys think I did the right thing by going to him?" I asked.

Alicia nodded. "Claire, you really didn't have another choice. Didn't you say he pretty much knew anyway?"

"Yeah, and he did," I sighed.

"I know this sounds weird," said Alicia, "but you know the old saying 'There's safety in numbers', well, I think in your case Claire, it's true."

"Which is why mom needs to know," Kass agreed.

I nodded in agreement too, but I still wasn't convinced on telling mom.

Kass put her hand on my leg. "Claire, she needs to know. I think mom is much stronger than we give her credit for."

"I know Kass," I said , "but that's easier said than done. I don't even know how to begin to tell her this."

"Did Major Silva say he would tell your mom?"

Alicia asked.

"No Mony, and I don't want him to. I feel like it's my responsibility, and it would come better from me."

A light knocking at the door interrupted our conversation. "Claire?" Mom said softly opening the door.

"Hey Mom," I smiled, "come on in."

"Claire, Johnny's here," she whispered. Our eyes met, and both grew wide. Her's in excitement, and mine in surprise.

Kass and Alicia squealed in delight, high fiving each other, and mom laughed at them. "Girls. Shhhh," she said.

"Oh my goodness, girl," Alicia said, playfully punching my arm. "I wonder what he wants."

I shook my head, still not knowing what to say. "I can't see him now. I look disgusting," I finally gasped.

"Mom, stall him for a moment please," Kass said standing up, and lifting me off the ground. "Come on, Alicia. We got this."

The girls went into makeover mode, taking my hair out of my messy bun. Kass powdered my face, while Alicia spritzed my hair with a curl booster shine. When they finished I changed into my favorite sweater, and threw on my black leggings. Kass sprayed me with my favorite body spray as I walked out of the bedroom. I took a deep breath and headed down the hall.

"What is he doing here?" I thought to myself, walking into the living room. Johnny sat on the couch alone, looking even more gorgeous than ever. He looked up

from the floor, his eyes locking with mine, and I knew instantly something was strange and different. I stopped by the door, too nervous to approach him. We stared awkwardly at each other for a moment. I'm sure he knew exactly what my face was saying. You pretty much get what you see with me. I started twisting the bottom of my sweater in my nervousness, unable to say a word.

"Hi Claire," he said his voice shaking. That was a new one. I've never heard him sound nervous, or seem uptight about anything. Johnny always oozed confidence, and complete control.

"Johnny," I said unsure of how to respond.

"Can we talk out on the porch?" he asked.

"Sure," I said, walking to the closet to get my coat. I felt his stare boring into my back. I remained facing away from him, throwing on my coat, hat, and gloves. I turned to get a blanket off the chair, noticing that Johnny came in his uniform, as if he didn't have time to change after work. He threw on his skull cap, and followed me outside.

Our porch gleamed with thousands of twinkling Christmas lights. Kass and Kyle really overdid it this year, making our house look like a mini Las Vegas. I unplugged the lights around the door and windows for more privacy, just in case Major Silva's boys hadn't been relieved from their stalking duties yet. I found my usual place on the porch swing, but he kept his distance from me and leaned against one of the poles. I didn't say anything, remembering what Major Silva had told me about keeping everything quiet.

"Claire, I'll get right to the point," he said, his voice still nervous. "I was called off guard duty tonight to Major Silva's office. I met with him, and the General."

"The General of the..the whole base?" I stammered.

Johnny nodded yes. "They told me Claire. They told me everything."

I felt my body tense up, and my face flush red. I didn't know what to say to him. "I'm sorry, Johnny."

Johnny leaned off the pole, and began pacing in front of me on the porch. I don't think he even heard my apology. "I can't even...how am I supposed to believe any of this Claire? It sounds like something out of The Twilight Zone! How is it even...how can this be possible?"

"Johnny...I'm so sorry," I tried again. " It's not like I planned this...and I don't know how it's possible. Major Silva said they were going to try and figure it all out."

Johnny sat in a chair across the porch, restless, and obviously wanting to be as far away from me as he could. "I'm sorry Claire, but I can't wrap my mind around this. How can it be true? Everything I thought I knew about flight, has just gone out the window. And if it is true, how can I ever believe anything I've been taught, or reality as I know it?"

"It's true. I don't know what else to say, Johnny." I was unable to look at him and he was making me feel uncomfortable, almost like I was some kind of a freak show or disease.

Johnny stared at me, like he didn't believe me. "I need to see for myself."

"Johnny, maybe later…" I didn't think he could handle seeing me fly right now.

"No!" he insisted. "Show me Claire. Please."

I took a deep breath, knowing this wasn't going to be good. I reluctantly went to the only dark corner of the porch and popped myself into the air really quick, only about five feet up. I hung there for a moment, watching Johnny's face turn white, and feeling embarrassed and ashamed. I slipped back down to the ground, and quietly said something like, "That's pretty much it," as I sat down on the swing again.

Johnny came over to me in a daze, and sat on the swing by me.

"Are you ok?" I asked biting my lower lip.

"No Claire. No, I'm not ok. How could you keep this from me? Why didn't you tell me about it when it happened? We were supposed to be in a relationship. I mean, I was thinking about forever with you."

I looked up from the ground unsure of what I heard. *Forever with me?! How could he be thinking about forever with me? He left me when I needed him most.*

"What are you talking about? Forever with me? You left me… and what was I supposed to do?" My eyes welled up with tears. "If I had told, you would have probably lost your job, and any chance at being a pilot. I was trying to protect you."

"Protect me? Protect me by lying to me?"

I swallowed back my tears, trying not to cry, but a large tear rolled down my cheek. "I didn't lie. I just didn't tell you."

He sat back on the swing annoyed. I felt anger rise up in me. After all these months of trying to protect him, all the ups and downs, and drama I'd been through, I didn't feel like he had the right to be annoyed with me.

I stood up from the swing, and started walking to the door, but I turned around. I had one final thing to say.

"You know what, Johnny? Try walking in my shoes through all of this. You have no idea what I've been through. Oh, and thanks for asking me if I'm ok, and what effect all of this has had on me."

I walked inside of the house, and closed the door. Mom came from the kitchen, noticing my red cheeks.

"Claire, are you ok, sweetie?"

"Yeah mom, I'm fine. Don't worry."

"I guess things didn't go so well," she said hugging me.

"No," I said tears running down my face. "What a jerk."

Kass and Alicia appeared in the door of the living room. They came over, and wrapped their arms around me.

"Oh Claire," Alicia said. "Don't take it personally. He just doesn't understand."

"No Mony, he understands," I nodded knowingly at her, trying to not let mom know what we were talking about. Kass and Alicia stared wide-eyed at me. A light tapping at the front door caught our attention.

Mom patted my shoulder. "I'll get that."

She opened the door slightly, and I heard Johnny's voice. "I'm sorry to bother you again Mrs. Haley, but can I speak to Claire?"

"Just a minute, Johnny." Mom turned and looked at me.

"Go Claire," Kass said nudging me.

Mom nodded, and I walked to the door.

"Claire, I'm sorry," Johnny said. "Can we please start again. I didn't mean to be so self-centered."

I looked sideways at my mom, who continued to stand by the door, but out of Johnny's sight. *"Awww,"* she mouthed at me.

I walked out to the porch, and Johnny immediately wrapped me in his arms. "I'm so sorry Claire Bear. I don't blame you for not telling me," he whispered. " I know you didn't know what to do, anymore than I would have. Do you forgive me?"

I kept my face buried in his shoulder. I didn't want to move. I felt so safe with him holding me again. Johnny must have sensed my mood, because he held me tighter. At last he let go, and I looked up at him.

"I'm so sorry too. I was honestly just trying to protect you, Johnny."

Johnny kissed the top of my head. "I know you were. I'm sorry I overreacted, and let my emotions get the best of me. All of this," he sighed, "it's just not believable."

I could definitely understand that. Flying had become such a normal part of my world, that I forgot how abnormal, and unbelievable it was for everyone else.

We sat on the swing again. Johnny held me close, and wrapped the blanket around us. For the next half hour he asked me questions about the past six months, and I patiently answered every one.

"My goodness Claire," he said. "I can definitely say life hasn't been dull since I met you."

I smiled at him. "I don't think dull would be so bad right now."

Johnny laughed at me. "No, dull is no fun."

"Are you sure you're not in trouble?" I asked for the hundredth time.

"No, I'm fine," he smiled. "I haven't lost anything, and I'm not in trouble for having you there. In fact, Major Silva pretty much told me I was in charge of helping look out for you now."

I raised my eyebrows at him. "Oh really? And why would he give you that annoying task? "

Johnny smiled a mischievous smile at me. "Well, I might have told him we were together."

I laughed. "I told him we're not!"

"Well, too bad Claire Bear. We are. You're stuck with me."

I smiled at him. "So what happens now?"

"Well, Major Silva will meet with you and your mom tomorrow, and then go from there."

"Johnny, my mom doesn't know yet."

"I know, but you have to tell her Claire."

My face cringed at the thought of it. "I know, but I just don't think I can."

"Claire, it will be easier on her coming from you. I'll help you. We'll get Alicia and Kass, and we'll all tell her together."

My eyes grew big. "Tonight?"

Johnny nodded his head. "Tonight."

THIRTY-TWO

I'VE BEEN IN some pretty scary situations in my life, but I don't think I've ever been as nervous as I was that night. Sitting my mom down to tell her that I could fly, was about as nerve wracking as the night I found out I could fly. I had worked so hard to protect her, and make her proud of me. Now I worried all of that would be gone. I knew Johnny was right, though. It had to come from me. Having Major Silva tell her would be wrong of me, and make her not trust me even more.

Mom was sitting in her favorite armchair when I told her. It was my dad's armchair. I knew she felt a special connection to him when she sat there. Kass and Alicia sat on the couch close to her, and Johnny stood by me.

At first mom didn't believe me. I didn't think she would. In fact, if Johnny wasn't there, I don't think she would have believed any of us. Kass was right. She was a lot stronger than we really gave her credit for. Once we finally convinced her, (she didn't even ask to see me fly), her first concern was, of course, my safety and the effects the potion had on me.

"Mrs. Haley, I know how you're feeling right now," Johnny said to her. "I just found out today, myself. It just doesn't seem real."

"I just want Claire to be ok. I'm worried about her health." Mom grabbed my hand. "I was thinking, maybe we should go see Dr. Ryan tomorrow. She's been Claire's pediatrician since she was a baby."

"Mom, no," I said sternly. "I promised Major Silva no one else would know. It has to be kept between just us. The Air Force is going to monitor my health, and try to get me back to normal."

"But Claire, this stuff got into your bloodstream," Mom argued. "We should have had you checked out a long time ago. The hospital staff said your blood type was abnormal, and that could be very serious."

I sighed. I was so tired, and didn't want to argue with my mom. I knew she was concerned.

Kass sat by her on the arm of the chair. "Mom, look at Claire. She's totally healthy. It's been almost six months. I'm sure if something was going to happen to her, it would have already happened by now."

It was midnight before we were all done talking. Alicia had gone home at 10, and just Kass, Johnny, and I stayed up talking with mom. We finally got her a little more comfortable with everything, and she was eager to talk to Major Silva the next day.

I walked with Johnny out to his car. "So you promise you're coming tomorrow, right?" I asked him.

Johnny held me, and kissed me once more before leaving. What a night it had been.

"I'll be here, Claire," he assured me. "I promise I'll never leave you alone again. No matter what."

I didn't sleep well that night at all. I dreamed I was locked in a large building, that seemed like a hospital. Everything was really bright and white, and I kept trying to escape and couldn't.

I had my phone, and was trying to dial 911, but my hands wouldn't move.

I woke up around three in a panic, and was relieved to be staring at my ceiling. Mom must have had the same kind of night I did, because I heard her stirring around in the kitchen, and a couple of times she opened my door to peek in at me.

Mom let Kass and I stay home from school, and she took the day off work. At noon the doorbell rang, and Alicia came over, having gone to school for just half a day. Major Silva wanted to talk to Alicia and Kass too, since they knew about everything.

"Is Coach Alexander upset that you are missing practice?" I asked.

"Not terribly," she said. "The team has definitely been missing you. When do you think you'll be back?"

"Maybe after Christmas break. Depending on how everything goes the next few days."

"Are you nervous?"

"Yeah, but I'm also ready to get this over with."

Kass joined us in the living room. "So who all's coming?" she asked.

"I think just Johnny and Major Silva," I said.

"How's your mom?" Alicia whispered.

"She seems ok," Kass said softly.

As if on cue, mom entered the living room, and turned on the fireplace. "Girl's, they're going to be here any minute. I want you to let me do the talking, ok?" I looked at my mom's tired eyes, an obvious sign she hadn't slept all night.

We all agreed. I would do anything my mom asked me at this point, just to make her feel better about everything.

Mom sat with us, and we talked again about the accident. She seemed extra concerned with the tattoo the potion had left on me. The sound of a car pulling in the driveway made me stop talking mid sentence. Kass got up and looked out the window. "They're here," she said looking at me.

Mom answered the door, and invited Johnny, Major Silva, and one more older soldier in. They were dressed so sharp in their dress uniforms, and each one removed their berets as they entered our house.

Johnny made the introductions. "Mrs. Haley, you remember Major Silva."

Major Silva shook hands with my mom, and smiled

warmly at her. "It's a pleasure to see you again, Mrs. Haley."

Johnny continued, "And this is the Commanding General of Ft. Campbell, General Collins."

The girls and I looked slyly at each other in surprise, as the general shook my mom's hand. Johnny glanced at me, smiling slightly. He then looked at Major Silva and General Collins. "Sirs, this is Alicia and Kass," Alicia and Kass shook their hands, "and this...this is Claire."

I walked nervously to the General, and stretched out my hand. He must have sensed my fear, because he immediately tried to set my mind at ease. "Claire, I'm so glad to finally meet you," he said, not letting go of my hand. "I'm sure you are in a state of shock as we all are. I just want to say, I'm sorry this happened to you, and we're going to do everything we can to help you out."

I smiled at him. "Thank you, Sir," I said quietly.

Mom invited everyone to sit in the living room, and Kass helped her serve coffee. Major Silva started the conversation, by again asking me if i was sure no one else knew about my flying power.

"I'm definitely sure no one knows. I mean, there is a rumor going around Clarksville about it, because of the guys who were chasing me…"

General Collins interrupted me. "Yes, we're aware of that. We've been following the story in the papers. After Major Silva told us about the accident, and the break in at the airfield, we started putting two and two together."

I looked at the ground, a little embarrassed of my actions. "I'm so sorry."

"Claire, I'm not trying to make you feel bad. I don't know what I would do if I were in your shoes either. This is just something that we're going to have to work through. In one way it's unknown, so it's scary to think about, but in another, it's completely astonishing and exciting, and none of us know what to do with it."

"None of us meaning who?" I asked.

"Well, Major Silva and I have people we have to answer to. In fact, we will be going to Houston to meet with them next week, and we'll take it from there. Claire, we would like to take you with us."

My mouth dropped opened, and I looked at mom.

"Of course, Mrs. Haley, we would expect you to accompany us," Major Silva added.

Mom, Major Silva, and the General discussed the trip at length for the next half hour. They explained to mom the purpose in going, and what we could expect. I would be given tests, and they would observe my flying abilities. It was decided that we would leave the following

Thursday on a flight out of Ft. Campbell, and Major Silva would be taking us.

The men stood to leave, but not before the General asked to see me fly. I looked at my mom, a little worried, because she hadn't seen me yet, and I didn't know if she was ready to. Mom nodded her approval to me. I wanted to do something cool, so as not to completely freak her out.

I walked to the corner of the room. I floated to the ceiling, laying flat against it, then did a flip, and slowly floated back to the ground. I heard a silent gasp from my mom, and looked over at General Collins who stared at me unmoved, nodding his head.

The General looked at Kass and Alicia. "Girls, thank you for your discretion in this. I just want to remind you, that for Claire's safety and yours, it is very important that no one finds out. At least not until we know what to do with all of it."

Kass and Alicia shook their heads in agreement. "Yes Sir," they both said wide eyed. No wonder why this guy was a general. His personality demanded respect without even asking for it. He was quite intimidating.

We walked the men to the door, and Johnny turned and looked at me. "I'll see you tonight," he whispered, winking at me.

I smiled and nodded at him, closing the door behind them. I turned and looked at Kass, Alicia, and mom, and we all stood there speechless.

THIRTY-THREE

I SPENT THE next four days busily catching up on my school work, and preparing to leave for Houston. Before I knew it Wednesday was here, and mom and I were being picked up by the same maroon car that had been stalking my neighborhood for the last week. I immediately noticed the the driver was the big football soldier I had seen meeting with Major Silva the week before. As my father used to say, "*Oh, how the tide has turned.*"

We were driven directly to the tarmac at the airfield, where a small military jet was waiting. Major Silva greeted us at the plane and we boarded.

I held mom's hand as the jet lifted off the ground, and we took off from the air base. Neither of us had ever been on a plane before, but I knew well the rush of being lifted off the ground and it never got old. Mom, on the other hand, sat with her head back against the seat, looking straight ahead, completely terrified.

"Mom, its ok," I tried to reassure her.

We arrived in Houston 2 hours later, and I felt the balmy 70 degree heat envelop me, as we walked down the plane stairs. A black suv was waiting at the bottom, with two soldiers standing guard. Each saluted Major Silva and one of the soldiers opened the door for us. We climbed in and were immediately whisked away.

I looked out the window an hour later as we entered through two very guarded gates, to a large white building that almost resembled a hospital. I remembered my dream from a few nights ago. Major Silva must have noticed my nervous stare, because he reassured me it was not a hospital.

"This is more like a research center," he said.

That didn't make me feel much better. Mom patted my leg for reassurance.

The armed soldier led us into the building, where we presented our I.D's at a long counter, that resembled a hotel check in desk.

A lady dressed in a crisp green dress uniform, who had her red hair pulled back in the tightest bun I had ever seen, handed us two cards.

"Ok Major Silva, the 10th floor is where you will find your rooms. I believe they are expecting you all in the conference room on the second floor, after lunch. The cafeteria is just down the hall, here on the left."

I looked at mom, who in return stared back at me. I knew we were both thinking the same thing. We were going to be stuck in this compound for the next ten days.

We were led to an elevator, and up to the tenth floor, where Major Silva gave us our room key.

"Alright ladies," he said, "I'm in the room right beside you. If you need anything from me, day or night, just let me know. Ok?"

Mom thanked him, and we went inside the room to freshen up before lunch. I looked at my phone. It was already 11.

I heard mom gasp as she entered the room first. I joined her, in what seemed to be a five star hotel room. Everything was shiny, white, and gold in color. The room smelled of the fresh lilacs that adorned the tables, and a warm breeze blew in from the window that was cracked open. I walked to the window, wheeling my small suitcase, across the soft carpeted floor. Outside a large swimming pool sparkled in a bright blue below us. To the west, a lush garden path led the way to a large dome-like building, that had to be at least 10 stories high. A row of airplanes, including one that looked like a shuttle, sat on a tarmac behind the dome, lined up in perfect formation.

Mom joined me at the window and was equally impressed. "Is that a shuttle?" she asked in wonder.

"I think so," I laughed, and immediately began snapping pics to send the girls and Johnny. I had really wanted Johnny to come with us, but Major Silva thought it would be too suspicious if he came too.

Mom and I rested for a few minutes, then changed into nicer clothes for lunch and our meeting we had with some "officials."

Major Silva knocked on our door 30 minutes later, and we headed downstairs to the cafeteria. I noticed that he had changed into a dress uniform. He looked so sharp.

The elevator door opened to the smell of food down the main hallway, that sparkled on the freshly waxed gray tile. The cafeteria was bustling with service men and women in uniforms, standing in the food line and filling up the 20 plus round tables that filled the large room. Maybe it was just me, but I thought I heard a slight hush cover the room and felt eyes

staring into me. I walked behind Major Silva, and could have sworn I heard someone mumble, "That's her."

I could barely eat the salad and mostaccioli we had, even though it smelled amazing. I noticed mom had barely touched hers too. We were so nervous about the meeting ahead. Neither of us knew what to expect. Major Silva tried to calm our nerves by asking me about my flying adventures. I was glad to share my stories with him, but I had to be careful not to say too much, and worry mom even more. If she knew where I had been, and what I had done, she would be even more nervous than what she already was.

Major Silva seemed to really enjoy listening to me. I think I reminded him of Bryan, and the miracle in me he had created.

"If only Bryan could see you now," he had said.

At 1 pm, we were escorted to the second floor of the building. We stepped off the elevator to another receptionist waiting at a large mahogany and gold desk. I looked down the hall that stretched both ways. A plush red, white, and blue carpet lined the floor, and several small crystal chandeliers hung from the ceiling. Each office had a mahogany desk and secretary outside of it. This place was high class.

"We are here for a meeting with Chief Master Sergeant Bryant," Major Silva stated.

"Ok, Sir. They are expecting you," the Secretary said, and took us down the hallway to the last room.

Major Silva led the way into the room. A long conference table stretched out in front of us, and 10 men, all in their dress blue uniforms stood around the table quietly talking amongst themselves. When I walked in, all conversations stopped, and the men looked at us, sizing me up to see exactly what they were dealing with. I was so grateful to have Major Silva with us. He was so confident and shook every person's hand.

Chief Master Sergeant Bryant, who was clearly in charge, introduced mom and I to every officer. There was no way I could remember all their names, and what to call them respectfully.

He invited us to sit in the three tall leather chairs on the opposite side of the table. I sat in the middle chair, with mom and Major Silva on either side.

"Well Gentlemen, I'm not sure how to even begin a

meeting like this," Chief Master Sergeant Bryant began, tapping his pen on the pad of notebook paper in front of him. "This is one of those things where, as a trained officer in the military, all logic that you have ever known goes out the window." He looked over at me. "Claire, first of all, we want you to know that we are on your side in all of this. We are not going to do anything to you to put you in harm's way, or make you feel uncomfortable." I nodded in silence and he looked at my mom. "And Mrs. Haley, I can't even imagine how you are feeling right now. I know you are concerned for your daughter's safety and health, and I just want you to know as parents ourselves, so are we."

Mom nodded. "Thank you."

"You're welcome," he continued on. "So, I guess the first things first. Claire, we need to see exactly what effects this has had on you. If you don't mind showing us, please."

I looked at Major Silva, who nodded at me. I slowly got up from my chair and walked to the corner of the room, away from everyone. I flew the same way I had for mom, making it look more like a trick, so as not to freak everyone out. I went back down slowly, pausing a bit before I finally rested on the floor. Several of the men gasped, but I did my best to ignore them, and walked back to my seat. Major Silva patted me on the knee.

The room was silent for a moment, before Chief Master Sergeant Bryant spoke again. "That Claire...that was unbelievable. How long have you been like this?"

"Six months, Sir," I answered, a little more confident than I had been before.

"Do you mind telling us your story, starting from the beginning?"

I told the officers everything that had happened to me. This was my fifth time, and I had become so good at sharing it, I had the story done in less than 20 minutes. Every once in a while, one of the them would stop me, and ask me clarify something I said. I don't think it was because I wasn't being clear enough, I think it was because they honestly had a hard time believing me at all.

The officer, whose name I did remember, Dr. York, had the most questions for me. He kept asking me about my health, and how this had an effect on me. He was most intrigued, when I explained the cut with the potion and how quickly it had healed into a tat. He asked if he could get a closer look at it, and I walked up to the table to show him. Somehow, Dr. York had obtained my medical records, and began to ask me about my concussion, and most importantly, the results of my blood tests. Mom stepped in to answer those questions for me, and she had a few for him also. Dr. York kept answering her the same way, "I'm not sure Mrs. Haley, I wish I could answer that," or "We will figure this out together."

Chief Master Sergeant Bryant then turned their attention to Major Silva. They had a lot of questions for him about Bryan Kearney and all his research.

Another officer, who seemed to be more into the science side of all this, had a brown file box in front of him that I could only guess was full of Major Kearney's journals and the potion. I looked at it and thought back to last night when Johnny came over to see me before I left. He had kissed me, and then reached down and grabbed my hand. He opened it and put something inside. I looked down to see the small pink vial and gasped.

"Claire, put this in a safe place. Don't lose it."

I hugged him tightly. "Thank you, Johnny. Thank you so much."

His hand lightly rubbed across my face. "Well, you earned that one," he teased softly.

Major Silva was a pro in every way. He told his own story with Major Kearney, and answered questions from the panel for over an hour.

It was close to 5 pm when Chief Master Sergeant Bryant finally began to close the meeting. He gave us all an itinerary of the next few days, and what we could expect. My days were going to be full of blood work and observation.

Mom and I returned to our room exhausted. I took a long hot shower, and let the craziness of the day sink in. When I came out the TV was on low, and mom had fallen asleep without even changing her clothes. I took a plush blanket from a chair and covered her with it. I layed down, and immediately fell asleep.

THIRTY-FOUR

EVERY MORNING WE started at 7 am sharp. I bounced between floors, each of them a different point of study. The fifth and sixth floor was the hospital floor, where my health was monitored and blood was drawn daily. Dr. York was so kind and gentle with me, and careful to make sure mom and I knew every step he was taking. He went over my blood work with me, as he tried to figure out the strange blood type I had now. Everything else was completely normal, and he even complimented me on my overall health.

The seventh floor was a large science lab. It was very guarded, and I was only allowed on this floor in the company of the man in charge of the research in my case, Commander Whitley.

My favorite part of the whole itinerary was the dome. They gave me a blue jumpsuit to wear there, and I later found out it was the same uniform the astronauts wore! It had NASA on the side, and they even had my name embroidered in white thread above the pocket. Chief Master Sergeant Bryant always accompanied me to the dome, not because he had a real reason to be there, but I think just because he liked to see me fly. They tested me flying with objects, and I was surprised to learn I could carry quite a bit of weight up with me.

By the third day, I was feeling more comfortable. A lot of the people called me by name, and seemed genuinely excited we were there. In the afternoon I would go swimming, and at night I would play pool with some of the guard soldiers in the game room. They taught me how to play poker, and I got pretty good at it. By the time I left, I had won over 30 dollars off them.

Everyday I texted Johnny, pretty much anytime I had a break. I kept him informed on everything that was going on. I missed him so much, and I was counting down the days until I could see him again.

On my last day there, Friday, December 16th, we all met in the conference room again. Chief Master Sergeant Bryant went over Dr. York and Commander Whitley's findings. Basically what he told us was that I was perfectly healthy, even with the strange blood type which they named "0c." Dr. York gave my mom explicit instructions that from now on for my own safety, I was to be taken to a Doctor at Ft.Campbell only. My health records would be sent to him and sealed, and I was to consult with him for everything that went wrong with me. Even the simplest cold.

Commander Whitley read his staff's findings on the potion, and reported that my case would be on going. He encouraged me to stay out of the sky, reminding me that although it didn't look like I would be grounded anytime soon, they still had no idea when, and if this would wear off . The look on my face must have said 'no way', because my mom elbowed me, and looked at me as if to say *"you better listen young lady."*

Chief Master Sergeant Bryant walked around to the front of the table and leaned on it to talk to Major Silva, mom, and me. "Mrs. Haley and Claire, I know it wasn't easy for you to come here, not knowing us or what was going to happen, but I want to thank you for your patience with us. We have learned so much from you, Claire, and I just want you to know that we are here for you. I will be checking in on you, and we will be keeping an eye on you. If you ever feel in danger, or sick, or anything out of the ordinary, just contact Major Silva, and they will take care of you. I have 100% confidence in General Collins, and his staff at Ft. Campbell."

"Thank you," mom and I said in unison.

"Just remember," Dr. York chimed in. "This has to stay as hush as we possibly can keep it. I know it's tempting to tell others, but you just can't."

"I understand," I agreed.

Chief Master Sergeant Bryant stood up and walked towards the door. "Ok Claire, before you leave, we have one more thing we need to do, so if you'll just follow me, we'll take care of it."

"I thought I was done," I said laughing at him.

"Come on, just one more thing," he said waiting for me at the door.

I looked at my mom who was grinning mischievously. I followed him out the door, mom and I wheeling our suitcases through the hall, and downstairs into the bright sunshine. We walked the garden path to the dome, and circled around the building with my mom, Major Silva, and the rest of his command behind us. We turned the corner, and there sitting against the western sunset was the biggest Chinook I had ever seen. Lining the path to the chinook was all my new buddies I had made here. Everyone from the Doctor's staff, to the cafeteria workers, and my poker friends, lined the path that lead to the Chinook. They all cheered and clapped as soon as I came into view. I stopped, trying to catch my breath, feeling so overwhelmed by their kindness.

"So, how about a ride to the airport, Claire?" Major Silva asked.

My mouth dropped open, and immediately tears blurred my eyes.

"Seriously?" I asked, not knowing what to say.

"Seriously," Chief Master Sergeant Bryant laughed.

I hugged him in my excitement. "Thank you Chief Master! Thank you so much!" I looked at him more seriously. "I sincerely mean it. Thank you for all you've done for us."

"You're welcome, Claire," he smiled.

Major Silva, mom, and I shook the hands of each of the command members, then headed toward the helicopter. I high fived hands all the way down the line, while they all called out 'best wishes' and' good luck' to us.

We boarded the Chinook as the blades began to turn.

"Do they all know what I was here for?" I asked Major Silva.

"No way," he laughed. "The less people who know about this, the better for you."

I felt the floor beneath me tremble, as the engines roared louder. We were given headphones to put on, to cover the noise of the helicopter. With Major Silva's permission, I pulled out my phone and began recording our lift off. I caught a moment of worry in my mom's face as we left

the ground, but then she relaxed and seemed to enjoy herself.

"Oh my goodness! This is so amazing!" I yelled into my mic as we headed north towards the airport. I nudged my mom. "Look mom! This is my view when I'm flying," I said looking at the ground below.

The Chinook had us at the airport in 20 minutes, and we were able to immediately board our plane from the tarmac. On the flight home, mom fell asleep, and Major Silva and I talked about the week and what would happen now. I was to meet with him once a week, so that I could continually be monitored since no clear answers were found the last ten days.

"Claire, have you given any thought as to what you want to do after High School?"

"Well, I'm not sure," I sighed. "I actually thought about becoming a teacher, but everything's changed now. I just want to be able to help my mom and Kass, no matter what."

Major Silva smiled at me. "You know, the Air Force is always a good start in life. I mean, you're stuck with us now anyway, so you might as well make money and go to school while you're at it."

I smiled back at him, because the thought had already crossed my mind.

"If you do decide to, you know under your special circumstances, you can stay at Campbell so we can keep a better eye on you."

"That's definitely something I would consider," I said. "I will have to talk to mom about it, though. I feel like I've kept enough from her already."

Major Silva laughed. "Definitely, no more keeping stuff from mom."

THIRTY-FIVE

THE NEXT DAY I woke to Kass sitting on my bed. I looked at the clock. It was already 11.

"Hey sleepy head," she said smiling at me. I was so glad to see her. "Get up! Alicia will be here in an hour to get us."

"What?" I said rolling over and putting my pillow on my head. "Where are we going?"

"Duh!" she said pulling the pillow off. "Christmas shopping! We have one week until Christmas, and everybody will be here! Plus we want to hear all about Houston!"

I rolled over and looked at her. She was smiling so big at me. I slowly sat up and rubbed my eyes. "I need to shower Kass."

"Well, come on! Snap to it!" she ordered.

An hour later, Alicia and Lexi pulled into the driveway, and we were off to Governor's Square Mall, our home away from home.

Alicia and I were shopping in our favorite bath and lotion store, while Kass and Lexi ran across the hall to the bookstore.

"Claire, I want to hear all about Houston, but I know we can't talk about it in front of Lex," she whispered. "Do you think I can come over after we're done shopping?"

"Sure," I said, "but there is a lot I can tell you in front of Lex. Don't worry. I'll fix it."

Around 5, we finally crossed the last person off our Christmas list. Kass and I had a lot of people to buy for. Our older sisters were coming home, and we would have 13 people at our house on Christmas day. I was beyond excited to have my whole family under one roof, and even more than thrilled for them to meet Johnny. He was spending Christmas with us.

We were starving, so we headed for a soup restaurant. After we ordered, and Lexi began asking me about my trip. I managed to truthfully explain to her where I was, without giving away any information.

"So what were you doing in Houston?" she asked.

"I was down there touring an air base," I answered. Kass and Alicia looked at me skeptically. "I actually have something to tell you guys."

Kass folded her arms and sat back in the booth. "And what would that be, Miss?"

I laughed at her, and paused for a moment. "So, I'm pretty sure that after I get out of high school, I'm joining the Air Force."

Alicia stopped slurping her soup, and they looked at me surprised. Lexi gasped in excitement, "Claire, that's so awesome!"

"Thanks Lex!" I looked at Kass and Alicia, who were still staring at me in shock. "Well?"

Alicia smiled. "I think it's great, Claire. As long as no one is...what's the word I'm looking for..forcing you to," she said emphasizing the word, "forcing."

"I promise you guys. This is completely my choice. You know how fascinated I've always been with aviation. Plus, I might be able to serve in the Special Forces."

Kass snorted a little laugh, and I threw a wadded up napkin at her. "It's not funny Kass," I said, unable to scold her without laughing. "and listen, not a word about this to anyone. I'm going to surprise our family on Christmas."

That night Johnny came over to hang out, while Kass, Alicia, and I were wrapping gifts. I told them all about Chief Master Sergeant Bryant and his command staff, the compound, my new poker abilities, and the Chinook ride.

Kass and Alicia hung on to my every word, but Johnny seemed a little distracted. "So all that research and we still have no idea of its effects on your body, and how safe you are going to be flying?"

"Johnny, I'm fine. My blood work is fine, and I'm

still able to fly, no problem. I'm not some simple mystery that's going to be solved overnight." I sat closer to him and wrapped my arm around his waist. "Think about it. They have three different scientist, and their experiments, that span 7 decades, all wrapped up in my body to figure out."

Kass pulled a long string of ribbon from a roll. "Claire, did they say that you're not allowed to fly?"

I looked sheepishly at the ground.. "Well,...not exactly. They didn't say I couldn't, they just suggested that I do it under their supervision."

Johnny smiled, shaking his head. "Let's be real, Claire. I don't think anyone is going to be able to keep you out of the sky."

Alicia winked at me. "Well, I'm sure they are going to keep an eye on you, and it makes me feel better knowing you'll be under their care."

I smiled at Johnny, but inside butterflies turned in my tummy thinking about Major Kearney, and the way he died. I still hadn't told anyone what Major Silva had said about his death. If I told mom or Johnny, they would never let me leave the ground again.

Later, I walked with Johnny out to his truck, as a light dusting of snow began to fall. He stopped at his door and pulled me close to him. "Claire, I'm sorry if I was a little cold in there tonight. I'm just so worried about you. When you were in Houston I had a lot of time to think, and I just don't know what I would do if something ever happened to you."

I looked into his eyes, creased with worry. "But you will be with me a lot now, and I'm going to be constantly monitored, especially when I'm in the Air Force."

Johnny lightly placed his hands on my chilly red cheeks. "Hmmm...," he said. "I don't know if I'm ready to share you with everyone yet."

I stood on my tiptoes and pushed my lips to his. He leaned down and returned my kiss. "That's not going to be a problem," I said trying to catch my breath when he finally let go.

He squeezed me tightly one last time, and jumped in his truck to leave. I watched as he

pulled away. I felt my arm tingling, and looked down to see my tattoo lightly glowing. I rubbed it and smiled. My tat glowed the most when I was flying, and when I was with Johnny. Two of my most happy times in my life.

THIRTY-SIX

CHRISTMAS EVENING OUR house was bursting at the seams. Our kitchen was busy with my mom, aunts, and sisters all squeezed in, trying to get dinner together. The smell of ham, cinnamon, cedar, vanilla cookies, and the burning fireplace swirled in the air and melted together, blanketing the house with the magical aroma of the Holidays. Johnny and Kyle, joined my brother-in-law and Uncle in the living room watching the game. I was in charge of the mashed potatoes, because my mom said she enjoyed my secret recipe, which was simply milk, butter, salt and pepper, and sour cream.

We all sat at our large dinner table later that night, and just enjoyed being with each other. I was so happy to be with my sisters again, and hear all that was happening in their lives. When I introduced them to Johnny, I immediately noticed their approval. My sister

Tessa, sat beside of me and grabbed my hand under the table. "He's a keeper," she whispered with a wink.

"Thanks, Tess," I smiled back.

We were just starting dessert when I decided to make my announcement. I dinged my glass, like I had seen someone do in the movies, and stood up. "So, I have an important announcement to make." The room went completely quiet, except the soft sound of a Dean Martin Christmas carol, and the fire place occasionally popping. "So...well, first of all I want to say how thankful I am that we are all together this Christmas. Our family is the greatest gift we can ever have, and

I'm so thankful for my family." Everyone awed and smiled in agreement. "Ok, so I'm hoping that next Spring you all can make it back home again, because that will be my swearing in date...I'm joining the Air Force."

Everyone gasped, and then began to congratulate me. My Uncle Mike piped up from the other side of the table. "Well, that's good to know," he said in his thick southern accent. "For a minute there, I thought you were having a baby."

We all laughed, and I'm pretty sure Johnny blushed.

"That's a long time away, Uncle Mike," I assured him.

By midnight, my sisters and I were sitting at the

kitchen table in our PJ's catching up. Everyone else had gone home or to bed, and we snacked on leftover ham and a veggie tray.

"Were you guys surprised with my decision?" I asked them.

Dani threw a mini tomato at me. "Well, to be honest Claire, I was starting to think like Uncle Mike. I didn't know where that was going."

"Oh please Dani!" Tessa laughed, then turned to me. "We know Claire better than that." She leaned in closer to me, like she was trying to get information from me. "Although, I have to say Claire, there is something so different about you."

Kass looked at me, smiling snidely. "It's probably Johnny," she said. "What do you guys think about him?"

"Definitely a keeper," said Dani.

"I think he's adorable," agreed Tessa.

Dani grabbed my hand. "Claire, dad would be so proud of you. You know how incredibly patriotic he was."

I nodded my head, smiling. It was so hard not to tell my sisters what was really going on in my life. Maybe someday I could. Maybe someday my flying power could be known, and everyone wouldn't make a big deal out of it. I'm sure when the Chinook was invented, everyone thought it was strange and impossible, that 33,000 pounds of metal could be lifted straight off the ground and even hover there. I could do the same as a Chinook. Maybe I could become the norm. At this point, I knew anything was possible.

On a hot summer morning, a year to the exact date of my accident at the hangar, I stood with 200 other young recruits at Lackland Air Force Base in Texas. After 8 and a half grueling weeks, I finally graduated from the Air Force training camp. Chief Master Sergeant Bryant had flown my whole family, plus Alicia, Johnny, Kyle, and Shawn down to watch me. Being a military secret, had its perks.

My family greeted me at the west edge of the field. I welcomed all the hugs and photos, especially from my Johnny. He grabbed me and held me tight. I had dreamed about being wrapped in his arms again for the last 8 weeks.

Chief Master Sergeant Bryant joined us, as families slowly began to clear the field. I couldn't believe he had traveled all the way from Houston to see me graduate. "You made a fine choice joining us, Claire. I think you're going to be glad you did."

"Thank you Chief Master Sergeant Bryant," I said saluting him and then shaking his hand. "I'm a little bummed to leave the friends I've made here, but I'm excited about being at Campbell, and close to my family."

Shawn put his arm around my shoulder. "You're lucky to get stationed at Campbell, Claire. That don't happen too often."

I nodded my head in agreement with him, while Major Silva looked at me, sideways, smiling.

"We're glad to have you aboard, Claire."

"Well, I'll see you in Houston in a couple of months, AB Haley," Chief Master Sergeant Bryant said as he walked away with some of his crew.

"Houston?" Johnny whispered as we walked behind my family off the field.

"Quarterly Evaluations. They are pretty serious about continually checking me."

The next night I laid in my own bed, so excited to be home on a short break before everything started for me at Campbell the next week. My mind was so full. A year ago today, I realized I could fly. My thoughts went again to the feeling of lift off, and free falling to the earth. My heart pounded in my chest just thinking about it. I looked down at my rings, and noticed their faint glow. I hadn't flown in two months.

I sat up in bed, and listened. It was 1 am and everyone was exhausted from the day. I couldn't stand it anymore. I got up and threw on my chucks, tee, and favorite leggings. I tiptoed to the kitchen, and out the slider door to my launching spot. The night sky seemed more majestic than ever to me. Each star popped brighter against the black bliss, than any night I could remember.

I focused on the evening star, and shot up into the warm night. "Go, Claire!" I said to myself as I climbed higher and higher, towards the stars. Oh, how I had missed this. At last I reached my favorite height of 500 feet. I layed back as content as I could be, and watched as the clouds floated over me, sometimes blocking the bright moon above. I waited, hoping just maybe I could catch a shooting star, or see a plane flying over.

The sound of sirens sliced through my thoughts. I looked down to see 4 sets of lights; two sets from a couple of squad cars, one from an ambulance, and the final from a firetruck. My curious brain began to race.

"Don't do it, Claire," I warned myself. I bit my lip, and twisted the bottom of my shirt, unable to curve my curiosity. Pulling my hair back into a tight pony I paused for a moment, like mom taught me to do, to avoid a "fly by the seat of my pants" reaction.

I ran my hand over my tat, that was now glowing a very bright pink. Like I said at the beginning of all this, I don't claim to be a Superhero, but neither do I claim to be perfect. I stretched my arms out before me, and chased after the sirens, into my future.

THE END

About the Author

Cynthia L. McDaniel, is a Clarksville, Tennessee native, who resides in Northwest Indiana.When not writing, she enjoys spending time with her family, being outside, running, watching her son play football, and shopping with her daughter. Sky Walker is Cynthia's first Young Adult novel. She loves to meetand connect with her readers, and other authors.

You can find her on Goodreads, on Facebook at @CynthiaLMcDanielauthor, or on Instagram @cynthialmcdanielauthor.

Hey There, You!

Thank you so much for reading my book! I hope you enjoyed reading it, as much as I enjoyed writing it. Your support means the world to me.

This book is a dream come true for me. One I thought would never happen, but here I am!I just want to encourage you to chase your dreams. Anything is possible!

XOXO,

Cynthia

Made in the USA
Columbia, SC
09 March 2019